THE BELLBOTTOM INCIDENT

THE BELLBOTTOM INCIDENT

THE INCIDENT SERIES #3

A NOVEL BY
NEVE MASLAKOVIC

The characters and events portrayed in this book are fictitious. Any similarity to real persons, living or dead, is coincidental and not intended by the author.

The quotes in chapters 15 and 27 are reprinted, under fair use, from *The Sirens of Titan*, Kindle edition, RosettaBooks, © 1959 Kurt Vonnegut, Jr. The quote in chapter 19 is reprinted, under fair use, from *Slaughterhouse-Five*, Kindle edition, RosettaBooks, © 1969 Kurt Vonnegut, Jr.

This is a Westmarch Publishing book.
www.westmarchpub.com
ISBN-13: 978-1942458036
ISBN-10: 1942458037

WESTMARCH
PUBLISHING

for Libby and John

PART ONE:
SALLY

1

A girl lost in time. A list of numbers that would shut down the time-travel lab. And a death.

Only the first of those things was my fault. The rest just sort of…happened.

Let me back up a bit, to the evening I found out that Sabina had jumped back into the past. No, to that morning, a crisp Saturday dawn. Because what happened then set it all into motion.

Nate had driven to the house in response to my text message alerting him that rumors about Celer's ancient Roman pedigree had started to seep out online. I would have called them wild rumors, except that they happened to be true—we *had* rescued the dog from the first-century eruption of Vesuvius, along with Sabina, the teen daughter of Celer's owner. Pedigree was entirely the wrong word, though. Celer was a gray-brown animal of no particular breed, a shopkeeper's companion.

As to why we were in Pompeii at all—well, in my capacity as science dean's assistant at St. Sunniva University, a school nestled in Minnesota's lakes and hills country, I was called upon to help when a problem in the Time Travel Engineering (TTE) lab came up, which happens more often than you'd think. The SpaceTimE Warper (STEWie) was a tangled knot of mirrors and lasers in the oversized lab on the west side of campus. The contraption had sent a few companions and me on an unexpected voyage to ancient Italy. One of my fellow travelers had been Nate Kirkland, chief of campus security and a newcomer to our town of Thornberg.

We'd returned from that foray into the past with an extra person. The thing about time travel is that there are rules, four of them—no, more than rules, *unyielding cornerstones*—one of them being that History cannot be altered, down to the course of a single person's life. *History protects itself.* Had Sabina been slated to live through the eruption, to make it out alive as pumice and lava overtook her hometown, we wouldn't have been able to link hands with her and use the Slingshot to get us all home. It was that simple.

For the six of us from the twenty-first century, Pompeii had been what we at the university called a *ghost zone*, a well in time you did not want to fall into, as you were unlikely to make it out alive. The person Sabina had bonded with the most was a twenty-six-year-old TTE grad student, Abigail Tanner. Abigail had no family of her own and was quite happy to be guardian and mentor to Sabina, an arrangement eased by her working knowledge of classical Latin. I had invited the pair to live with me rent-free, which is how I'd become Aunt Julia to a thirteen-year-old girl.

For the past four months Sabina had gotten to know modern life in all its glory and shortcomings. Cell phones. Chinese takeout. Chemistry class. Being a teenager was hard enough, and when you're the only one in the world whose mother tongue is Latin—well, it's that much harder. The immigration paperwork Nate had procured for her listed Italy as her place of birth, though Sabina was no more able to speak Italian than I was able to converse in Old English. For the method of entry into the country—the options were land, sea, or air—we had put down *air*, as it was the closest thing to spacetime warping.

In my defense, I had been distracted by other matters. There had been my ex-husband's failed attempt at blackmail, which had ended badly. The hold Quinn had over us was that he knew Sabina's true background, that she wasn't a typical immigrant from modern Italy. We had dodged a bullet with Quinn (quite literally in my case), but Sabina had been a bit quiet since. We had tried to shield her from the details, but the threat had left some scars.

Then there was the *other* distraction, this one a good one. From the front steps of the house, I watched as Nate pulled into the driveway, and went to meet him. He hopped out of the Jeep, gave me a long kiss, and said, "Chilly this morning. Is Celer ready? My grandmother will look after him until the gossip dies down. I think they'll get along just fine."

I had met Mary Kirkland and was the recipient of both her hospitality, in the form of one of her famous meals, and her sage advice, so I knew this to be true.

Celer, whose name was pronounced with a hard *k*, had come outside with me and was lounging in the shaft of sunlight streaming into the open garage. "It will only be temporary anyway," I said to the dog, as if he could understand me. One of his eyes was half-closed and the other on Nate's dog, Wanda. The spaniel, having jumped out of the Jeep, was sniffing a walnut discarded in a flower bed by a squirrel, energetically wagging her tail all the while.

Nate pulled away from me as Abigail joined us in the yard. She gave Nate a friendly wave and took a seat on the steps where I had been waiting just moments ago.

Nate greeted her, then turned back to me. "Julia, why did you ask me to bring Wanda?"

"I—we were hoping you could leave Wanda with us for a few days. To keep Sabina company. Also, so I can pretend Wanda is Celer if anyone takes the Twitter rumor seriously."

"Will that work?"

"I researched it over breakfast," I explained, watching Wanda, who had a royal bearing and a silky chestnut-and-white coat, push the walnut around with her nose. "Cavalier King Charles spaniels trace their lineage to exactly six mid-twentieth-century dogs. Meaning she could not have been brought back from 79 AD with genetic certainty. She's too pretty and refined."

"Got it."

"It's not exactly ethical to lie, but if it will protect Sabina from being outed as an ancient Roman and the blast of publicity that would ensue…"

Instead of agreeing with me as I'd expected, Nate turned to where Abigail was silently following our conversation from her seat on the front steps. "What do you think, Abigail?"

She and I had already hashed out the pros and cons over breakfast, and Abigail had reluctantly agreed to my plan. "Well, sooner or later we'll have to tell the world who Sabina really is, but I guess swapping the dogs will buy us some time."

"What did Sabina say about it?" Nate asked.

"She's sleeping in," Abigail said.

"Sleeping in?" Nate repeated in some disbelief. After helping her father in his store for so many years—and having been in indentured servitude before that—Sabina was accustomed to waking up before first light.

"I asked her to give it a try. That's what normal teens are supposed to do on the weekends, right?" Having grown up in a series of foster homes, Abigail had never been a normal teenager herself.

"Well, I certainly did my share of sleeping in on the weekends," Nate said.

"Me too," I admitted. "It seems like a long time ago. Let's let her sleep. Besides, why worry her? She has enough on her plate. The Twitter rumor is just Quinn's way of sending us a message. No point in worrying Sabina. The Internet will move on by school time Monday—a day or two at the most, isn't that the rule?—so she probably won't even hear about it. We can come up with some excuse as to why Celer is at Mary's, that he needs more vet shots or something."

Mary Kirkland lived in St. Paul, a two-hour drive away. It was a thin story, but Sabina was in the unenviable position of having to accept everything that was to her unusual as being normal *here*. I felt a slight pang of guilt but pushed it aside.

Nate's brow had acquired a dark furrow at the mention of my ex-husband. He nodded. "All right then. I'll drop Celer off at my grandmother's, then swing back here later with Wanda's bed and grooming brush. C'mon, Celer."

Celer gave Nate a *humph* sort of look at being forced to move from his sunny spot but climbed into the passenger seat of the Jeep anyway.

"Don't worry," Nate told him. "Kunshi will take good care of you."

Abigail went back into the house, closing the door behind her softly so as not to wake up Sabina. Nate hopped into the Jeep. "Wanda likes to be walked three times each day," he instructed me.

"Three?"

"Four would be better. A good mile each time. One of my retired neighbors helps me out with that during the workweek."

"I didn't know that. All right, will do." As he snapped in a dog safety restraint and received an outraged look from Celer in return, I added, "When you bring Wanda's things later, do you want to stay for dinner—and, er, breakfast? Abigail and Sabina are planning on pizza and a movie. I could pick up a bottle of wine and some Swedish meatballs from Ingrid's for us."

"It's a date. I'll bring dessert."

"Can you make it something good and not, you know, fruit?"

"What's wrong with fruit?" We always teased each other about our opposite predilections for food—Nate opted for healthy choices, and I preferred taste to nutrition. Shaking his head at me in mock disapproval, he said, "I have a pecan pie in the freezer. Will that do?"

"And vanilla ice cream?"

"And vanilla ice cream."

Holding Wanda's collar as a precaution against her running after the Jeep, I watched Nate back out of the driveway. It felt good to have outwitted Quinn. I didn't think he was a real threat anyway. He was just needling us a bit, making sure he didn't get into any trouble over the fallout of his miserably failed attempt at blackmail. It would all pass in a day or two, and we'd swap the dogs back. Everything would return to normal, or what passed for it. We were three adults—four, counting Quinn—who were playing games, making decisions as if Sabina's opinion mattered not at all.

Sabina rolled out of bed at around nine thirty, embarrassed to have slept so late. She didn't complain when we explained that Celer had been sent to Mary Kirkland's house for a few days, but she was quiet all day, even when dutifully helping me walk Wanda.

The call came later, when I was sipping a refreshing cup of tea at the kitchen table, having just spent a good twenty minutes rolling a ball along the living room carpet for Wanda to chase after. Sabina was next door doing homework, and Abigail was on her way back from campus with pizza for the two of them. As for my part of the house, a plateful of Ingrid's Swedish meatballs was warming in the oven, and I was expecting Nate's footsteps outside the front door any minute. I thought the phone might be Nate calling to say that he was running late.

It wasn't Nate. It was Professor Mooney.

"Julia, we have a problem."

I set the cup down. Xavier was not calling at dinnertime on a Saturday evening to tell me that we needed to order more staplers for the lab or that STEWie's generator required a new part. What had gone wrong in the TTE lab this time? Another case of attempted murder? Had someone—again—used STEWie for a joyride into the past? I was ready for anything.

"Sabina—she came here tonight. She's gone, Julia."

"What? Where?"

"Back in time."

I hadn't been ready for this.

2

"That's impossible," I said, almost knocking over the teacup as I scrambled to my feet. "She's next door, doing her homework. I can hear the TV—the Weather Channel is on. Abigail went to get some work done on her thesis and is picking up a pizza for the two of them on her way back from campus. They're thinking of catching a movie later," I added, as if that settled matters.

Wanda had jumped up from under the table when I did, anticipating more playtime, and was hovering around my feet with her tongue hanging out.

"Hold on, Dr. Mooney, I'm going next door to check."

"Julia—"

But I was already out the back door, cell phone in hand, with Wanda at my heels. The mother-in-law suite shared by Sabina and Abigail had a separate entrance from the back deck. I knocked, as I always do—it was my house, yes, but it was their living space— then, when there was no answer, I peeked in through the window. The curtains were drawn, but a crack in their middle allowed me to see inside. The TV was on louder than usual and was showing some kind of blizzard disaster story. There was no one on the couch watching it.

"Julia?" Professor Mooney's voice crackled faintly through the phone in my hand.

The door was not locked. Wanda and I went in and I turned off the TV, then called out, "Sabina? Abigail?" and received no answer. The suite consisted of a small living room, where Abigail slept on the sofa, a half kitchen, Sabina's bedroom, and a bathroom. All were easily checked and all were empty.

An odd impulse led me to slide open the closet in Sabina's bedroom. She wasn't inside, of course, but I glanced around, as if the neatly organized shelves might hold a clue to where she was.

Her Pompeii clothes, a simple dress and sandals, were not on the top shelf where she usually kept them.

Almost tripping over Wanda, who had quieted down a bit, as if picking up that something was wrong, I turned and took a good second look around the room. The walls, covered with photos we had taken in Pompeii and lists and notes Abigail and I had crafted to help Sabina acclimate to modern life, told me nothing. Her bed had been made—she excelled at keeping up with her chores, which had always made me uneasy rather than pleased. Like I said, she had toiled away much of her young life as an indentured servant, then as helper in her father's shop, so it would have been refreshing to see her bedroom messy once in a while.

"Huh," I said.

"Julia?"

I picked up the square wooden frame from the bedside table. What was usually in it was a snapshot, the same one that was on my desk at work, of Sabina with her twenty-first-century family: Abigail and me, Nate, Xavier, Helen, Kamal, and Jacob, all of us at our Fourth of July picnic two months ago by Sunniva Lake.

The frame was empty.

I sat down on the bed, wrinkling its crisp sheets. Wanda jumped up next to me, and I didn't even have the heart to tell her to get down.

She was gone. Sabina really was gone.

3

Pedal to the floor, I drove my aged Honda down Thornberg's quiet streets to campus. Abigail, who had shown up at the house balancing a pizza box on her bike handlebars, was next to me in the passenger seat. She had left the bike and the pizza in the garage, both of us still not quite believing that Sabina wasn't on some impromptu stroll around the neighborhood. I had texted Nate to meet us at the lab.

"Wait a second," Abigail said as a red traffic light temporarily halted us. "Tell me again what Dr. Mooney said."

"Just that she has jumped back in time."

"To where? How?"

I had no answers. "Did you know she came to campus today?"

"No, I didn't."

"I wonder how she got into the lab without anyone noticing…And, more importantly, how did she know how to work STEWie?"

"Well, the thing is, Dr. Mooney has been letting her help with his Slingshot experiments."

I hadn't known that. Sabina often spent her after-school hours in the grad student office where Abigail had her desk, doing her homework, or just wandered the campus people-watching—and, apparently, hanging out in the time-travel research lab. As the light turned green and I slammed the pedal to the floor again, Abigail added, "Damn. Do you think she figured out that the real reason we swapped Celer and Wanda was to protect her?"

"And decided to jump back to Pompeii, no longer wanting to be used as ammunition for Quinn to blackmail us with?…I don't know. But it couldn't be pre-eruption Pompeii she jumped to, could it? She was already there then."

"Oh, no."

"What?"

"What if she jumped back straight into the eruption, or its aftermath?"

Well, that was an awful thought. I shoved it aside as we pulled into the parking lot. "Whatever happened, we're going to get her back. That's all there is to it. Even if we have to check every nook and cranny of History to find her."

We hurried into the TTE building. Oscar, the security guard, gave us a friendly wave. Used to the various comings and goings in the TTE lab, he didn't seem surprised to see us there on a Saturday night. Time travel does not fit neatly into a nine-to-five schedule, but then again neither does Oscar, who hardly needs any sleep and spends most of his day at his post.

"Julia—Abigail—hold up."

It was Nate, who must have pulled into the parking lot right behind us. I guessed that my text had reached him en route to my house—he was in slacks and a nice shirt, his hair still a bit wet from a shower. As he joined us in the hallway, the police radio on his hip crackled (he was always on call) with a bit of mundane campus business. It was Officer Lars Van Underberg checking in to say he'd put a stop to a student prank involving a dozen dorm mattresses and some fun-loving seniors. Nate instructed the officer to stand by in case we needed him. Our eyes met over Abigail's head as she typed the security code into the small panel to the right of the lab doors, but he said nothing. What was there to say?

The three of us filed into the TTE lab. This was where STEWie researchers worked on turning legend and myth into textbook material. A typical week in the lab could yield anything from video footage of the construction of the Mayan pyramids to details about Winston Churchill's boyhood.

Xavier Mooney was at one of the workstations, his shoulders stooped in his lab coat as he pondered something on the computer screen. He was alone. STEWie's basket, the one that had taken Sabina away, must have been gone for a while—send-offs into the past generated so much heat that cryogenic equipment under the floor was necessary, and the lab was already back to its usual chilly state. But it wasn't the cold that sent a sudden shiver down my spine; it was a feeling of foreboding, one the fleece jacket I'd grabbed on my way out into the crisp late-September evening could do nothing to ease.

"She left a note." Dr. Mooney nodded toward a piece of paper taped to one of the blackboards, above a collage of photos taken on previous STEWie runs. "The basket took off an hour and thirteen minutes ago...No, fourteen minutes," he amended, checking the timer he had set running on his computer screen.

Nate pulled down the note in one sharp movement, read it, and passed it to Abigail and me. Writing English by hand was a skill Sabina was still working on, so she had typed up the note on one of the lab computers, where the spell-checker was her friend, and printed it out. Abigail read it aloud:

BEST THING TO GO. IF STAY, ONLY MORE
TROUBLE WILL BE. THANK YOU FOR
FRIENDSHIP AND HOME.

Sabina had added an additional line below:

SEND CELER TO ME, YES?

I felt tears well up in my eyes and didn't bother blinking them away.

"It doesn't say where she jumped to," Nate pointed out.

The professor spun around in the barstool-like lab chair to face us. "Seventy-six. That's where she went."

"You mean Pompeii of 76 AD?" I asked, confused by this new bit of information. "A couple of years before the eruption? How can that be? She's already there."

The professor tugged at the strands of his graying hair. He was that rare breed of academic—beloved by students and colleagues alike. He took the note back and explained in the affable manner that was the hallmark of his lectures but felt a bit strained, given the circumstances, "Helen is away at a conference, so I thought I might as well get some work done. It took me a while to notice something was wrong. The lab felt a little warm, but I didn't think much of it—I was already sweaty from biking—and my attention was elsewhere." He gestured toward the workbench. "Whereas STEWie was what you might call old-generation time-travel equipment—large and clunky were the best descriptors for the nested array of mirrors and lasers that filled the oversized lab—the Slingshot was portable and the next thing in time-travel technology. Since our time in Pompeii, Dr. Mooney had focused his energies on perfecting the device, which at first glance looked like the junkyard edition of a laptop. He was tinkering with a new version, 3.0, and had taken apart the prototype, Version 1.0, which had been damaged by a direct hit from a bullet. Its parts lay strewn all around the worktable.

He went on. "Then I saw the last entry in STEWie's log. Sabina may have thought she was going back to the ancient Roman world, but no, it was not *that* seventy-six, and it wasn't Pompeii either. She's still on campus. Only in near time. The year 1976."

4

I breathed a small sigh of relief—1976 wasn't that bad as these things went. She'd find the campus somewhat different, but she would be safe. There would be buildings for her to take shelter in, water fountains to quench her thirst, people she could turn to for help.

"Hold on," Nate said. "Are you saying she arranged this alone? How is that possible, Professor?"

"The system was ready for Steven's run tomorrow. For his ongoing series of experiments in 1976," Dr. Mooney explained. "She must have misinterpreted the date."

Steven Little was one of the two junior professors in the TTE department. I knew all about his research, and none of it had anything to do with Sabina.

"All right, so the system was set for 1976," Nate said, then followed up with the same questions I had asked Abigail: "But how did she know how to work STEWie? It's not just a matter of simply stepping into the basket, is it? There are generators and things that must be turned on. And how did she get into the lab in the first place if no one was here?"

"It's my fault." Dr. Mooney got up to tape the note back on the blackboard, as if it belonged there with the other historical documents and photos. "I've been giving her free rein in the lab. She's so bright and has a real aptitude for math and physics—but, more to the point, I reasoned that she has a *right* to know how time travel works. It saved her life and brought her here, after all. And so I've let her help me with a test run on occasion. No, nothing like that," he said, noticing our shock. "I don't mean I've let her step into the basket. Of course not. She's only assisted me in sending the mobile robot on quick STEWie runs and in testing the Slingshot around campus."

He didn't need to explain why he himself could not step into STEWie's basket again, not for the adventurous, uncharted kind of time travel in any case. Dr. Mooney had been grounded in the present by an immune system illness that put him at risk when traveling to places and times before the advent of antibiotics. He was one of the original minds behind STEWie, the other two being Gabriel Rojas, who was on a well-earned sabbatical after having been wrongfully accused of murdering a handful of people, myself included, and Lewis Sunder, who was now behind bars for his attempt to commit the crime of which he'd accused his colleague.

The lab ceiling light caught the reflective stripes on the professor's pants, which went along with his usual method of transportation—Scarlett, his red bicycle. "I would send her on foot with a GPS unit to wherever I was planning to jump, and she'd help me gauge the Slingshot's accuracy. That sort of thing. I never thought..." He didn't finish the sentence.

"You gave her the security code for the lab door?" Nate asked, not unkindly.

"Of course not! She was a favorite visitor here, and we all always tried to make her feel welcome—well, not Steven, but that's just how he is. Giving her the code would have been a completely different matter, Chief Kirkland. I'm not sure how she got in, but she must have seen Steven's run listed on the roster"—the roster hung on the wall just inside the lab door—"and misinterpreted the destination." Dr. Mooney griped, as if it mattered at the moment, "I've asked Steven before to write out his dates fully in the roster, but he seems to expect everyone to know the specifics of his research."

"It's not your fault, Xavier," I said, "it's mine. I shouldn't have insisted that we keep the story from getting out. I wanted to give her more time." Or maybe I didn't want Quinn deciding the when and where for us. "Actually," I admitted, "I had hoped that we could avoid it altogether, that the matter would stay known only to the TTE staff and Chancellor Evans."

"If it's anyone's fault, it's mine." It was the first thing Abigail had said since we'd walked into the lab. She pulled herself to her full height (all five foot and change of it) and crossed her arms over her chest. I hoped she didn't blame me. This being-an-aunt thing was more complicated than I had anticipated. It was hard to know when to offer help and advice...and when to butt out. "I should have noticed that Sabina was unhappy. I'm her guardian and I'm responsible for her well-being."

Nate looked from me to Abigail and back. "I think we all wanted to protect her. Anyway, there's no use crying over spilled milk. We can ask her how she got the code for the door once she's safely back."

"Wait," I said. "You don't think someone...wanted her out of the way, do you? Gave her the code and encouraged her to go? Someone who knew her real background." I didn't get an answer, but then, I hadn't really expected one. I was just thinking out loud. "How surprised she must have been to find herself not in Pompeii but in a strange time period. I can picture her wandering around campus, trying to pin down the year, but once she did so...shouldn't she have jumped back already? She can't *want* to stay in 1976." I had been glancing toward the mirror-laser array, expecting to be hit with a warm *whoosh* as the basket returned onto STEWie's platform with Sabina in it.

Dr. Mooney gestured wordlessly toward the shelf above his workstation. A small device about the size of a cell phone sat there next to its identical backup. "She didn't take the Callback."

We all knew what that meant.

Sabina couldn't come back. She was stuck in 1976.

5

"She didn't take the Callback?" Abigail asked, her face falling. "She must have had no intention of returning, no matter what."

I put a hand on her shoulder and wanted to tell her not to take it personally but didn't know how to frame the words.

"Has anyone called Dr. Little?" Nate said, now fully in his campus security chief mode. "We need him to go on his run to 1976 as soon as possible. Tonight."

"I couldn't reach him, Chief Kirkland," Dr. Mooney said. "His phone must be off so as not to wake Piper. I texted him as well, but no response yet."

Steven Little was not only a junior TTE professor but the father of a six-month-old baby girl, Piper.

"I'll send Officer Van Underberg to fetch him." Nate turned aside to deliver the order into his police radio.

Abigail peered at the STEWie log over Dr. Mooney's shoulder. "Are those Dr. Little's notes? Let's see…He set the system for one o'clock on October 29, with the intended destination…the Open Book sculpture, it looks like. Well, that's good, at least. I was worried Sabina might have jumped into subzero January weather."

"My old lab coat is missing from the lab locker," Dr. Mooney said. "But it won't help her if it's a cold or snowy October. It's just light cotton."

I involuntarily looked in the direction of the locker, as if it could yield some answers. "She took your old lab coat along? I wonder why—she must have known it wouldn't belong in the ancient world. Did she take anything else from the lab?"

"Not as far as I could tell."

"The Fourth of July photo from her room is gone. And her Pompeii clothes," I explained. This was making no sense. Sabina had donned her old dress and sandals in anticipation of returning to the ancient world. But why had she brought the modern lab coat and photo with her?

Nate rejoined us, saying, "Van Underberg is on his way to Dr. Little's house and will bring him here as soon as possible. We need to get going. The clock is ticking fast in 1976."

His words made my stomach sink a bit. A second rule of time travel is that clocks carried by researchers touring the past tick faster than clocks do in the present. Much faster. One hour in the past equals just over two minutes in the lab. I glanced at the timer on Dr. Mooney's computer screen. Sabina had been gone an hour and twenty-five minutes now. I did the math in my head. She'd been in 1976 for a day and a half—alone, frightened, probably cold and hungry. I could see Abigail thinking the same thing and tried to put a positive spin on the situation. "As you said, Abigail, at least it's October and not the depths of winter. And she's on campus—there are far more dangerous places and times she could have ended up in, war zones and other ghost zones I don't even want to think about."

"Yes, it should be fairly straightforward to get her back," Dr. Mooney said, though something about his tone told me that he thought nothing of the sort.

My stomach sank further. As time travel went, jumping back thirty-some years was a blip on the scale of human history. On the other hand, one could never know what to expect when attempting to navigate History's alleys. What if we didn't manage to find her? Or, if someone *had* purposefully given her the code, what if they stood in our way and made sure we *couldn't* find her?

Nate was in full take-charge mode. "Let's leave as soon as Dr. Little gets here. I'll grab some water, a blanket, and a first aid kit."

"Uh, Chief Kirkland—" Abigail began as Nate turned toward the lab doors. Dr. Mooney intercepted Nate by putting a hand on his shoulder. "You can't go."

"You need me to stay here until we leave?"

"I mean, you can't go after Sabina."

"Why not? Surely STEWie has cooled and recharged by now. Is it the double basket issue?" He was as impatient to get going as I was.

Dr. Mooney shook his head. "That's not the problem. Your basket will return because Sabina's is already there, but you can use hers to jump back home. Chief Kirkland, she traveled to 1976. What year were you born?"

"Nineteen seventy-one. Dammit. Of course."

"You can't travel to a time period in which you already exist," the professor reminded us.

And there it was, a subheading of History protecting itself, one Sabina had perhaps forgotten in her eagerness to return to her home town of Pompeii.

Abigail, who was the youngest person in the room, said, "I can go to 1976 just fine, so that's one."

"And you're two, Julia," Nate said. "You were born in 1977, weren't you?"

Dr. Mooney, who had sat back down at the computer, took his attention away from the screen to give me a look. "Were you? I always assumed you were younger than that, Julia. Sorry, that came out rude."

"No harm done. I've been told often enough that I'm baby-faced. Just the other day someone assumed I was an undergrad and quizzed me on the whereabouts of a dorm party."

"What month?" Dr. Mooney asked.

"My birth, you mean? I was an April Fool's baby—April 1, 1977."

"And Sabina's gone to October of the previous year. You would have already been conceived by then."

"Well, yes, I would have."

"Why is that a problem?" Nate asked. "It's called the birth date cutoff, not the conception date cutoff."

Having volunteered for Dr. Little's study, which was designed to answer the knotty problem of just when the cutoff happened, I already knew the answer.

"The birth date is more of a rule of thumb—an approximation, if you will—when it comes to time travel." Dr. Mooney sat up a bit in the lab chair, again slipping into his professorial mode, even under the stressful circumstances. "For most time travelers the cutoff seems to fall somewhere between conception and birth, but we think it's closer to the conception side of things than the actual birth event. Dr. Little's experiments aim to explore the matter, though he's had no luck so far in figuring out the pattern. Dr. Little's run—the one Sabina stepped into—was intended to send him into that unique period in his own life."

"So I might be able to go, and I might not?" I asked.

"The only way to be sure is to try. In which case, Julia, you might want to change your outfit. I'm not sure a fleece jacket and those athletic pants"—beneath my fleece jacket, I had on a tank top and yoga pants, having been just about to change into something nicer for the date with Nate—"will do for 1976. You too, Abigail."

Abigail was way ahead of him. Leaving Dr. Mooney to ready the equipment and Nate looking stunned by the news that he was grounded in the present, I followed her out of the lab and into the travel apparel closet across the hall.

It seemed wrong to bother with something as pedestrian as clothes with the clock ticking, but we would need to blend in if we wanted to move around freely—assuming I managed to make it to 1976 at all. *Blend in* was the third of the time-travel rules, the last one being *There's always a way back*. Abigail, whose hair was back to its natural blonde this week, short, and just below her ears, headed to the corner where modern clothing hung on hangers. The closet was loosely organized by century and geographical area, with shelves and boxes overflowing with everything from ancient Greek tunics to medieval cassocks to disco pants. Abigail, who was more familiar with medieval cassocks than disco pants, began rifling through the modern clothing uncertainly.

"Don't beat yourself up about not noticing that Sabina had snuck into the building," I said, taking a guess at what was gnawing at her.

"I had my nose buried in my work, trying to weave the notes and photos I took on that last run into a coherent thesis chapter. You know, the ones of Marie-Anne Lavoisier sketching Antoine's apparatus."

Under different circumstances, the wording might have made us both chuckle. Of course, the apparatus in question was a piece of chemistry equipment. The notes and photos were from an eighteenth-century run.

"If Dr. Mooney didn't give her the lab code—you didn't give her the code, did you, Abigail?"

"Certainly not."

"Let's see, the seventies…jeans and wide-collared shirts…Then maybe one of the other grad students or Dr. B did. Gave her the code, I mean." Dr. B—Erika Baumgartner—was the fourth of the TTE professors, a junior one like Dr. Little, and Abigail's advisor. I couldn't imagine her acting that unprofessionally, however. "I wonder why Oscar didn't say anything to you about her being here when you left the building."

"I told him I was headed to pick up a pizza. He must have assumed that I was coming right back for a late night at the lab. I've certainly done that often enough in the past."

I grabbed a couple pairs of bellbottom jeans from the clothes rack and turned to find that Abigail had dug up a set of leg warmers. I shook my head at her. "Not those—they're from the eighties. Here." I handed her the smaller of the jeans. She was petite and thin, and I was more what I liked to think of as average sized, both in height and the other dimension. Next I found us both loose-fitting peasant blouses and, as we hurriedly donned the jeans and blouses in the changing area, said, "I suppose I should let Dean Braga know what has happened." I was not looking forward to that call. Dean Isobel Braga, formerly of the Earth Sciences Department, was my boss. By quiet consensus, we had never gotten around to telling her about Sabina's real background, and the dean was, I was very sure, not going to be happy about that. She already disapproved of what she called *past irregularities* in the lab.

Abigail took a look at herself in the floor-to-ceiling mirror and rolled up the sleeves of the shirt, which was a bit large, as were the jeans. My clothes fit just fine. As Abigail rummaged around for a belt to keep her jeans up, I made the call. The dean didn't answer. I breathed a sigh of relief and, as I was pretty sure that she would see a text message immediately, left a voice mail instead on her desk phone. With any luck she wouldn't get around to checking her messages until Monday morning, by which time we'd hopefully have Sabina back safe and sound, and the dean would not have to be told of the matter at all.

Abigail and I finished up by donning a couple of black woolen coats—I figured our modern sneakers would not be that noticeable under the long jeans—and hurried back across the hall, almost bumping into Dr. Little on his way in. The young professor was in pajamas and slippers under a plaid robe, having left his house in haste after being roused from bed by Officer Van Underberg. The good officer was right behind him, concern written all over his face. He was very fond of Sabina. We all were.

I hoped that Dr. Little wasn't going to have a problem with me joining the search-and-rescue party. Abigail was a TTE grad student and had plenty of STEWie experience up her sleeve. I had some, too, much of it hard earned, but that had not seemed to matter to Dr. Little when I popped into his office during the summer. He had sent a note to Dean Braga requesting several STEWie roster spots, and in it he'd mentioned that he was seeking volunteer research subjects.

"You were born in the first half of 1977?" he had asked when I showed up in his office to volunteer.

"Yes, April 1."

"You look younger."

He didn't make it sound like a compliment. He added, "When I asked for volunteers, I meant people in the science departments—professors, postdocs, senior graduate students."

"I'm in the dean's office. That counts."

I could almost see the phrase *But you're just the dean's assistant* hovering on Dr. Little's lips.

"As a general rule I prefer that those who step into STEWie's basket with me have *some* technical knowledge," he finally said. "Obviously you've been on the Pompeii run"—this was before the incident with the runestone and its accompanying fourteenth-century run—"but that hardly counts."

Given that we had barely made it back in one piece, it counted quite a lot in my opinion. I decided not to belabor the point and instead said, "I'm a quick learner. I'll attend a workshop."

He tried another tack. "You should know that some of the questions we need answered by each volunteer about their family history"—*we* included him and his two graduate students, Tammy and Lee—"are, by definition, *very* personal. After all, we are trying to find the link between birth date, conception date, and the historical cutoff for time travelers."

"Shoot," I said. "Ask me anything. Father's name, Soren Olsen. Mother is Missy, maiden name Donovan. They met here at St. Sunniva as freshmen and married at the end of their senior year, soon after I made my appearance in the world."

Dr. Little, who could hardly be called insightful, looked up from the volunteer form he had opened on his computer screen. There were several pages of questions, it looked like. I was pretty sure my parents wouldn't mind if I provided details about their younger days, and if they did, I was confident I could convince them that it was for the greater good and the advancement of scientific knowledge. Which it was. As for any *personal* matters…well, there was one, but I wasn't about to spell it out for Dr. Little.

He was frowning at me. "I find that when people volunteer for these things, they often have an ulterior motive. The goal of the study is not for you to run around in the seventies digging around in your parents' lives. If you want to do this because you have unanswered questions about your parents' past, it would be best just to talk to your folks. Unless—I'm sorry, are they still living?"

"They are. They live in Florida," I explained, as if that was of any interest to him. "They are in charge of a retirement community there and—"

He held up a hand. "Just as long as you understand that STEWie cannot be used to resolve personal issues."

That was unfortunate, because, like I said, there *were* things I wanted to know. Perhaps there would be a way of getting around that. I'd worry about it later. "Got it," I said.

"I've sent the questionnaire to the printer," he said in a voice that suggested he was only humoring me and had just wasted six sheets of paper. "Fill it out, and I'll let you know if we need you."

Needless to say, I never heard back about the study.

Well, I was going now, and he would just have to accept it.

We all tumbled into the lab at the same time, Abigail and I looking like we were on our way to a theme party. Dr. Little wasted no time before asking, "How long has she been gone?"

"Ninety-five minutes," Nate said at once, as if he and Dr. Mooney had just done the math again. "Forty-two hours and counting in 1976."

"Almost two days! Dammit. This is what comes of letting teenagers roam around the lab."

This was directed at Dr. Mooney, who didn't seem to take it personally. "Sabina is hardly a typical teenager. What was I supposed to do? Turn her out of the lab and send her to the mall?"

"It would have been safer."

I wasn't so sure I agreed with Dr. Little about that. What would Sabina have learned from hanging around at the mall? How to fall into debt by spending money she didn't have? That she could never be thin enough or pretty enough? Not for the first time, I thought about how strange our culture must seem to her.

"And how did she get in?" Dr. Little asked.

"I couldn't tell you. None of *us* gave her the security code for the door."

The two professors—one gray haired with life-earned wrinkles around his eyes, the other young and underslept with bags under his eyes—stood facing each other, as if in some kind of academic standoff. Abigail, even though graduate students occupied just about the lowest rung on the academic ladder, had no problem speaking up when the occasion called for it. "We're wasting time. Julia and I are ready to go."

Dr. Little turned his displeased stare in my direction—the volunteer study aside, there was no love lost between us, as he thought I interfered in the TTE lab doings far more than what my title should have allowed. I stared him down and he nodded. "Give me two minutes—I have my to-go bag and seventies clothes in my office."

"Please, can I come along?" Officer Van Underberg's caramel-colored mustache was wrinkled in consternation. "I'd like to help."

"Sorry, three people is enough. The larger our group, the more attention we'll draw," Dr. Little called out as he headed out of the lab at a brisk clip.

A few minutes later he was back, and we all assembled by STEWie's platform, which stood raised off the ground and supported a steel frame that represented the basket's dimensions. The basket itself, the component of STEWie that would travel with us into 1976, was invisible. We were taking Slingshot 2.0, the only one in working condition, so we would be able to make small spacetime adjustments as needed.

Dr. Mooney was bent over his keyboard. "I've adjusted the coordinates by forty-eight hours to account for the two days Sabina has already been there."

"We can't jump to the exact same point she did, greet her as she steps out of the basket and into 1976?" I asked.

He shook his head without looking up. "Those two days are already part of her own past and can't be changed. You'll be arriving on October 31, 1976. That's a Sunday. I left the destination unchanged—the Open Book."

The Open Book was a large stone sculpture on the green fronting the student cafeteria. As he climbed up onto STEWie's platform, Dr. Little explained why he had chosen this destination for his study. "I figured there would be a lunchtime crowd, which would allow me to arrive on campus unnoticed."

Abigail and I followed him up onto the platform. Nate hesitated, then climbed up as well. "Since the birth date cutoff is only a rule of thumb, I figure there's a chance."

Dr. Little gave him a disapproving look, as though he personally begrudged such an unscientific attempt to circumvent one of History's key rules. "Kirkland, no one has ever managed to travel *past* their birth date. It won't work."

"No harm in trying." Still, he passed me the blanket, bottle of water, and the first aid kit he had dug up in the lab stores.

As the lab equipment started whirring to life, I asked, "Do we know how cold it will be? Should we have grabbed an umbrella, or hats and mittens for ourselves and Sabina?"

Dr. Little shook his head curtly. "I checked the campus weather database. October 31 will be dry and sunny, with a midafternoon high of thirteen degrees."

Officer Van Underberg gasped from his position just outside the laser-mirror array.

"That's Celsius," Dr. Little said with an implied *of course*. He adjusted his hair, which he had been letting grow to more seamlessly blend into the seventies, over his coat collar. It was, along with the beard that was undergoing the same process, still a work in progress. "About fifty-five Fahrenheit, so reasonably warm for fall. Unfortunately, last night's low almost reached the freezing point. Let's hope Sabina found shelter somewhere." He sounded not unfeeling about it; rather, it was clear that he was attempting to prepare us for anything. Like Abigail and I, he had changed into bellbottoms. Above them he was wearing one of his trademark button-down vests. It was a denim one that was a slightly lighter blue than his jeans, with two pockets and four buttons. Under it he had on a white T-shirt, and a short coat covered the whole ensemble.

Nate thought of something. He took the two-way radio off his belt and passed it to me, then nodded at Officer Van Underberg to give his to Abigail. The officer hurried over with his radio and passed it to Abigail like a good-luck charm. Nate explained of the radios for us, "They can work without a base station if you're not too far from each other. In case I get left behind."

"*If* you get left behind?" Rousing Dr. Little out of bed had made him grouchier than usual, though he was no more a fan of Nate's than he was of mine. The pair were neighbors and a troublesome property-line tree had caused some tension between them. "You *will* get left behind."

Setting the watch I'd borrowed from the costume room to one o'clock, I heard Nate say calmly, "Dr. Little, why don't you give your bag to Abigail? In case *you* get left behind with me."

"I'm pretty sure that I'll arrive just fine. I'll still be a good six months away from being born." Still, he grudgingly pushed his duffel bag into Abigail's arms. It held his travel gear—this typically meant local currency, a map, snack food, water, camera, a notebook, that kind of thing, perhaps a sleeping mat and blanket for extended runs.

"Abigail," I said, "if I get left behind, too…"

Her eyes met mine above the duffel bag. "Don't worry, Julia. I'll find her."

6

A pleasant fall day, with the sun high up in the sky, greeted only three of us. History had weeded out Nate. I had expected it, but it was still jarring. I had never made a journey into the past without him, and I'd come to depend on him in more ways than one.

No Sabina either. I don't know why I'd expected her to meet us, as if she would have spent two days waiting by the book sculpture, but in the back of my mind I guess I had.

I blinked in the bright sunlight, then let out my breath, which I had been holding in anticipation of being left behind. With my next breath, I took in the familiar scent of the campus—the sweetness of the decomposing fall leaves, sharp cooking smells from the nearby student cafeteria, pine needles…and a couple of less familiar ones. Car exhaust fumes and cigarette smoke were rife in the air, and cigarette butts and pop and beer bottles littered the ground by my feet. I resisted the urge to bend down to clean up the mess and instead reached out to touch the sculpture itself, which looked new, unweathered by thirty-plus years of alternating hot and cold seasons. Shaped like a large letter V laid on its side, it was a portrayal of a half-open paper book, its marble pages chiseled with famous quotations. (*A room without books is like a body without a soul.*) The three of us were inside its seven-foot pages, where we were sheltered from curious eyes.

"I *told* Kirkland he wouldn't be able to come and that I would arrive just fine," Dr. Little said smugly as he took his duffel bag back from Abigail.

"And you were right." I peered out from behind the sculpture. Students, individually and in clumps, were making their way across the plaza toward the cafeteria for lunch. We heard the campus clock tower across the lake chime one o'clock.

Leaving the blanket and water tucked under the sculpture in case Sabina returned, we emerged unhurriedly, as if we belonged on campus on the early afternoon of Sunday of October 31, 1976. Caution really wasn't necessary. If it wasn't all right for us to be seen, if our presence was likely to interfere with anyone's path or the course of their day, then History would not have let us leave the shelter of the Open Book. We crossed the small green to the paved plaza. The campus, as familiar to me as the back of my hand, was both the same *and* disconcertingly different. The two-story Hypatia House, where I worked, was in its place farther up the lakeside path, which was no surprise as it was one of the original nineteenth-century buildings. The trees fronting it stood in a different configuration, though, and had shed most of their fall leaves. In the other direction, down by the bend in the lake, I could see that construction had begun on a future campus eyesore, the square cement building destined to house the English department. No work was being done on it at the moment, however, it being Sunday. Just a quiet autumn day on campus.

Only one of the Science Quad buildings was missing—the balloon-roofed building that would eventually become the Time Travel Engineering lab. Its spot was occupied by five stories of stained concrete that looked to be a dorm. Perhaps its occupants were the ones responsible for the late-night party that had left the Open Book littered with trash.

Somewhere nearby, in the physics building some ways up the lakeside path or in one of the graduate student dorms, were a young Xavier Mooney, Gabriel Rojas, and Lewis Sunder, only a couple of years into their PhDs. The thought sent a tingle down my spine.

I had forgotten that October 31 would be Halloween, of course. Decorations—skeletons and ghosts and such—hung here and there in dorm and office windows. I wondered what Sabina was thinking about this strange ritual.

We didn't see any sign of her dark locks or Xavier's white lab coat, if she was indeed wearing it, among the students crossing the plaza, so we turned toward the cafeteria. It looked just as it did in the present, except that the posters in its large windows advertised different current events and campus happenings. One called on supporters of Jimmy Carter's presidential run to gather for a rally tomorrow evening, a second urged everyone to get vaccinated for the swine flu, and a third spread the news of a Halloween party at a dorm whose name I didn't recognize, St. Olaf's.

I cupped my hands so I could see into the sunlit cafeteria window—one of the students eating lunch inside gave me a startled look back—then turned to face the others. "Let's split up and check the nearest buildings. Abigail, why don't you check inside the cafeteria? Dr. Little, do you want to take the computer science building? Of the three of us, you'll probably blend in the best there." This was the closest of the science buildings. "And I'll poke my head into the Registrar's Office next door."

We headed in three different directions.

"Over here."

It was Abigail, waving at me from around the back of the cafeteria.

I joined her, with Dr. Little right on my heels. He reported, "Nothing at the computer science building—I checked all around and even in the back parking lot, in case Sabina was forced to stay out of sight by History. Obviously I couldn't go into every office and classroom."

My story was similar. "I went into the Registrar's Office—it's hardly changed at all. I even looked in the nonpublic areas where the student records are kept, but she was not there…Did you have any luck, Abigail?"

"I did. Look."

She opened her palm. In it lay Sabina's lunula. The orange-brown amber, crafted into a crescent-moon shape, sparkled in the sunlight. It was Sabina's one link to home, and she always wore it as a lucky charm. In Pompeii it had hung around her neck on a leather strap, but she'd switched to a silver chain after a few snide comments from the other girls at the Thornberg high school.

Abigail explained that she had poked her head around in every corner of the cafeteria. There hadn't been anything of interest until she checked the restroom. "It was on the floor of the women's restroom, by the couch. The clasp is loose. I've been meaning to get it fixed for her."

"So she must have spent at least one night, maybe both, there," I said. "I'm so glad that she was able to get out of the cold and find shelter. Hopefully she managed to get some food, too, after they locked up the cafeteria for the night."

"There's a couch in the women's restroom?" Dr. Little asked, his brow slightly furrowed. "Why?"

"There are two, as a matter of fact," Abigail said. "The restroom is roomier than it is in the present. I think part of it will be converted into a kitchen freezer or something."

"Women's restrooms often do have them…or at least, they used to," I explained absentmindedly. "For nursing mothers mostly, or if you're pregnant or have bad menstrual cramps and need to sit down for a bit—well, not *you*, Dr. Little, but you get the idea. I wonder if that's where the term *restroom* comes from."

Abigail carefully slid the lunula into her pocket. Dr. Little watched her do it and said, "If Sabina was here last night, she can't have gone far."

"I hope so," I said, remembering the odd tone of Dr. Mooney's voice when he'd said that finding her should be straightforward.

"Why do you say it like that?" Dr. Little challenged me. "Obviously she must have immediately understood that she wasn't back in 76 AD. She should have known that we would come get her. The prudent thing to do would have been to stick close to the Open Book."

He didn't know Sabina as well as Abigail and I did. She was not one to sit around and wait, not when there was a new place to be explored. She had much of her father's personality. Secundus had opted to stay in Pompeii to look for his mother and try to protect his shop rather than flee town on foot, as many of Pompeii's inhabitants did. We had never found out what happened to him, or his mother, Faustilla—whether they had met up and fled to safety or perished.

I attempted to explain. "It would have been the prudent thing to do, yes, but remember that the details that anchor this decade for us—bellbottoms, smoking on campus, Jimmy Carter and Gerald Ford election posters—would mean nothing to her. To her eyes, the campus would only appear slightly different than it does in the present."

"She must have been both curious and puzzled," Abigail said.

"All right, so she wandered off," Dr. Little said.

We all realized that a methodical circuit of campus to check every single building and every single room would take impossibly long. We needed a better way.

"Maybe she's trying to find us," Abigail suggested. "Here, I mean. In 1976. Not me, obviously, but—well, maybe even me if she hasn't figured out yet how far back in time she jumped, as you say, Julia."

I nodded. "Yes, in which case she'd look for us where she expects us to be—the campus security office for Nate, Hypatia House for me...There's no TTE building for her to look for you, Abigail...but perhaps she's gone to the physics department to find Dr. Mooney."

"If she tried all of those already and didn't find us, then the lake," Abigail said. "It's where she likes to go when she needs to think."

Sunniva Lake sat smack in the middle of campus, and Sabina often sat on its reeded shores when she got pensive. The lake's gentle waters reminded her of her demolished seashore home.

"Let's check all those places," I suggested.

"I would argue that that's a waste of time," Dr. Little said. "You said that those places are the ones she would have gone to first, two days ago. Why would she still be there?"

"Well, we have to start somewhere. Abigail, why you don't make a circle of the lake? And once again, Dr. Little, you'll probably blend into the physics department crowd more easily than us. I'll swing by Hypatia House and the security office. Then we can meet back by the Open Book. In an hour, say?"

Abigail and I had the radios Nate and his officer had given us, but we would have no way of reaching Dr. Little. Nothing could be done about that, however. Something occurred to me. "Oh, and Dr. Little? I've been meaning to ask—will we get time-stuck less frequently here than we did in Pompeii? No one seemed to care that I was poking around the Registrar's Office."

Dr. Little fought off a tired yawn and confirmed my suspicion. "Yes, you should find it easier to move around."

"Because the strands of History aren't as deeply woven as they are in far time?"

"Partly, but that's balanced out by the fact that many of the far-time strands are dusty and irrelevant. The reason is simpler. We blend in. We're not from so far into the future that we do not belong."

"What could be keeping Dr. Little?"

Abigail and I had managed to keep in touch via the radios, though we had encountered interference, a testy voice instructing us to get off this frequency, as it was reserved for campus security. Abigail had done a full circle of Sunniva Lake, heading from the Science Quad down to the future English department at the lake's south end, then up the other side past the tower clock, the library, and the dock, and back to her starting point at the Open Book. I had visited Hypatia House and then the security office, which was still where it was in the present, near the south parking lot. After turning off my radio so Abigail wouldn't try to reach me at an inopportune moment, I had walked right in. I mumbled a weak cover story about having lost a wallet, looked around to see if they had Sabina anywhere, and left. The only bright spot was that the young officer who had promised to keep an eye out for my wallet had been a young and handsome Dan Anderson (in his late twenties, I guessed), our campus security chief before Nate took the job. It had been nice to see him at his prime, before old age ushered him into retirement and a gardening hobby.

The blanket and bottled water were still there at the Open Book, where the basket—invisible, patient—waited to take us back home.

After cooling our heels for a good fifteen minutes past the allotted meeting time, Abigail and I decided to look for Dr. Little.

The lakeside footpath, tree-shaded in spots, took us to the Chemistry and Physics Annex. Marie Curie's name would be appended to the building's name one day, but for now its title was strictly utilitarian. The physics side of the annex was connected to its concrete twin by a glass-encased walkway appreciated by professors and students alike in the winter. It looked just the same as it did in the present, though the glass of the walkway was perhaps a little cleaner. Graduate students catching up on their research over the weekend trickled in and out of the coupled buildings, book bags on shoulders.

Dr. Little was in the courtyard between the two halves of the annex, on a bench by a small fountain under the walkway. He was asleep, his duffel bag by his feet.

I put a hand on his shoulder, and he jerked awake.

"Sorry, it wasn't my fault. I sat down to get a pebble out of my shoe and found I was time-stuck," he said with no hint that he was aware of the irony of getting time-stuck right after he'd explained why we weren't likely to. Like Abigail and me, he had retained his modern footwear under the bellbottom jeans—a five-toed sneaker on each foot—which I knew he preferred for walking. "I found that I couldn't get up at all. There were two students talking—Good Lord, are they still there? Don't they have work to do?" A male and a female student were chatting by the front doors on the physics side of the building. "What could possibly take so long?" Dr. Little's tone suggested that he felt graduate students should have more important things to do than socialize.

Abigail and I had taken a seat on either side of him. I tried to get back up, but my bottom might as well have been glued to the bench.

"Guess we're all stuck now," Abigail said.

After a good ten minutes of waiting, punctuated by Dr. Little's irritated sighs, the pair finally disappeared inside.

Abigail jumped up. "It's okay now."

Dr. Little tentatively got to his feet, reached for his duffel bag, and slung it across one shoulder. As we headed toward the physics entrance, he explained, "I've visited this current iteration of campus twice already while working my way closer to my birth date. The grad student offices are in the basement. The stairs are at the end of this hall." He led us down them into a dingy, windowless hallway.

"This must be it," Abigail said of the third door down.

The door didn't have a list of names, only a piece of paper nailed to it that said *If Physics Students You Seek, Look No Further.*

Abigail raised a hand to knock. She rapped softly first, then, when there was no response, more sharply.

There was still no answer. She sent a shrug in our direction and turned the handle. The door swung open with a gentle creak, and we filed inside.

The grad student office was larger than I had expected, but the dozen desks packed into it made it seem cramped. All of the desks were unoccupied at the moment. There were coats hanging on a rack by the door, as if several students were there for the day but elsewhere in the building, either in labs or in the physics library on the top floor. A large blackboard stood in one corner and held equations and a sketch. After a few seconds' consideration, it dawned on me that the sketch represented an idealized version of STEWie—there were circles where the mirrors would be one day, wiggles for lasers, a square box for the generator, and a small oval for the basket. Abigail—and also Dr. Little, which was a little out of the norm for him—let out chuckles of delight as soon as they noticed it. Abigail took out her cell phone and snapped a picture of the blackboard.

"Abigail, you brought your phone along?" I chided her.

"I figured no one's gonna see it in my pocket. Hey, this must be Dr. Mooney's desk, look," she exclaimed. The professor was a bit of a father figure to her, which no doubt fueled her interest. She bent down to examine a pair of mismatched conga drums nestled under the wooden surface. The drums were the start of a collection whose gems would one day include a didgeridoo from far-time Australia and many other musical instruments collected by Dr. Mooney on his journeys in time.

"Gabriel and Lewis must have desks in here as well," I said, looking around. "I'm guessing *that* one is Gabriel's, judging by the neatly stacked books. And that one is Lewis's—who keeps a picture of themselves on their own desk? Of all the—"

"Shh, someone's coming," Dr. Little interrupted me, then continued in a low voice, "We better get out of here."

We tried, but it was a no-go. History, very firmly, did not want us to leave by the door we had entered, probably because voices were approaching in the hallway outside. We felt a wall of *something* push us deeper into the office, gently but decisively, toward a corner where there was a second door I hadn't previously noticed.

"There's another exit," Abigail whispered.

We quickly tumbled through the second door only to find ourselves shut in a closet.

7

Abigail flicked on her cell phone light. We were in a cleaning supply closet, which some quirk of building design had placed in the grad student office. Sharing the small space with the three of us were a vacuum cleaner, a mop and bucket, and a large can, into which discarded paper, food wrappers, and other trash had been dumped in a decidedly non-recycled fashion.

"…and then she told me she wasn't interested in dating because she's too busy with classes. Besides, I'm not her type, she said. I guess she doesn't like physics students. The lunch only went downhill from there. It was very short, needless to say." From the first audible word, I knew it was a young Xavier Mooney speaking. I would have recognized his voice anywhere.

"I don't think I've met this Isobel," another voice said, accompanied by the thump of textbooks hitting a table. This one was undeniably Gabriel Rojas's. "Have I?"

"I don't know. She's a geology student."

I had met her. She was my boss, a professor of geology turned dean of science. Xavier was very definitely not her type, though not for the reasons he imagined. Back home, Dr. Braga was away for the weekend with Mindy, her longtime partner, for a visit to Mindy's family in Chicago.

"I even put on a suit and tie to impress her. Honestly, I don't know why I bother. Never mind that, though. Something occurred to me during lunch. What if we're thinking too small with our Time Machine?"

"Elaborate."

"The plan is to try and sell them"—he didn't say who—"on the concept of sending an object on an infinitesimal jump into the past, a nanosecond or two. But, to be quite frank, that's just boring."

"No jump into the past is boring," Gabriel said in his usual cautious fashion, the one I was familiar with from countless department meetings.

Abigail, next to me, was positively twitching with excitement as she eagerly took in every word. Dr. Little was crouched, peering through the closet peephole. I tapped him on the shoulder and he moved aside to let me take a look. I brought my eye to the keyhole. There they were, young Drs. Mooney and Rojas. No, that was wrong; they weren't doctors yet, I reminded myself. But they certainly were young. Gabriel, thin and scrawny in a plain white T-shirt, had his elbows on the table and looked lost in thought, as he often did. Xavier's feet were propped up on his desk, which connected to Gabriel's back-to-back, and he was indeed wearing a tweed suit, though he'd loosened the tie as he leaned back in his chair. They both looked like they needed a good haircut, and there wasn't a trace of the gray that would one day prevail.

They both had mustaches! I had to hold my lips tightly together to contain a laugh.

Xavier took off his tie and waved it in Gabriel's direction. "I didn't mean boring in a technical sense, I meant from the bigwigs' point of view. Hear me out. What if we go *bigger*, promise a jump of days, weeks, months back in time? Hell, why not *years*? And not an object but a person! That would get their attention, wouldn't it? And don't talk to me about risk or energy expenditure," he added before Gabriel could reply. "Those are just details, my good man, details."

"But we can't guarantee a weeklong jump. We can't even guarantee a nanosecond one."

"Yes, but we might as well think big, don't you agree?"

"Hmm…I don't know if I'm comfortable promising results which we're not sure we can deliver."

"Isn't that how the game is played? After all, if we already knew *how* to do it, that it would work for sure, we wouldn't need their money. We'd be writing papers and filing patents and so forth."

As Gabriel pondered the ethics of this, I felt someone elbow me in the side. It was Abigail, wanting a closer look. I moved to make room for her. "Xave," Gabriel finally said after a while, "I think the prudent thing to do when seeking funding is to at least try to sound like your project isn't straight out of a story by Asimov…But maybe we should ask Lewis his opinion."

"I did, on the way back here. He thinks it's best not to mention the words *time* and *travel* together and stick instead to talking about warping spacetime. He's being all *political* about it."

"He's probably wise."

"He insisted that we not call it the Time Machine in our funding proposals. He suggested the Spacetime Warper."

Gabriel tested the phrase. "The Spacetime Warper. It doesn't exactly roll off the tongue."

"It doesn't, does it?…Wait, I got it. How about this? We take the *s*, *t*, and the last *e* from *spacetime*…and the *w* from *warper*. That gives us STEW."

"The STEW machine. It sounds a little mushy but could be worse."

"Better yet, let's call it STEWie."

"Now that I like."

"Let's remember to tell Lewis about it."

Lewis Sunder, I knew, would soon abandon the project to seek a safer topic for his own degree. Years later, when Xavier and Gabriel achieved fame and the promise of a Nobel Prize, he would regret the move, even though by then he would have a prestigious position of his own as the university's dean of science. But that was years away. Much hard work lay ahead before STEWie would grow from a blackboard sketch into a working lab with a cement-and-steel home. Even then, years of false starts would follow, progress held back because they kept trying to jump into near time, after they'd already been born. The first successful run, in summer of 2010, would be to the sandy dunes of 1903 Kitty Hawk to watch a breakthrough in aviation take place, one that paralleled the astonishing breakthrough Dr. Mooney and Dr. Rojas had just made.

"In retrospect," Dr. Mooney had said to me once, "Kitty Hawk was not the best site. The sandy dunes offered little cover, and we weren't able to get very close. Not to mention all that time wasted on attempting near-time runs. They required less energy, we reasoned, and would be safer and easier to pull off as a demonstration. Little did we know…"

I wished I could tell the pair to try Kitty Hawk at once.

"It maddens me that we have to suck up to pencil pushers," I heard Xavier say, his voice muffled by the closet door. The young Xavier Mooney, brash and full of himself, reminded me of someone—someone besides his older self, that was—and I suddenly realized who: Junior Professor Steven Little, with whom I was currently rubbing elbows in the closet.

"Science should be pure, free of all that red-tape stuff. I don't mind the teaching part, but the rest of it…"

Gabe agreed. "You said it, man. Is that the time? I spent the whole morning in the library and forgot to eat breakfast. Time to grab something before I keel over. Hey, are we still on for going as Einsteins tonight? We are? All right, I'll see if I can dig up a suit. See ya later, Xave."

We heard the office door open and close. The three of us had our ears glued to the cupboard door, which seemed sturdily shut, but it turned out that History was the only thing holding it in place. As Gabriel's footfalls receded down the hallway, the door burst open under the force of our combined weight, and the three of us fell out onto the linoleum floor of the grad student office.

Xavier looked up from a stack of papers he had started grading, probably homework from one of the classes he was TA-ing. "How did you three get in there? Is this some kind of undergrad prank? Never mind, I don't want to know. This office is off-limits to undergrads. How about you use your fancy sneakers to walk out the door?"

As we picked ourselves up off the linoleum, he added in Dr. Little's direction, "Though *you*, at least, look like you might be a grad student."

Dr. Little swatted at the knees of his jeans, which had acquired a layer of dust in the closet. "I'm not a student—I already have my PhD." I sent him a look. What was he doing? I'm sure it was quite a strange and thrilling sensation to meet an older, more famous colleague at a time when that colleague had been no more than a newbie, but still.

"Physics?" Xavier inquired.

"No, computer science and engineering."

"Ah. Well, then you and your friends are in the wrong place," Xavier said, his tone and words reminiscent of what Dr. Little might have used himself in similar circumstances. He nodded toward the door and gave his attention back to the papers.

Abigail moved closer and tapped him on the shoulder. "We are looking for a girl."

"In the janitor closet? Besides, who isn't?"

"No, you misunderstand me. A girl has gone missing."

Xavier put the pen down and studied the three of us for a moment. "A student?"

"No, she's…a visitor to campus," I explained. "It's a long story."

This was all quite strange. How could we be having this in-depth conversation with the young Xavier Mooney? What, had he developed selective amnesia and forgotten to mention it to us back at the lab?

"I'm Julia," I introduced myself, still feeling quite odd about the whole thing. "I'm not a student either, nor is Abigail here—or, well, actually she is…"

"Not a student, huh, Julia? Are you single?"

"What?"

He looked me up and down and I almost said, *Dr. Mooney, are you feeling all right?*

"Do you have a picture of this girl you're looking for? I could show it around, ask if anyone has seen her," he offered, sounding as if he was only doing so to impress me. Great. He and Isobel would not end up together for the aforementioned reason, but he would, in a few years, fall in love with a young linguistics graduate student, Helen Presnik, who was now a good friend of mine and a senior professor in her own right.

I decided it would help matters if I thought of the man in front of me as the young and upcoming academic Xave and not as the older and mellower Dr. Mooney. After all, the Dr. Mooney I knew was quite different; he played his musical instruments at office parties and was kind to everyone who came by his lab, whether it was a newly arrived freshman or Chancellor Jane Evans herself.

I attempted to give a physical description of Sabina. "We don't have a picture, I'm afraid, but she's just about my height, with dark hair and eyes, strong shoulders, sandals, and a dress the color of wheat. She's possibly wearing a white lab coat," I added.

Not just any white lab coat, but the very one hanging on the back of his chair, I was startled to see. It looked crisply white and new.

I felt it was important to mention one more thing. "She is, uh, mature for her age." Sabina had experienced a growth spurt over the summer, but that wasn't it. While she was thirteen, she wasn't a *modern* thirteen but rather like Juliet in *Romeo and Juliet*, only without the Romeo. Kids stayed kids longer nowadays. Sabina's peers in 2012 were middle-class high schoolers whose biggest worries were what their friends were saying about them on Facebook and how to fudge the book reports they had no interest in writing. Sabina had already worked two jobs. Her family had been preparing to marry her off to a shopkeeper's apprentice when the volcano disaster had struck. In some ways she was more of an adult than Abigail and I were. I concluded my verbal snapshot of Sabina by saying, "She's from Italy, so her grasp of English is a bit sketchy."

Abigail seemed to come to some sort of snap decision. She reached into her coat pocket, but carefully, as if she expected her hand to be pulled up short by an obstruction. It wasn't.

There were a lot of things about this scenario I had trouble wrapping my head around. One, I still couldn't believe we were talking to the twentysomething Xavier Mooney. Two, I couldn't believe that Abigail was about to show him her smartphone, a small, sleek twenty-first-century device that was bound to look straight out of *Star Trek* to him. But most of all, I couldn't believe that History was letting her do it.

But it was…and it did. Abigail methodically thumbed through the phone's photos (some of which no doubt showed Xavier himself) until she found a close-up of Sabina. She stuck the phone under Xave's nose.

Xave had been watching the proceedings wide-eyed. His feet now hit the floor. He got stood up and took the device.

Abigail had taken the picture at Sabina's birthday party, on the back porch of the house, with Celer lounging by the girl's feet in the warm sunshine. The paper hat on Sabina's head, which I had made, said *Happy 13th Birthday (again!)*, which was an in-joke. We had jumped from August of 79 AD to May of 2012, and it had seemed simpler to double celebrate her mid-July birthday than to have her lose almost a full year.

"Haven't seen her," Xave said of the picture. He was clearly more interested in the phone itself. Turning it over in his hand, he asked, "What is it?"

"A smartphone," Abigail said.

"A *smart* phone?" A look of curiosity and something close to satisfaction spread across his young face. "Hotdog! I knew it—our Time Machine idea will work. You're from the future!"

8

Abigail and Dr. Little had moved to one side of the room and launched into a whispered argument about the possible ramifications of what had just transpired. I heard Abigail say, "But Professor, if there *were* any ramifications on future events, I wouldn't have been able to show him the cell phone at all, right?"

"True, but that is not how we do things, haphazardly and without forethought. I object strongly. In the future I'll expect you to—"

"It worked, didn't it?"

"Yes, but that's hardly the only consideration, is it?"

Meanwhile the *other* professor (I couldn't help but think of him that way, even in his much younger incarnation) was still turning Abigail's phone over and over in his hand. "Where is the antenna? And the keys to work it? Does it sense thoughts somehow?" he mused.

It very definitely was not the moment to explain about touch-screen technology or the concept of a band antenna wrapped around the edge of a phone. When Abigail and Dr. Little rejoined us, Xave gave the phone a last look of wonder before handing it back to Abigail. "Have you really come to look for a girl? Because if you're here to try and prevent some future apocalypse, I'm ready to help. Tell me. I can handle it. What will it be? Nuclear war? Have the Soviets invaded us? Or is it some kind of global epidemic? Swine flu? The Philadelphia thing with the Legionnaires? That new hemorrhagic fever near the Ebola River?" Something seemed to occur to him and he went stiff, as if at military attention, and squared his shoulders. "It's us, isn't it? Gabriel, Lewis, and me. We are going to damage spacetime with our experiments, and you're here to fix things by killing us before we have the chance. That's it, isn't it? All right, I understand if it must be done…"

Dr. Little held up a hand. "Whoa. No to all of that. We really are just here to look for—that is to say, on the track of…" His face scrunched up as he tried to speak through History's latest blockage and trailed off.

Apparently Xave was not to know Sabina's real name yet. "Call her Sally," I suggested.

"Thank you, Julia. Yes, we're here to look for, er, Sally. She spent at least one night in the restroom in the student cafeteria, probably two," Dr. Little said. "That's all we know."

We would seriously need to sit down with Dr. Mooney—the future one—and have a conversation about this when we got home. Why had he never mentioned meeting us in 1976? An unsettling thought flew across my mind. Had the present-day Dr. Mooney known what Sabina's fate would be…and elected not to say anything, not even a reassuring *You'll find her*, because we wouldn't? Maybe something awful happened and he wanted to tell us but couldn't, since the events were locked in—we had to jump to 1976 and go through with the whole thing, as it was part of his past and had already taken place.

Xave's eyes followed Abigail's movements as she slid the phone back into the pocket of her jeans. "I have so many questions for you."

"We can't answer them," Dr. Little replied curtly.

"I'm going to guess based on that *smart* phone that you are not from this century. How far into the future are you from? The year 2000, just at the turn of the millennium? Or later? 2025? 2050? Any takers? Ballpark? And does everyone in the future wear those five-toed slip-ons?" Xave asked of Dr. Little's shoes.

"As I said, we can't answer your questions," Dr. Little repeated.

"Not even who's going to win the election next week? Gabe and I have a bet riding on it. A dollar each."

We didn't bother replying to his attempt at levity.

"I guess I'll just have to wait to find out who wins—I'm voting for Carter. I'd like to see a peanut farmer in the White House. All right, then. If I'm not to know what's going on or why you're really here, so be it." He gave a small shrug of acceptance. It was very much like Dr. Mooney to take an unexpected event like three time travelers stepping out from a janitor closet and into his office in his stride. He added, "Hey, can I at least tell Gabe about this?"

"Best not to," I said. "Sorry we can't say more, but we *do* need your help."

He sat back down at his desk. "To find this Sally?"

"Yes."

"Then I'll ask around and see if anyone has seen her."

"It might be worth checking at the dorm that's in the middle of the Science Quad," I suggested. Abigail had already gone inside, of course, but she hadn't checked every room. It was possible someone had taken Sabina in.

Xave's head flicked up at my suggestion. "You mean St. Olaf's? Why there?"

The correct answer to that was because St. Olaf's Hall was the site of STEWie's future home. We had already revealed too much about the future. I said, "Sally has a particular reason for going there."

"A *particular* reason? Boy, you are being mysterious, aren't you? Well, that's easy enough in any case—St. Olaf's is where I live. Can that little device spit out the photo of her, like a Polaroid? No? All right. Let me finish grading these papers—I need to get them back to the students by tomorrow, but all the math errors are just depressing me…Where was I? Yes, let me finish these, and then I'll ask around. Where can I find you?"

"By the Open Book," Dr. Little said as we headed for the door.

"I'll need some time. How about we meet up at five thirty, say?"

"Five thirty it is," I said.

"Catch you on the flip side."

I checked my watch. It was half past four, so we still had a good hour before meeting up with Xave. We had been poking our heads into various classrooms and residences and checking behind buildings. Just as we were about to go into the covered tennis courts, having strolled through the athletics pool facilities without attracting much attention, something occurred to me and I stopped.

"Hold on," I said.

Dr. Little and Abigail halted their step and turned to face me inquisitively.

"The house. My house, I mean." My bungalow wasn't my bungalow yet, or even my parents', but I should have thought of looking there at once.

We set a course for Elm Street, which was a fifteen-minute walk from campus in the direction the sun was heading in its setting arc. Crossing a three-way intersection that in the twenty-first century had a traffic light but only stops signs here, we left the hubbub of campus behind and entered the neighborhood I'd grown up in. The cars parked along the residential streets paid tribute to the decade, but otherwise it all looked the same as it did when Sabina and I had walked Wanda earlier today home-time. Ranch-style houses and compact bungalows occupied small, carefully tended yards. Pumpkins, scarecrows, and other Halloween decorations lined the front porches, and kids played outside on the low-traffic streets, waiting impatiently for dusk to arrive. We could hear them swapping costume ideas—the familiar ghosts and pirates, cowboys and princesses. The adults were also outside, raking the orange and red leaves, washing cars in driveways, gardening in the crisp fall day.

We turned onto Elm Street, which accommodated about half a dozen houses on each side and dead-ended in a small park. Mine was the third house on the right, with the front facing south. Even though I knew it would be there, I felt a stab of surprise at seeing the house. Instead of its home-time dusty blue with white trim, it was painted a hideous brown color.

"Eeek," Abigail said from beside me.

We strolled by the house, then looped around for a second look. The family occupying it—twin boys and their mother—was engaged in a window decoration project. They were taping up homemade paper skeletons. Their small dog yapped at us from the front yard. I assumed it was this family that would build the mother-in-law addition in the back for a relative in need of housing, because the addition wasn't there yet. Other details jumped out at me on the second pass: the weeping willow that would one day shade the front of the house, now scrawny and only head-high; the kids' matching bicycles carelessly left on the lawn; the mailbox across the street, freshly painted white.

"It's weird how much the house looks the same, except for that hideous brown, of course," Abigail said as we reached the corner and stopped under the sign that said *Elm Street* in one direction and *Cottonwood Way* in the other.

Dr. Little shook his head. "There's no sign of Sabina here. We should head back to see if Mooney has any news for us."

I held up a hand. "Hold on for a moment. I have an idea."

I turned back toward the house—there was no sidewalk, not then and not in the present, just neatly trimmed yards meeting asphalt—and took the stone path to the bungalow's front door. The mother, who was juggling tape in one hand and a drooping paper skeleton in the other, looked up at my approach. "Thank you, but we don't need any magazines. Or vacuum cleaners. Or encyclopedias."

"What? No, I'm not selling anything."

"And we already have a church."

"Not that either. I just—I wanted to ask if a girl stopped by your house sometime between mid-day Friday and today. She would have been a few years older than your kids, a teen."

She paused in the act of taping, and the skeleton's paper head drooped further. "I don't think so, but I'll ask. Mikey, Jimmy," she called out, "has a girl been by?"

The two kids, who were now wrestling a large pumpkin into place on the small front porch, called back with an indifferent "No, Mom," delivered in chorus. They were by the kitchen window, a square one that had always stuck and was impossible to open. It was half-open now, giving me a glimpse of the small fridge and kitchen cabinets inside. The wallpaper behind the cabinets was a medley of teapots—beige, pink, and white teapots. That wallpaper would become a family project for my parents and me—one Christmas vacation when I was in middle school, we had rolled up our sleeves and tackled it, peeling and scraping off each cutesy teapot segment over the course of a few days. At the end, we had painted the kitchen a cheery yellow.

The woman looked at me kindly. "Is she a runaway?"

"Not exactly. Just…lost."

"Do you want to leave a phone number in case she does stop by?"

I shook my head.

"Well, good luck finding her, honey." She resumed taping the skeleton.

I turned to leave. Emotions flooded me, memories of my own family taping up Halloween and Easter and Christmas decorations in those very same windows. My parents now lived in Florida, where they were in charge of a community of retirees not much older than themselves, but this was 1976. And in 1976 Mom and Dad were at St. Sunniva University, seniors embarking on a key year in their lives that would end in marriage and my birth—not in that order. I had been so worried about Sabina that I'd forgotten that I might run into them, even though it had been my main purpose in volunteering for Dr. Little's run in the first place.

We left the house behind us and headed back to meet Xave, crossing from the quiet suburban streets back onto the vibrant and busy campus. It dawned on me that it was highly unlikely that I *would* run into my parents. Even in 1976, the school probably had a body of at least a couple thousand students. Still, I couldn't help but keep an eye out for two special people in my life once we passed the first of the signs directing visitors to campus parking lots and various departmental buildings.

My musings had slowed me down—Dr. Little and Abigail were ahead of me, having already crossed the three-way stop sign intersection, and I picked up my pace. Or tried to...

Instead I ran smack into one of History's invisible walls, right at the curb, at the exact spot Dr. Little and Abigail had just passed before crossing to the other side of the street. It was like there was a *fourth* stop sign just for me. I watched as a bright red, two-door convertible with a young man at the wheel rounded the corner at a speed far exceeding the posted limit of thirty-five miles per hour. The driver ran the stop sign, as if he had taken the turn many times before and couldn't be bothered to heed the rules anymore. Had I stepped out onto the street, the car would have mowed me down.

I watched as the convertible sped away, the driver's shoulder-length blond hair buffeted by the wind. Then I was free. The whole thing had lasted maybe thirty seconds. I hurried across the road to catch up with Dr. Little and Abigail.

"There you are, Julia," Abigail said. She had clearly missed the whole incident.

"Sorry, I got time-stuck. Which was better than being struck by the car that just ran the stop sign."

I could almost see Dr. Little's ears perk up, though he seemed more interested in the scientific ramifications of what had happened than he was in my continued safety. "Ah. The opposite of a ghost zone, if you will. History protected you. If you had been splattered all over the pavement, it would have affected the driver's day, that of the ambulance personnel, and so on."

"Yes, and mine, too."

"Well, I'm glad the car didn't mow you down," Abigail said, a concerned look on her face.

"For a second there I thought I'd hit the wall because History was sending me back...you know, because of the matter you're studying, Dr. Little."

Dr. Little shook his head. "If History wanted to send you back, Julia, it wouldn't strand you by a stop sign. It would channel you in the direction of STEWie's basket by the Open Book, which is where we're heading anyway."

"I'm older than you by what, a month or so?" I asked as we resumed walking.

"Twenty-eight days."

"So I will be the first one to go, if these things happen in order."

"They may not. As you have just seen, History can be unpredictable. Let's pick up the pace—Mooney said to meet him at five thirty. It's past that now."

There was, however, no one waiting by the Open Book to meet us.

9

"He'll come," Abigail said after we'd waited by the sculpture for a good half an hour, during which time the sun had sunk under the horizon and the campus street lamps had started to flicker on. Students were gathering for some kind of rally in the plaza, but there was no sign of *our* graduate student. "He said he would, and Dr. Mooney always keeps his word, right?"

He usually did, this was true. "I imagine he'll show up if for no other reason than that he must be so curious about what we could tell him—this must be the most exciting thing that's ever happened to him. Speaking of which…Dr. Little, has Dr. Mooney ever said anything to you about having met us in the past?"

"No."

"And you, Abigail?"

Abigail shook her head. She was seated with her back against the sculpture with her knees drawn up. For some reason my mind interpreted the image in the fading light as if she were a Lilliputian leaning against a normal-sized book rather than a normal-sized person leaning against a large book.

"Well, he never said anything about it to me either," I said. "So what do we make of that?"

Abigail stuck up her chin. "He must have had a good reason."

"Humph," was all Dr. Little said.

I was with him on that one. I didn't like being kept in the dark.

Dr. Little was also on the ground, cross-legged on the grass. He had stepped into STEWie's basket already dog-tired from the triple pressure of being a new parent, teaching, and conducting research. The catnap in the physics courtyard had helped temporarily, but he was back to looking beat. I fought back a yawn myself and the impulse to lie down on the grass for just a brief moment. By now it was past midnight in our internal clocks. And here? I checked my watch. It was 6:15. Dusk came early in the fall.

"Why is no one doing what they're supposed to be doing?" Dr. Little complained after we had waited a while longer in silence. "Sabina is wandering around instead of waiting where she could easily be rescued. Mooney isn't here even though he said he would be. This is why I don't research *people*."

He meant historical figures, which is what almost every other professor and graduate student in the TTE department studied, in addition to doing their more technical work. I understood why he felt that way, even if he had phrased it strangely. He wanted his heroes to remain heroes. The more information the STEWie program gathered on a historical figure, the more *human*—and therefore imperfect—an image emerged. For example, a research team had recently happened to confirm that Beethoven was quite fond of cheap wine…*If you want your heroes to remain heroes, you best not look too closely*. It was the unwritten rule of time travel. Probably life itself, really.

"I don't know why Xavier Mooney didn't come, but for all we know Sabina could simply be time-stuck somewhere on campus," I said. The blanket, water bottle, and first aid kit had remained undisturbed, so we were fairly certain she hadn't come back to the Open Book and left again. "Once it gets completely dark, maybe she'll be able to emerge from her hiding spot, wherever that is, and make her way back here."

"And what's your hypothesis about Mooney, then? He's forty-five minutes late." The young professor fought off another yawn, as if irritated with his own body's behavior as well as that of the people around us. We were all hungry—the granola bars and water we'd shared while waiting had not gone far, and we had done a lot of walking. Dr. Little had budgeted for a short run, and in my haste to get going, I'd left my shoulder bag, which always contained an abundance of snacks, behind in the lab.

"I guess he must have changed his mind about coming for some reason, or got held up at his desk. Either way, I don't think there's any point in waiting here any longer. The cafeteria is where Sabina found shelter before, so she may come back for the night." I bent down to pick up the blanket, water, and first aid kit.

Abigail reluctantly got to her feet and dusted off her bottom. "I guess if the professor were coming, he'd have shown up by now."

Dr. Little pulled himself up too, but more slowly.

"You want me to carry the duffel bag for a bit?" I offered.

As if I had said something to impugn his manhood, Dr. Little heaved the bag up on his shoulder. "I'm fine. Let's go."

"I think I just saw her—well, a person in a white lab coat—going in *that* direction. Did you see her, Julia?"

Dr. Little gave Abigail an unconvinced look, clearly not sharing her excitement. "Lots of white coats on campus. Could have been a researcher coming to the rally straight from a chemistry or medical lab."

"Sorry, Abigail," I said, "I was looking in the other direction." I scanned the plaza crowd where she had pointed, in the direction of St. Olaf's Hall. Judging by the homemade cardboard signs the students were holding, it was a pro-Carter rally urging people to vote in the upcoming Tuesday election. Someone was getting ready to make a speech, but for the moment everyone was still milling around, making it impossible to determine whether Abigail really had glimpsed Sabina in Dr. Mooney's white lab coat. Complicating matters further, many of the rally attendees and those crossing the plaza by foot or bicycle were in Halloween costumes. "Why won't everyone stand still?" I complained. "Watch out for that bicyclist, Dr. Little!"

Dr. Little, standing with his feet apart, didn't bother moving. "I'm pretty sure History will not let me be hit by a cyclist, Julia. Just like it stopped you from being run over."

That may well have been true, but I still adopted a more careful approach, stepping aside to dodge the bicyclists weaving across the plaza around the pedestrians. I was still staring in the direction in which Abigail had thought she'd glimpsed Sabina, trying to see over people's heads, when a bike bell chimed behind me. I turned quickly, ready to jump out of the way again.

It was Xave, streaking across the green toward us, his head bedecked with a white wig. He came to a stop next to us and hopped off his bike, a red one that seemed to be an early version of

51

Scarlett, his future bicycle, as though parts from it would be incorporated into its successor.

"Where have you been?" Dr. Little demanded loudly, so as to be heard over the increasing chatter of the crowd.

"And a howdy to you too."

"You're an hour late."

"No, I'm not. We said half past five."

I double-checked my watch. It showed just about six thirty. Dr. Little checked his, which showed the same.

Xave looked from Dr. Little to me. "Don't you have daylight saving time in the future and all the annoying changes it entails?"

Dr. Little's mouth turned downward. I heard him swear under his breath as we moved toward a less busy spot by the cafeteria. "Right. It's October 31—DST ended last night. I still had my original run date in mind."

Xavier—the older one—had sent us forty-eight hours ahead of Dr. Little's original coordinates. Instead of being one o'clock when we'd arrived, apparently it had only been noon.

"I should have remembered that," Dr. Little continued in the tone of an academic mortified to have gotten something wrong. He adjusted his watch, and I did the same with mine. "We wasted the last hour of daylight waiting for Mooney to show up."

We had, but it was no one's fault. I said as much. "We rushed here to 1976 without much planning. And Steven, you haven't been getting enough sleep since Piper was born."

"That's no excuse." I couldn't tell if he was glaring at me because I had used his first name or what.

Xave raised an eyebrow at us. "So this is what time travel is like, huh? Girls lost in time. People bickering over an hour here and there."

"It does mess with your head," Abigail conceded.

"Far out. I'm looking forward to it."

"Well?" I demanded. "Did you ask around the physics building and St. Olaf's Hall?"

"I did."

"And?"

He shook his head at us. "No luck. Sorry."

We digested the news silently.

Xave regarded us for a moment, then said, "Look, it seems to me that what you need is a good meal and some rest, and then we can put our heads together and see what to do about finding Sally. Why don't you join me for"—he raised his voice as a speaker started shouting into a microphone, eliciting an approving roar from the crowd—"DINNER?"

Dr. Little gave him a frank look and shouted back through cupped hands. "It's not that easy...We can't exactly go WHEREVER WE WANT."

"History might STOP you, or something like that?"

"I CAN NEITHER CONFIRM OR DENY THAT. No more questions, MOONEY."

"Well, what would you do in my place? I'm burning with CURIOSITY."

"Sure, we can join you for just dinner," I said quickly as the speaker went temporarily quiet, getting in the words before Dr. Little had the chance to disagree. Xave had a point. We wouldn't be doing Sabina any good if we fainted from hunger. Besides, the cafeteria was where we wanted to be anyway, the likely place Sabina would return to as night fell, wherever she was at the moment.

Xave had locked his bicycle into an empty spot in the rack by the front doors. "Fair warning—the cafeteria food is really bogue," he threw over his shoulder as we followed him inside.

"Did he say *bogue*?" Abigail whispered to me. "What does that mean?"

"From what I know of cafeteria food, it can't mean anything good."

Long rows of green plastic tables, which had thankfully been changed out at some point before my arrival at St. Sunniva as an undergrad, formed the eating area of the cafeteria. Students sat at the mostly packed tables engaged in lively conversation over their dinner trays, except for a loner here and there reading a paperback. There was a somewhat larger number of women than men, which was not a surprise since the school had only turned coed in 1968 and I knew it had taken a good decade for the numbers to even out. No one had a laptop or a tablet or an e-reader or a smartphone, which was not a surprise of course, but I couldn't help but notice that it made for a more social setting. The only electronic device in sight was a radio blaring in one corner. I coughed. The place reeked of cigarettes. Still, they didn't mask the cooking scents wafting from the kitchen, and I suddenly realized how ravenous I was.

Xave pointed the three of us to a table that had just emptied, then came back after a minute to ask, "Scarily fried chicken or dismembered sausage links?"

At first I thought the attributes were related to the bogue quality of the food, but then I remembered it was Halloween. The staff must have chosen to get creative with their menu. "Fried chicken, I guess," I said.

Abigail nodded. "Same for me."

"Your wish is my command, ladies," Xave said. He turned to Dr. Little, who had slid his duffel bag under the table and taken a seat across from us. Dr. Little wrinkled his nose. "Isn't there anything...lighter? A vegetable would be good."

Dr. Little had grown up in California and earned his PhD at Berkeley before coming to St. Sunniva. He was not the only vegetarian in the state of Minnesota; they were just grossly outnumbered.

"Time travelers can't be choosers, but I'll see what I can do. I don't suppose you have any...funds to contribute? I'm just a poor graduate student."

Dr. Little dished out some cash from his travel wallet, and I said, "I'll help you carry, Xave." He and I got into the food line, exchanged some light chitchat about the election while waiting, and came back with fried chicken (which was a strange orange color), mashed potatoes (green), and corn on the cob (with pitchfork-shaped holders).

Abigail hesitated before digging in. "I hope Sa— Sally comes back here. It's getting really dark out there."

I was worried too—where could Sabina be?—but forced myself to eat. After all, none of us would be thinking clearly if we didn't nourish ourselves. The food coloring made for an unappetizing appearance, but it didn't change the taste of the chicken and mashed potatoes. Just standard cafeteria fare. Dr.

Little, who had stuck with the corn and mashed potatoes, seemed to be enjoying them just fine.

After a moment of quiet contemplation, Abigail dug in as well. "How's the chicken tonight?"

Gabriel. Gabe was dashing in a dark suit, with the upturned collar of the white shirt underneath tightly pinched by a tie. His hair was slicked and tied back to look short, and his mustache had been combed to a bushier version. I glanced from him to Xave and it sank in that their costumes were supposed to be of a young and an older Einstein. Gabriel was the young Einstein. Xave—dressed in a sweater, casual droopy pants, and the white wig—was the older Einstein; he had even dyed his mustache white, which I had somehow failed to notice. It wasn't bleached but covered in some kind of a white paint. I found myself hoping it was nontoxic food coloring, as it had started to flake as he ate.

Gabe had addressed the question to his friend and fellow grad student, all the while avoiding any eye contact with the rest of us. I studied him above my fork. This was strange. If I didn't know better, I would have thought History was making sure he didn't register our presence, but that made no sense. It was supposed to be the other way around. *Our* movements were supposed to be limited while we traveled, not those of the locals.

Xave waved his fork at the three of us. "Gabe, meet Julia, Abigail, and Dr. Little. They're visitors. You're not allowed to ask them anything."

Gabe didn't appear to have a problem with that request. He seemed too weighed down by what I suddenly understood was his own social anxiety to care why he wasn't expected to talk to us.

Xave told him, "The chicken's not awful."

Focusing on a spot on the floor, Gabe replied, "I'll be back with my tray," and left.

"Gabriel's a bit shy," Xave explained, and waved hello to a female student passing by our table. She waved back at him.

I opened my mouth to comment that we all knew Gabriel Rojas but thought better of it. It struck me that while we'd been able to fill one of STEWie's inventors in on the bare bones of our situation, we probably wouldn't be able to interact much with the other, if at all. Xave was a doer, his confidence in his pet project unshakable, so our presence was only confirmation of what he already knew with certainty—his time machine idea would work. Gabe, on the other hand, was a thinker, a worrier, a tight knot of social and other doubts. He obviously didn't like meeting new people, something he would mostly outgrow in his professorship, with his shyness morphing into excessive politeness in social situations. Learning where we were really from and that we had gotten here using a device he would have a hand in designing— well, that would have deeply affected the mild-mannered graduate student and sent History on a different path. Which explained why we'd been stuck in the janitor closet in the graduate student office earlier.

"Hey, before Gabe gets back, let me ask you this. The three of us—Gabe, Lewis, and I—we haven't been able to figure out how fast time streams for travelers relative to their home-time. Does it stream in parallel? Just nod if I'm correct…Faster? Slower?"

I saw Dr. Little bite his lip, as if to fight back the urge to show off his superior knowledge on the subject by giving a detailed answer, one involving the use of pencil and paper and lots of diagrams and equations. Gabe came back and took a seat on the side of Xave that was opposite to the three of us. The friends launched into an in-character discussion—Gabe, as the young Einstein, was arguing for the cosmological constant, whatever that was, while Xave, the older Einstein, was arguing against it. We heard the terms *field equation*, *spacetime*, and *relativity* bandied about with abandon.

Dr. Little just stared across the table at the two grad students as if jealous of the success and fame that awaited Xave and Gabe, and simultaneously disdainful that they were wasting time on Halloween fun instead of applying themselves in the lab. He caught my gaze, cleared his throat, and went back to eating.

The fried chicken and mashed potatoes were heavy and I fought off a yawn. We were all experiencing the time-travel version of jet lag, which really needed a name, I thought. *Time-travel lag*, perhaps. We had jumped from early evening home-time to one o'clock—no, noon—local time, which meant that it felt far later for us. I fought a follow-up yawn and transferred my attention to the students streaming into the cafeteria, keeping an eye out for Sabina.

There was no sign of her, but then someone else came in.

I dropped my fork into the tiny mound of green mashed potatoes left on my plate and instinctively started to rise to my feet, but History sent me right back down.

The *someone* was my mother, Missy Donovan, before she became one half of Mr. and Mrs. Olsen. She was in a group of five or six students who seemed to be using the cafeteria as a shortcut; having streamed in through one door, they were immediately heading for the other. Mom's blonde hair had been blow-dried into a big and puffy feathered look, a la Farrah Fawcett. Her cheeks were plump and smooth, and there was a spring in her step I hadn't seen in a long time. A moment later she was gone, the far door of the cafeteria having closed behind the group.

"Julia?" Abigail asked. "Something wrong?"

"Hmm? Nothing. Just saw…a familiar person. Not Sally," I said quickly, before Abigail could get her hopes up.

I went back to eating, but not before I did a quick mental calculation, counting back from my day of birth, April 1 of 1977. My mother had five months to go in her pregnancy. Did that mean she was aware of it already? It wasn't anything I had personal experience with. If she knew, was she being responsible and all that? No. She'd had a cigarette in one hand and had taken a leisurely puff on it as she walked, before passing it on to another student. Maybe they didn't know that kind of stuff was bad in the seventies? The campus ban on smoking was a good twenty years away. I had never seen her smoke—she must have given it up after I was born.

I also couldn't help but notice that the person she'd passed the cigarette to was not Dad but some other student, a tall, broad-shouldered guy with dark hair. Granted, I'd only gotten a quick glimpse of his back, but Dad was more of an average height, blond, and had a different line to his shoulders.

There was something else. Seeing my mother, I had felt odd, shaky, as if I had instantly come down with a bad bout of the flu and it had narrowed my breathing passages. The feeling—so brief I couldn't be sure it wasn't just my imagination—passed as quickly as it had come on.

Abigail and I stayed behind as the cafeteria slowly emptied and the kitchen staff cleaned up. Dr. Little, who couldn't function any longer without sleep, had headed to Xave's room in St. Olaf's Hall, having taken one of the two-way radios. Xave was going to leave for the dorm Halloween party with Gabe after letting Dr. Little into the room.

Abigail and I slipped into the women's restroom as soon as the janitor had finished up inside. We waited in silence until all sounds of activity died down and the lights in the building turned off one by one. The rally outside had lasted a good while, but even the most strident Carter supporters had other places to be on a weekend night.

"Let's prop open a side door so Sabina can come back in," Abigail suggested, her face shadowy above her cell phone, which we were using as a flashlight.

We peered out of the restroom and slipped into the hallway when we determined the coast was clear.

Looking for an object to prop open the cafeteria doors with, I spotted a magazine someone had left behind on one of the green tables. I rolled it up—it was *Mad*, with some kind of *Star Trek* spoof, the *Star Trek Musical*, on the cover. "Oh, that's a collectible. We should bring it back with us," Abigail suggested. I cracked open the back cafeteria door and stuck the magazine into the small space. Cold, fragrant autumn air wafted in, mixing with the smell of cleaning chemicals, which had lingered after the janitor and the kitchen-cleaning crew left for the day.

There was nothing to do but head back to the restroom and wait. "Guess it's all right to turn on the lights now," Abigail said. "I don't want to completely drain my phone battery."

The couches were in the front of the restroom, set in an L-shape and offset from the plumbing part by a wall. Abigail took the smaller couch, a two-seater, while I took the other. We made ourselves as comfortable as possible, our heads pointed toward the bend of the L. I offered Abigail our blanket, the one Nate had sent with us, but she shook her head and curled up under her coat.

I folded the blanket into a pillow and lay on my back, staring up at the tiled ceiling. We had decided to leave the overhead light on, a small beacon to Sabina under the door. The tiles were a creamy white and there were sixteen of them, with lights set into four middle ones. As tired as I was, I was too wired to sleep and I suspected the same was true of Abigail. I heard her give a little sigh, but it was a sound of dissatisfaction, not of sleepiness.

"Julia?" she said.

"Yes?"

"Do you really think someone did let Sabina into the lab? Watched as she wrote the note, helped her into the basket?"

Having had time to think about it, I'd decided that it was unlikely. I said as much and explained my reasoning. "No one who belonged there and knew the door code would have made the mistake of misinterpreting the date. He or she would have known that STEWie was set for 1976, not the first century."

"True. Unless they didn't care where Sabina was jumping to, just as long as she jumped somewhere." Abigail was silent for a moment, then said, "I'm not saying it was him, but Dr. Mooney did seem a little *odd* about the whole thing back in the lab, didn't he?"

She had said it in a quiet voice, as if mortified to be voicing suspicions about her beloved professor.

He *had* sounded odd, but we now had an explanation as to why. "I'm pretty sure it was because he remembered meeting us in 1976 but didn't want to say so for whatever reason. I believe him, though; I can't imagine he gave her the code. Maybe Kamal or Jacob or one of the other students did it without realizing how she'd use the information." I decided that it might be good to talk about other matters to get our mind off Sabina, so I asked, "How's your thesis going, Abigail? You said you've been working on a new chapter?"

Her thesis topic was Marie-Anne Lavoisier, wife and lab partner of the eighteenth-century chemist Antoine Lavoisier and a chemist in her own right—she of the apparatus sketching.

Abigail propped herself up on one elbow to face me. "The thesis? Slow, I guess. I've been writing Chapter 4, but I'm not happy with the first three and want to redo them. I'm thinking of overhauling my outline and choosing an entirely new approach to presenting the work...My defense is scheduled for early in the spring and I have all the historical data I need, so I'm done with my STEWie runs. Which is good, I guess."

"But you're not sure how to weave the results into a solid thesis?"

"No, that's not it."

"You wish you'd chosen a different topic?" This was pretty much guaranteed with all grad students at some point in their career, sometimes even long after they'd graduated and left school.

She laughed outright at that and said, "Well, yes. A topic more hands-on, perhaps, not involving people. Now I sound like Dr. Little. No, the real problem is that when I finish the thesis and graduate, my funding will stop."

And there it was. It was a simple statement that spoke to a far larger story, again a familiar one. Abigail supported herself with a research assistantship from Dr. Baumgartner. Since there just aren't enough postdoc and junior professor spots to support all graduating PhDs, most leave for teaching or research jobs at other schools or institutions after graduation or, more likely, enter the corporate workforce. It's a problem every grad student faces as his or her graduation date nears—what to do next?—and more than one student dealing with this conundrum had been known to drop by my office for a sympathetic ear, a cookie, and a list of alumni for networking. In general, the students tended to want to stay in academia, since that was all they had ever known. But it wasn't realistic, not for all of them. I wanted Abigail to be one of the ones who could stay, if that was what she really wanted to do.

"Has Dr. B said anything about a postdoc for you?" I asked.

"Not yet."

"But you do want to continue on?"

"Well, wouldn't you? I've been lucky enough to get to use STEWie for my research. The prospect of working anywhere else, where I might not be able to time-travel, seems so—I don't know—boring? Even if the salary is larger and the health benefits better. But now that I'm responsible for supporting Sabina, maybe I do need those things. A steady job with a good salary and benefits, I mean. I didn't used to worry about such material goals, but now...Plus I don't want her to have to move or change high schools."

So it wasn't just the money that worried her. A career in academia entailed relocation from position to position as funding necessitated, at least until the holy grail of tenure was achieved. Thornberg had a five-year high school, grades eight through twelve, giving Sabina plenty of time to get acclimated before having to move on. Or that had been the plan, at least.

I sat up on the couch. "You know you can always count on me, don't you? Nate feels the same way—we're Sabina's honorary aunt and uncle. And Helen and Xavier might as well be her grandparents, they dote on her so much. Kamal, too; he's like an older brother."

Kamal Ahmad was Dr. Mooney's senior grad student and one of Sabina's biggest fans.

"Thanks, Julia. It's going to be all right, you know. I have a feeling we'll get her back safe and sound. We can figure everything else out later." Nestling back into her coat, she asked, "So who did you see? Or is it *whom*? During dinner, I mean."

"It's whom. And I saw my mother."

"Wow, your mom. I mean, I never knew my parents, so I have nothing to compare to, but I can imagine that it had to have been weird and strange."

"It was. Do you hear that?"

Muffled voices were audible outside, the sound drifting under the closed restroom door. We rose to check, but it turned out to be nothing more than already-inebriated Halloween partiers crossing the plaza. We heard the faint chime of the midnight hour on the campus tower not long after.

"So it was strange to see your mother," Abigail prompted me once we were back on the couches, like two patients undergoing simultaneous psychotherapy.

"I got an odd vibe, like History was clearing its throat, reminding me that I can't stay here much longer. Just wanted to mention it in case I suddenly have to run out." Dr. Little had told me that if History decided to send me home, I'd feel a sudden tightening in my chest, as if the air was getting thin in all directions but the one leading to STEWie's basket. It had felt like that for just the briefest of moments, then it stopped.

"It could just be a reaction to seeing your mother when she was young," Abigail suggested half jokingly.

"Not only young, but younger than I am now."

"So…?"

"Hmm, what?" I was lying on my back again, looking up at the creamy white ceiling.

"There's something else that's bothering you about your mother, right?"

"Well, there's…a personal matter I was hoping to look into. My brown eyes and hair, if you must know."

At this, Abigail pushed herself back up on one elbow and looked over at me. "Why, what's wrong with your hair and eyes?"

"Nothing, other than the fact that my parents are both blond and blue-eyed, as befitting their Norwegian roots."

She raised an eyebrow in my direction. "You know you can change your hair color, right? I do it every other week practically. As to eye color—I'm far from an expert, but I don't think two blue-eyed parents always equals a blue-eyed child, just usually."

"I like the brown. I just don't like the potential implications."

"Is that why you volunteered for Dr. Little's study?"

"How do you know about that?"

"I saw the form you filled out. It was in the recycling bin. So are you wondering if you're adopted? Did you ever ask your parents about it?"

I took a moment before replying. My parents had driven up to see me after our return from Pompeii, obviously thrilled to hear that I was alive and well. After a somewhat harried morning spent ensuring I had enough instant coffee in the cupboard and clean guest sheets, I'd heard them open the garage door, for which they still had the code. I went outside to greet them and gave them both hugs. They were looking a little older—I had not seen them in eight months by the calendar—but they looked tan and healthy enough.

"We never did think you were dead, Jules," my mother said at once. "Kept expecting you to come back every day…and you finally did."

"It sounds as if you had quite an adventure. Where is the Roman girl?" This from Dad as they followed me inside. "I want to ask her about gladiator fights—what they were like and if there was betting and stuff. You didn't get to see one, did you? Maybe get video of it?" He gave me another hearty hug around the shoulders.

I explained that Sabina was not there to greet them, as Abigail had taken her to the mall to buy her clothing and other necessities—Sabina had arrived in the twenty-first century with only her dog and the clothes on her back, so she needed everything: tops, pants, dresses, shoes, undergarments, pajamas. It was a long list. I expected that they would be gone the whole afternoon.

Mom elbowed Dad—"You can ask her about gladiator fights later"—and pushed a potted plant into my hands. Had I been gone so long they'd forgotten about my tendency to kill all flora in my care?

"It's not for you," my mother reassured me. "We thought Sabina might like a present from Florida. It's a lemon tree that she can grow in her room. We also got her a pair of sunglasses and a beach towel for when you visit. I would have gotten a bathing suit, but I didn't know her size, so I left it for—"

I held up a hand. "Slow down, Mom, there's plenty of time to buy her presents for birthdays and such." I set the tiny lemon tree on the kitchen table and offered them pop from the fridge. "Sabina and Abigail should be back for dinner, and you'll both get to meet them then."

Dad's eyes lit up. "Dinner? Should we go to Ingrid's for lingonberry pancakes?"

They didn't have lingonberry pancakes in Fort Myers.

Mom elbowed him again. "It could be that Julia is cooking for us. Are you, darling?" she asked a little apprehensively.

"The possibility never crossed my mind. Ingrid's it is."

My Pompeii adventure had left me pensive, perhaps even obsessed with the big mysteries of life—time, history, death—and personal ones as well. The question had been burning on my tongue for their whole visit, but how was I supposed to broach the subject of genetics, hair color, and paternity over lingonberry pancakes?

I answered Abigail truthfully. "I did try to work it into the conversation once, but they didn't seem to notice. And asking outright felt too much like I didn't trust them. When I was younger, I researched it a bit and found an answer I liked—that eye and hair color follow complex patterns of inheritance, and hidden traits can sometimes skip a generation or two. So you're right: blond parents can have a brunette, brown-eyed child…but it's very rare. I decided

I was that rare case and that there had to be a dark-eyed, dark-haired ancestor deep in the family tree. Then I got the opportunity to time-travel."

"I've heard about this phenomenon from other people, how it's easier to broach a subject with just about anyone on the planet than with your own parents. To me it seems like it would be easier just to ask, but what do I know? I've never had that particular relationship. Did she have a pregnancy belly?"

"What, my mother, you mean? In the cafeteria?"

"It's what you need to know, right? It would settle the question of whether or not you were adopted. Or was it too early in the pregnancy?"

"I couldn't tell either way. She had a coat on. And, well, she was a bit chubbier than she is in the present."

"If we get a chance, we can spy a bit on your parents after we find Sabina. Your birthday is on April 1, so let's see…" She counted nine months back on her fingers. "July of this year would be the time to look and see what they were up to. That was what you were hoping to do when you volunteered for Dr. Little's study, wasn't it?"

"I don't know what I was hoping to do," I answered honestly. "Have you—forgive me for asking this—have you ever wanted to use STEWie to find out who your own parents are?"

"Of course. Who wouldn't? All I was told is that something in their life circumstances prohibited them from raising me. Growing up and moving from foster family to foster family, I always pictured them—and I know this is silly—as secret agents. Their line of work involved too much danger and international travel for them to take care of a kid…As I said, I know it's silly, but I still imagine them keeping an eye on me from afar. As to using STEWie to find out— even if it were allowed, I'm pretty sure reality would not live up to my imagined scenario."

It was a strange conversation to be having in the pitch-dark of the restroom. (We had turned the light off after deciding that Sabina might be spooked by it rather than enticed.) I thought again of my own parents, who called every weekend to see how I was doing, and all my personal problems suddenly felt so very small. I had just gotten a postcard (my parents were the only people I knew who still sent them) telling me they were on a Key West cruise with some of their charges and were planning on driving up for a visit before winter set in.

Abigail cleared her throat. "I suppose everybody must have *something* personal they'd wish to check on or bear witness to or whatever."

"Except for Dr. Little." We chuckled again at that, but in the back of my mind I wondered if the young professor was as uninterested as he seemed. You never know with people.

Apparently Abigail had had the same thought. "Did you notice the strange thing about his study?"

"What strange thing?"

"He wants to zero in on his personal cutoff date in History, compare the results with volunteers with similar birth dates, and look for a pattern."

"Right. So what's strange about it? It sounds like a legitimate research topic."

"His methodology for himself differs from what he's doing with his volunteers. For his own runs, he started in September 1976 and intends to use STEWie to edge closer to his birth date in April."

"And…?"

"It's not the most efficient and cost-effective method."

I sat up on the couch again, though I couldn't see her in the dark. "Hold on. What would be more efficient?"

"The approach he's using for the seven volunteers he enlisted for his study. Start with a person's birth date—a STEWie run guaranteed to fail, thus saving energy and resources—then shift the arrival date back day by day until History allows the person to jump. Or he could run a binary algorithm between his birth date and his date of conception. You know, start at the halfway point and see if the run takes, then halve the next time period, and so on."

"That is strange, I suppose, that he's using a different algorithm for himself than for his volunteers…Perhaps there's a technical reason for it. But wouldn't it be funny if it turned out that he was curious about something, too, for all his protestations?" I slid back down into the couch. "His family's all the way in California, though, so it probably has nothing to do with them. He did seem very familiar with the layout of the physics building—perhaps he's researching some finer point of STEWie's development and it's legit after all."

"That's what I was thinking—that he's got a side research topic that he doesn't want to tell people about for fear of his idea being stolen."

"Well, he wouldn't be the first."

"Speaking of ideas, I still can't get over that blackboard in the physics grad student office. Young Dr. Mooney and Dr. Rojas are certainly nothing like I would have imagined. I pictured them as being very serious and focused. Also, *mustaches*?"

We shared another chuckle over this. Then, in somewhat of a change of topic, Abigail added, "Too bad Nate couldn't come with us. He would have enjoyed seeing them. But then he's already here."

And so he was. I did the math. "He's five years old and living up in Duluth with his grandparents while his parents finish up college. His mom had him while she was still in high school, did you know that? It was a bit of a scandal apparently."

"Huh. I thought I was the only one with a weird childhood."

"Everyone's childhood is weird…Even if it felt idyllic at the time, when you look back and think about things you realize it wasn't always as idyllic as it seemed. That doesn't stop the nostalgia, though." Then I remembered that it was Abigail I was talking to. I wished I had a box of cookies to offer her. "Of course, most childhoods aren't as weird as yours, I suppose."

"Don't worry, I get what you're saying. Besides, I think Sabina has us all beat when it comes to weird childhoods."

"She does, doesn't she?"

As we drifted into silence, I rubbed my eyes and didn't manage to suppress a yawn—the time-travel lag had kicked in with a wallop. Still, I fought to stay awake, my senses attuned to the sound of footsteps in the hallway. Meanwhile, Abigail's breathing had turned to a soft snore. There were plenty of other sounds, too: Halloween-related joviality drifted in from outside, the large fridge in the food-prep part of the cafeteria crackled occasionally, and the water pipes made mysterious noises, as water pipes tend to do. I started making a mental list of what we should do if Sabina didn't appear by morning. We'd broaden our search beyond campus to all of Thornberg, tape up posters telling her to come back to the Open Book, enlist the help of campus security…

The next thing to happen was a voice crackling in through the two-way radio. Groggily, I fought the coat to retrieve the radio from one of its pockets.

It was Xave. He sounded a little hoarse but jaunty. "Morning! I'm a little worse for wear"—*crackle*—"what a party it was."

The transmission was garbled with interference.

"More importantly"—*crackle*—"found—"

"Who's on this channel?"

"Your—"

I sat up, pressed the button on my end, and commanded, "Can you repeat that, Xave? Over."

"I said, *I think I found your Sally.*"

PART TWO:
THE
BOOK
CLUB

10

Abigail and I grabbed our things and hurried out of the cafeteria, attracting odd looks from arriving kitchen staff, but eager to see Sabina. The plaza was deserted in the chilly dawn of a new day, other than for a few volunteers setting up a polling station outside the Registrar's Office for tomorrow's election. At the other end of the plaza, St. Olaf's Hall looked out of place in the Science Quad next to department and classroom buildings. As we went up its brick path, the administrator in me noted that the steps leading to the front door were not handicap-accessible; if the building had been of any historical significance rather than just a five-floor cement block, a ramp could have been added and the front door widened. Instead, new student housing units would go up on the east side of campus and the building would be torn down. But that was years in the future. For now it was here, stained cement and all.

We went in through the unlocked front door. There was no hall monitor in the small common area just inside, only three students asleep in easy chairs, all of them still in last night's Halloween costumes. An old-fashioned-looking TV with a rabbit-ears antenna showed only silent static.

Following Xave's directions, Abigail and I took the stairs to the fifth floor—the elevator had an *Out of Service* sign taped to it—and knocked on the door that bore the number 510, then entered after Xave shouted out a peppy, "Come in!"

Abigail and I looked around the room.

"Where is she?" I asked.

Xave was draped over his desk chair, his legs stretched out on either side, his head resting on its back like he was a tired thinker. The room was otherwise empty.

Dr. Little came out of the bathroom, drying his hair with a towel. "Ah, there you are."

"You said you found her, Xave. Where is she?" I repeated. I almost bent down to check under the bed.

"Sally? I did," Xave said tipsily from under the puffy Einstein wig. His breath stank of beer and cheese. "Or at least I *think* I found her."

Dr. Little took over. "She must have come here to St. Olaf's yesterday evening, after Abigail caught a glimpse of her in the plaza, leaving. If only we hadn't wasted that hour by the Open Book doing nothing…I don't know if she came here looking for help, or if she was drawn to the spot because it will one day house the Time Travel Engineering lab."

"It will? Really?" Xave said, almost toppling off his chair in surprise. Luckily, in his state the odds were good that he wouldn't remember hearing that particular fact.

Dr. Little ignored the interruption. He looked alert, like the night's sleep had been restful, and there was a fresh T-shirt under his denim vest. Abigail's clothes and mine were rumpled from spending the night on the restroom couches, and I hadn't even thought to bring a toothbrush along, but I didn't care, not if we were on the verge of finding Sabina. He went on: "Besides being co-ed, this dorm is mixed between senior undergrads and grad students. The women undergrads are on the first two floors, and the men are on the third and fourth. The top floor, where the rooms have private bathrooms, is reserved for grad students like Mooney here who—"

"Can't afford to live off campus. Also, no car. Hold on, my visitors…from the future…" the professor-to-be said, stumbling a bit over the words. "Let me close the door so that no one overhears your…*futuristic* stuff." He rose up from the chair, staggered where he stood, and leaned over to shut the door Abigail and I had left open in our hurry. He tumbled back into the chair, almost missing it, and murmured something about needing coffee. Besides the desk, with its stacks of textbooks and notebooks, Xave's tiny room held a bed, a floor lamp, and a dresser. There were posters on the walls (one of Jane Fonda as Barbarella, another of the periodic table) and a pile of dirty clothes not too well hidden under the bed. The trash bin by the desk needed emptying and was overflowing with empty snack bags and candy wrappers—Xave had a bit of a sweet tooth, which would contribute to his health problems in later years.

"It seems a woman senior took Sally in for the night," Dr. Little went on, still with the same maddening deliberation. "There were people going in and out of the dorm all day because of the Halloween party downstairs in the recreation room, so I suppose Sally wouldn't have stood out—lots of people needed a place to crash for the night. What did you say was the senior's name, Xave, the one who took Sally in?"

"Gil—Gilb—why can't people have simpler names?" Xave finally spit out in one long breath, "Gilberte Dubois. Canadian. Room 104. The undergrads share rooms. Gilberte's roommate, Jenny, said a freshman wandered in sometime during the early evening. They guessed that she was a foreign exchange student."

I wanted to know everything. "Are we sure it's her? Did Jenny say what her name was? What did she look like?"

"Jenny said that she—the freshman, not Jenny—was wearing a joke Halloween costume. An ancient Roman scientist. A lab coat over a dress and sandals. A Roman *scientist*," he repeated, chuckling over the concept.

"Never mind the costume. Then what happened?" I asked.

"Jenny and Gilberte lent her a pillow and blanket for the night and let her use Jenny's bed." Xave added in a slow afterthought, "Jenny wasn't interested."

"In sleep?" Abigail had gone to perch on the edge of the windowsill, as if needing to sit down to keep her impatience at bay. "Jenny was at the party all night?"

"She was, but I meant in going out with me. I asked her to join me for a breakfast coffee, but she said no." Xave looked saddened by the memory.

Even if I hadn't known for a fact that he would end up finding somebody who was perfect for him, no matter their later marital issues, I wouldn't have been interested in his dating problems at the moment. I breathed a sigh of relief. "So she's in Room 104 downstairs?"

We had found her. It was over. I hadn't solved the mystery of my parentage, but that could wait for another day.

"I didn't think she'd come here." Dr. Little. said, still standing immobile. Why wasn't he gathering his sleeping mat and other things from the floor so we could pick up Sabina and be on our way? Was he time-stuck in the open bathroom door, towel in hand?

Apparently not, only dissatisfied with himself. "I should have instigated a search of the premises last night. My lack of sleep contributed to a poor handling of the problem. I apologize. I assumed she'd go back to the cafeteria restroom to sleep. It seemed logical."

I didn't bother reminding him that like he himself had pointed out, people rarely act on logic and more often on what feels *right*. Coming to St. Olaf had felt right to Sabina.

Xave's white Einstein wig had slid over his forehead to the bridge of his nose. His head was down on the back of his chair again. I thought I detected the faint sound of snoring from underneath the wig.

"It doesn't matter," I said to Dr. Little. This was no time to coddle his bruised academic ego. "Let's go get her. Room 104, you said?"

He shook his head. "You're not understanding."

"What are we not understanding?" Abigail asked.

Xave gave a half snore, which woke him up. He mumbled from under the Einstein wig, "They've all gone…Udo's book club."

He wasn't making any sense. More worrisomely, neither was Dr. Little. I looked from one to the other. "What book club? What are you two talking about?"

Dr. Little draped his towel over the bathroom doorknob. "The students in the dorm's book club—they've gone away…and Sally left with them."

"Where did they go?"

Xave's Einstein wig slid to the floor and his head shot up. He said quite lucidly, "Udo, Gilberte, and the others left bright and early this morning on a midterm break to parts unknown. Your Sally is not on campus anymore."

11

"We'll just have to get a car ourselves and go after her. Dr. Mooney—I mean Xave—do you own a car?" I turned to him before remembering that he had already mentioned that he didn't. "Well, we'll have to get one somehow. Or a bus or taxi, if we can catch—"

"That's linear thinking," Dr. Little cut me off. He still looked pained that he had failed to discover that Sabina had been so close, only four floors down, and angry at himself for having missed something obvious—for the second time in as many days. I guessed that he was worried about looking foolish in front of Xavier Mooney, who would one day have a vote as to whether tenure would be offered to our young professor from California. I doubted Xavier would judge Dr. Little on an incident that had happened thirty-some years in the past and which he had never once mentioned. But it did make me wonder yet again why he'd never said anything about meeting the three of us.

"You have a better idea?" I asked Dr. Little as I joined Abigail and him by the window, where he was rolling up his sleeping mat.

"Obviously we have to go after her," Dr. Little said, maneuvering the mat into the duffel. "Just not in a car or bus."

For a moment I thought he was suggesting that we find a helicopter or plane, but Abigail caught on to his meaning. "The Slingshot."

"The what?" Xave asked from across the room.

Dr. Little shot him a look, and Xave met his stare through half-closed eyelids. "I do believe I'll go downstairs in search of that cup of coffee. I can tell when I'm not...*wanted*."

Once the door had swung shut behind him, I nodded. "I get it. We'll jump ahead and catch up with—did you say it was a book club?—wherever they have gone." Xave had said *parts unknown*, but

I assumed it was just a figure of speech. With Slingshot 2.0, we could instantly meet up with the book club; it would only be a matter of calculating the coordinates. We had located Sabina; we just needed to jump ahead to meet her. Only…

"What is it, Julia?" Abigail asked.

"Don't you two think it's odd that Sabina was able to hitch a ride?"

"You're worried she'll never be heard from again because she got into a strange car? What could be safer than being in the company of a book club, for heaven's sake?" Dr. Little said.

"It's just…a bad feeling." I knew he didn't think much of feelings in the context of time-travel mechanics, so I attempted a different explanation. "As a time traveler, she shouldn't be able to interact quite this much with the locals, should she? I mean, we did in Pompeii, but that was because most of the town did not have long to live, as awful as that sounds. And *we* fit into near time, but she doesn't, not yet."

"I wouldn't read too much into it. If there's one thing I've learned, it's that just as you can unexpectedly become time-stuck, the opposite can happen as well. You waltz with ease into a situation in which you have no logical place. Sometimes the bold move accomplishes what the stealthy one can't. Sabina walked into St. Olaf's and everyone mistook her for a freshman in a Roman costume. Could anyone have predicted that?"

Abigail had a different explanation. "Weren't people in the seventies on drugs much of the time—LSD and so on?"

"Well, I don't know about *much* of the time," I said.

"Maybe everyone is just so used to being in a haze and seeing weird things that a person showing up out of nowhere is no big deal. Speaking of which, you don't think Xave is high on something, do you?"

"Just alcohol," I said.

"Did you know LSD stands for lysergic acid diethylamide and is made from a rye fungus?" Dr. Little said in an educational (but not very helpful at the moment) note. "It is rather unfortunate that Mooney chose last night to get inebriated. He just kept repeating that they—the book club members—were headed to a tree."

"I'll get him back," I said. "He's probably downstairs—I noticed a coffee pot by the TV."

He wasn't downstairs. He was slumped against the wall just outside the room, on the hallway floor with his knees drawn up, snoring.

"Gone east," he mumbled when we tried to shake him awake. "Tree."

I left Abigail and Dr. Little to the task and went downstairs to fetch coffee. The three students in their Halloween costumes were still asleep in front of the old-fashioned-looking TV. I reached for one of the mugs stacked on a tray next to the coffee percolator, then changed my mind.

The door of Room 104 was shut. I hesitated, then raised a hand to knock, figuring that asking Gilberte's roommate, Jenny, where the book club had gone might be faster than trying to sober up Xave. History had other plans for me; my knuckles barely grazed the wood, hard as I tried. There was an ABBA poster on the door, with the members of the Swedish pop group paired off on a park bench, Anni-Frid and Benny smooching and Agnetha and Björn side by side. The poster seemed to mock me, as if it were underlining that I was misplaced in time.

I went back to plan A—sobering up Xave. I softly walked past the sleeping students to the humming percolator, which one of them must have turned on before drifting off in an easy chair. The mugs looked reasonably clean, if mismatched and slightly dinged. Just typical dorm items.

I carried the mug back up the four flights of stairs to find Xave still slumped against the wall, gently snoring. Dr. Little was standing with his hands at his waist, like a two-sided teacup, tapping an impatient foot. Abigail turned up her hands at my approach. "Are we sure he's not high on something?"

I squatted down with the mug in my hand. Xave's eyes were soon open, though he was still a bit greenish around the cheeks. It took all three of us to pull him to his feet and steady him. Once we had Xave safely back inside his room and in the chair and he had imbibed more of the coffee, Abigail knelt down next to him. "Prof— I mean, uh, Xave. Where did they take Sally?"

He looked at Abigail with moist eyes and gave a small shrug, not of lack of concern but an indication of his limited knowledge of the matter. "East. Tree."

"The East Coast, you mean? But where?"

He shook his head.

Abigail's eyes were wide. I explained that I had no luck knocking on Jenny's door and voiced the problem. "The East Coast—that's like ten states and a thousand miles."

"Closer to fifteen states and two thousand miles, Julia." Dr. Little spotted a wayward hairbrush that had rolled out of his duffel bag and sprang on it. "We need a more precise location, obviously."

"Xave, did Jenny say anything else?" Abigail asked. "Try to remember. It's really important."

"Jenny…We talked about why I like physics and why she likes chemistry, which turned out to be the same reason—the building blocks of the universe…Then we got into politics for a bit and the election. She's voting for Ford—what are you gonna do?…What else? She likes Elvis…Hey, I should've asked if she wants to go to one of his concerts sometime. I don't know why I didn't think of that."

I was ready to shake him to get him to focus on the problem at hand, but Abigail guided him back with a gentler approach. "What exactly did Jenny say about Sally? Can you recall?"

"She didn't call her Sally—she just said a costumed freshman dressed as a Roman scientist." He chuckled at this again, but quietly, as if it hurt his head. "They took her in, offered her a bed, and that was when Jenny came to the party. I ran into her just as the party was heating up. Dawn. She was mad at her roommate, Gilberte, who couldn't be bothered to clean up her half of the room *before leaving for the week with her stupid book club.*"

The last bit was clearly a quote.

"So where did the book club go?" Abigail asked.

"Don't think Jenny knew. Wait. She did say that the Roman scientist girl wanted to get to the ocean, and that was why she decided to go with the book club."

"They're on their way to the ocean?" I said with a sudden uncomfortable feeling in the pit of my stomach. I met Abigail's eyes over Xave's head. Sabina had waited two days for us to come for her. When we hadn't, she had jumped at the chance to get to the ocean. It wasn't surprising. Sabina's frequent daydream—what I imagined her thinking about when she sat on the shores of Sunniva Lake—was to take a boat across the "big water" we had shown her on the map of the world, all the way to Pompeii. "Just for visit, yes?" she often liked to say, and we had promised her we would arrange the trip one day. She knew the town would be empty, but she wanted the chance to walk its stone streets once more, even if only as a tourist.

"Xave, you mentioned something about a tree before," I said.

His head shot up too fast and he said, "Ow. Yes, some kind of tree came into it."

"What kind of tree?" I asked as patiently as I could muster.

He shook his head at me.

"This line of questioning is doing us no good," Dr. Little said. "They're coming back in a week? Then the easiest thing is to jump ahead in time and meet them here."

"Won't work," I said.

Dr. Little sent a glare in my direction that was meant to remind me that I was just a dean's assistant. I shot him a look back and explained, "Sally is not going to return to St. Sunniva, not with the book club."

"Exactly," Abigail said.

Dr. Little stared at us as if we'd simultaneously gone mad. "Why on earth not?"

"Because of the ocean and the ships and everything. Just take our word for it." I tried to think clearly. "Can't we just use the Sling—the device we have at our disposal—to jump to early this morning and stop her from getting in the car in the first place?"

This time it was Dr. Little's turn to say, "Won't work. Even if we *could* jump to early morning—and we can't because we're present already, me in Mooney's room and you and Abigail in the women's restroom—there would be nothing we could do. It's already happened. She got in the car and they've all left. We need to catch up to where she is *now*, at this moment. Only we have no idea where they've gone."

We had hit an insurmountable wall. The three of us went silent as the enormity of the problem sank in, Xave watching us curiously all the while.

Despair swept over me. Had we saved Sabina from a quick death in the Vesuvius eruption only to have her die a slow one in 1976—homeless on the streets, perpetually time-stuck wherever she went, and in the end finally lost to an unknowable fate?

12

Having decided some questions were in order, I tried to think what Nate, being a police officer, would ask if he were here. I reflexively reached for my notepad before remembering that I didn't even have my shoulder bag, then grabbed a pen and lab notebook from Xave's desk. I sat down on the unmade bed, opened the notebook to a blank page, and readied the pen. Lists always made a problem more manageable. "Xave, tell us everything you know about the book club, no matter how unimportant it seems."

"Here, have more coffee while you talk." Abigail pushed the mug into his hands.

He took a slow slurp of the liquid. "It's a dorm club. They meet in the rec room downstairs."

"You called it Udo's book club. Who's Udo?"

"A senior. Udo Leland. Creative writing student. Third floor, I think."

"Does he have a roommate?"

"All the undergrads do."

"Well, then, his roommate should know where they went. What room is he in?"

Xave shook his head. "No idea."

"I'll go knock on doors," Dr. Little said and left.

I jotted down in an orderly fashion what we knew so far:

> *Gilberte Dubois and Jenny (last name?), Room 104 (where Sally spent the night)*
> *Udo Leland (book club leader), Room 3??*
> *Xave Mooney, Room 510*

I looked up from the page. Xave's head had started to droop, like he might doze off again in his desk chair.

"I'll get some fresh coffee," Abigail said. She grabbed the mug and left as well.

"Xave?" I said gently.

"Hmm, what?" Xave mumbled. "Right, Udo. He runs the book club. There are about nine or ten of them in the inner circle of the club. They meet on Friday evenings."

I jotted down *Friday evenings*. "Did all of them go on the midterm break? If any of the members stayed behind, maybe we can track them down."

"Couldn't tell you. It was a car caravan, if two vehicles make a car caravan. Do they? Or do you need more than two cars to call it a caravan? Hey...I just realized something."

I looked up eagerly from the notebook. "What?"

"Caravan has the word *car* already in it."

"Oh." I had been hoping he'd remembered some significant detail from the previous night.

Xave looked a little sad again. "Hmm...You know things about me, don't you, Julia? Am I going to meet anyone special? Or should I just give up and focus all of my attention on my spacetime-warping work? To be honest, I sort of do that already. It's the only way to do research, isn't it? You aren't pursuing a topic, it...it *consumes* you."

I knew this to be often true, having observed many an obsessed academic in my time as dean's assistant. As to the other—Xave wouldn't meet Helen Presnik for a few years, not until he was at a couple of stages further down the road in his career, in a junior professorship. The pair would get married, fight a lot, get a divorce, and then rekindle their romance after Pompeii. I have summarized their life together in a sentence, but of course there was much more to it—these events were just the bare bones of a flesh-and-blood life.

"It'll all work out, Xave," I said. "It really will. Now, what about license plates?" I wasn't sure what we could do if we had the vehicles' numbers but thought I'd ask.

"Hmm?"

"Of the cars in the two-car caravan?"

"No idea. Udo Leland drives a Ford Mustang, a red one. Everyone on campus knows it."

82

I certainly did. It was a bright red Ford Mustang convertible that had almost mowed me down in a three-way intersection just yesterday. All I could remember of the driver was his long blond hair. Had that been this Udo Leland?

"Whoever couldn't fit into the Mustang would have gone in the art bus," Xave explained.

I looked up from jotting down the makes of the cars. "Did you say the *art* bus?"

"It's a painted VW minibus. I've seen it in the parking lot—one of the undergrads in the dorm drives it." He added, "It's a midterm break for all of them, except for Udo Leland—he's going to be working."

This was new. "Working on what?"

"He's researching a setting for his novel or something, Jenny said. As I said, it has to do with a tree." The future professor did not sound too impressed with trees, as if he considered research that didn't have to do with time travel a frivolous pursuit. I had encountered this attitude in one guise or another in every circle of academia. Everyone thought their field was the one to be in: astronomers studied stars (stars!), physicists the rules that governed the universe (the universe!), anthropologists all of humankind (humankind!), and so on. The young Xavier Mooney was not immune to it.

"A novel, huh," I said. So this Udo Leland wanted to be a writer. "I've never heard of him, unless he later changed his name to Stephen King."

"Hey, I've heard of Stephen King. He wrote that book, *Carrie*, didn't he? I've been meaning to read it."

"And he'll go on to write a few more. Never mind that," I said as Abigail came back with the refilled coffee, a bit breathless from the stairs. She handed Xave the mug. As he slurped some more, I turned to Abigail and scratched my head with the pen, trying to think how to phrase my question. "If Dr. Little can't get anything out of the roommate and all else fails, can one of us jump back home and ask Nate to track down Udo Leland in home-time?" I tried to be careful, so as not to give away the year. "After all, he'd know where his own book club went in 1976."

Would that work? I wasn't sure, which is why I'd wanted to ask the question. Would talking to present-day Udo be pointless because the midterm break was already in the past and long over with? Or did we still have a chance to fix things as long as at least one of us stayed on Sabina's trail in 1976, like a temporal bookmark? The logistics were starting to confuse me. As the TTE grad students, including Abigail, were fond of saying, time travel messes with your head.

"Who's Nate?" Xave wanted to know, but I didn't bother replying.

Abigail seemed to understand what I was asking and tried to explain, but she didn't get far before she ran out of words—or, more precisely, her tongue became immobilized by History. "No one would have to stay, though one of us probably should, just in case we're wrong and Sally didn't leave with the book club after all. Whoever heads back to the lab will need to keep an eye on the clock. As you know, the clocks here run faster by a factor of…"

"Yes, I see. Because of the clock rate difference, whatever we do back at the lab would have to be done fast."

"Whoever goes back would have just minutes, really."

Xave had been looking back and forth between us as we attempted to carry on this stunted conversation, like a spectator in a tennis match that wasn't going terribly well for either side. The topic—the mechanics of time travel—had seemed to pull him back together. He downed the remainder of the coffee in a long gulp, shuddered, and set the mug on the table with a resounding *thump*. "Do you need my help in contacting this Nate?"

"Hardly." Dr. Little had come back in, having apparently had no luck locating Udo's room. He continued just as rudely: "What we need is for you to leave and let us have the room. That is, if we've decided to stop wasting time here and are ready to tackle the problem from the other end."

Nate was pacing back and forth in the lab. He was alone. We had been in 1976 from midday October 31 to the morning of the following day, but less than an hour had passed for him. He ground to a halt in response to the *whoosh* of warm air that signaled my arrival on STEWie's platform. His face fell when he saw that I was alone, but I didn't take it personally.

"You haven't found her?" he asked, lending me a steadying hand as I descended from STEWie's platform. Abigail and Dr. Little had stayed behind to inquire around the dorm, with Xave's help, about where the book club had gone. We had decided it would be best if I jumped to the lab, since I might find myself shuttled back at any moment anyway.

"We have," I explained. "She is with a campus book club."

"That's good news."

Since it had only been an hour, he was obviously still in the nice shirt and slacks he'd pulled on for the dinner we were supposed to have at my house. I was sure I looked very grungy after spending the day aimlessly searching around campus and the night in a public restroom. Nate didn't seem to care. He pulled me to him for a long kiss.

"There is a small glitch, however," I said once my feet found steady ground again...and not because of the time traveling, either. "The book club, they've gone on a midterm break and we have no idea where. All we know is that they are headed to the East Coast, to the ocean."

Since he, too, knew Sabina very well, he saw the problem at once. "And you don't think she'll want to leave the ocean."

"Sally—I mean Sabina—spent last night in someone's dorm room. Early this morning—November 1 in 1976—the book club members took off. We think they're probably headed for Georgia or Florida. Two vehicles, the first a red Ford Mustang, the second a VW minibus."

"Hmm...Sabina was able to hitch a ride with them?"

"I know, it's a bit weird. I don't like it. What if she just...disappears?"

"She's got a good head on her shoulders. She'll be fine."

"She's quite capable of sneaking onto a cruise ship going to Europe."

"That's true, she is," he said in a tone that could only be described as proud. "Hold on—don't the other students in the dorm know the book club destination?"

"It seems to be a bit of a mystery. Dr. Little and Abigail are asking around campus. All we know is that there's a certain tree that interests Udo Leland, the driver of the Ford Mustang and the book club leader. We were hoping you could talk to him in the present and ask him where they went all those years ago, in 1976."

"Will that work?"

"Dr. Little and Abigail seem to think so."

He slid into one of the workstations. "You said this Udo Leland was interested in a tree? He was studying to be a biologist or a botanist, then?"

"No, a writer. The tree had to do with the setting for his Great American Novel or something."

"I see. Udo Leland is an unusual name—tracking him down shouldn't be a problem. Let's see what we can come up with."

A disconcerting thought occurred to me as he commenced a Google search, but I held off on saying anything.

"Hmm…there's an Udo here and there, and many Lelands, but none are paired up."

"He must be somewhere."

"I'll keep looking."

"Okay."

"What?"

"*What* what?"

"It seemed like you had more to say."

I voiced the unsettling thought that had occurred to me. "If we don't manage to locate Sabina in 1976, that would mean she's here in 2012 as a middle-aged woman. What if we did a search on her name…and found her? It would mean that all of our efforts in 1976 are pointless."

"Then we should do a search for her name, if only to be sure."

"No…Wait. Yes, do it—I need to know. There was something odd about Dr. Mooney's demeanor earlier—where is he anyway?" I looked around the lab. The unfinished Slingshot 3.0 was still in its place in the middle of the worktable, next to the disemboweled Version 1.0, but the professor was nowhere to be seen.

"Dr. Baumgartner is on her way to take over guard duty for STEWie. She should be here any minute. Dr. Mooney had some things to attend to off campus."

"I bet he did. We just spent a day with him in the past."

"Really? He was, what, a graduate student then?"

"With a mustache. But that's not the only odd part. We talked to him and he figured out that we were from the future."

Nate frowned at this. "How's that even possible?"

"Well, he was a bit condescending and swollen-headed back then. I guess we merely proved that his high opinion of himself was correct."

"He's never said anything to you about having met you back when he was a student?"

"Never. We saw Dr. Rojas, too, but I'm not sure he took much note of us." The mild-mannered professor was still on his sabbatical, but I figured calling him up and asking him whether he remembered meeting us in 1976 would be a waste of time. Dr. Mooney was the person I wanted to grab by the collar and talk to.

Nate had given his attention back to the Internet search. "Hmm…"

"What?" I leaned over his shoulder to look at the search results.

"You'll be happy to know I'm not finding any hits on a Sabina Secunda Tanner."

I breathed a sigh of relief.

"Unless she's gotten married and changed her last name, of course," Nate added, ever the cautious police officer. "Or is still keeping a low profile and her personal information off the Internet, as we have taught her to."

The lab doors opened and Dr. Baumgartner hurried in, looking a touch irritated that she had been summoned without explanation. "Xavier said you needed me urgently. He didn't say why."

"Sabina is lost in 1976," I said simply.

Worry replaced the look of irritation on Dr. B's face at once. She was as fond of Sabina as the rest of us. "What? How did that happen?"

"Nate can explain later, but right now I need you to send me back—time is flying by in 1976. I came back to update everyone and to get a couple of overnight kits."

"Nineteen seventy-six?" I heard Dr. B ask as I exited the lab. "What on earth is going on?"

Overnight kits were always kept at the ready in the travel apparel closet. I chose two—Dr. Little had pretty much everything he needed in his duffel bag—and hurried back into the lab with a backpack on each shoulder, balancing the small stack of sandwiches I had grabbed from the vending machine in my hands. My few minutes in the lab would be hours back in 1976; I figured Dr. Little and Abigail would be hungry.

Nate steadied me by the elbow as I climbed onto STEWie's platform with the armful of supplies. "I'll get on the phone and get some official inquiries going. I've sent Officer Van Underberg to find Dr. Mooney. We need some answers."

"Send us a note through STEWie if you find out anything."

One of the larger mirrors blocked Dr. B's view of us and I wondered if we might sneak a kiss, but Nate looked a touch uncomfortable, so I gave him a platonic peck on the cheek instead. "For luck."

"Julia?" he said.

"Yes?"

"Be careful. I'm not sure I like the way this sounds, this book club outing with the mysterious Udo Leland at the helm."

13

Dr. B had sent me again to 1976 as swiftly as possible, but it was already evening back in November 1, 1976. A blast of cold air and lightly falling snowflakes greeted me at the Open Book sculpture. I radioed Abigail and Dr. Little, who radioed back that they were in Xave's room and that I should meet them there.

I slipped into St. Olaf's dorm past the hall monitor, who was busy flirting with another student, and made my way up to Xave's room on the fifth floor. All three of them were there. Xave was reclined on his bed, looking like his normal self again. (I remembered college, when all it took to bounce back from an all-night party or study session was a nap and a lot of coffee.) He waved a friendly greeting at me.

I learned that Abigail and Dr. Little had talked to Udo's roommate while I was gone. The roommate, Sam, was an electrical engineer. "I got the impression that he and Udo don't talk much. *Udo only likes people who do art,*" Abigail quoted the roommate. She was perched on the windowsill again.

This brought back college memories as well. Either you got on great with your roommate for the year, or you didn't.

"No one seems to know where the book club has gone. No one," Abigail continued. "It's almost as if Udo didn't want people to know."

"Well, he appears to have succeeded if that was his goal," Dr. Little commented from the desk chair.

"Too bad there's no electronic trail for us to follow," I said. "Tweets and such."

I swear I could see Xave's ears perk up. "What are *tweets*? Are tweeters trained birds—or perhaps programmable robotic ones?— and do they track people's whereabouts and report their location to the authorities?"

"Yeah, no," Abigail said.

"Which is it, yes or no?"

"People are all too eager to report their whereabouts themselves," I explained. "Everyone likes to share details of their lives, it turns out."

Dr. Little had mentioned that the seventies were considered the *me* decade, but I rather thought we had them beat. There really was no way to adequately explain the early years of the twenty-first century without living through them. And Xave Mooney would, of course, in due time. I hoped all the information we were letting slip wouldn't corrupt him into buying early stock in smartphone and social media companies.

"Hey, are those sandwiches from the future? I'm famished."

I had set the two backpacks I had brought with me on the bed next to him, and the sandwiches, too. "Help yourself. These two are ham, those two are peanut butter and jelly."

Xave waited politely as Dr. Little sprayed his hands with hand sanitizer, a proceeding he watched with interest. Abigail and Dr. Little took a sandwich each. Xave carefully reached for a peanut butter one. The vending machine fare consisted of pre-sliced white bread with a thin film of jam and an even thinner film of peanut butter. My guess was that he was going to be mightily disappointed.

He carefully unwrapped the sandwich and took a test bite. "Hmm. It's a little…bland, if you don't mind my saying so. Is it prefabricated somehow, created from some common source of nourishment?"

"It might as well be."

"Hey, where do I end up teaching?" he asked between bites. "MIT? Berkeley? Caltech? I know, you can't tell me that either."

"Julia, we've come up with a plan," Abigail said, having already downed her sandwich. She reached for the leftover ham one. "Anybody want this?"

Dr. Little shook his head at her. Xave said, "No, thanks. I'm still, uh, enjoying this one."

"What's the plan?" I asked.

"Some spying is in order. We need to find out when the book club last met," Abigail said. "You said on Friday evenings, Xave. Is it each Friday?"

Xave, having finished the peanut butter sandwich clearly more out of a desire not to offend us than anything else, wiped his hands on his pants. "There's a flyer downstairs by the front door."

In the present, he would have reached for his cell phone to check the book club webpage, blog, Facebook group, et cetera, but the norm was different in 1976. While we waited for him to return, I quickly explained that Nate was on the case in the present and that there were no search hits on Sabina's name, which hopefully meant we would be successful in our mission to catch up with the book club.

Xave popped back into the room as if he had taken the four flights of stairs two steps at a time (making me miss my college years, with their seemingly endless store of energy, yet again) and waved a flyer at us. In large block letters, it informed the public that *SERIOUS STUDENTS OF LITERATURE* were invited to congregate every Friday evening at 8.30 p.m. in the rec room of St. Olaf's Hall. Below that were two handwritten lists separated by a line down the middle. The one on the left chronicled the books the club had been reading month by month (a mix of modern authors like Kurt Vonnegut and Erica Jong, and classic ones like Tolstoy and Chekhov). The other list appeared to be a record of the book club regulars. First was Udo's own name, written down with an almost illegible flourish, as if Udo had practiced his signature until it looked satisfactorily author-like. It was followed by eight other names, each in a different handwriting style, starting with Gilberte Dubois's name. My eyes went further down and stopped: Missy Donovan, my mother, and Soren Olsen, my father.

"Julia, what is it?" Abigail asked, clearly noticing my surprise.

I tapped the list. "Small world. Missy is my mom and Soren my dad." My parents are avid readers—our house had always been littered with books—so I guessed it wasn't that much of a surprise when I thought about it.

"Interesting," Dr. Little said in a tone that suggested the opposite, and proceeded to wash down his sandwich with a swig from his water bottle.

During her college years my mother had lived with her parents in town, I knew, while Dad had taken up residence in a dorm on campus—"one of the old dorms" was how he'd described it to me.

St. Olaf's? I had never heard anything about a book club. I turned to Xave. "Do you know them? Missy Donovan and Soren Olsen?"

"Nope, but it's a big dorm. And not everybody in the book club is from this dorm—Udo tends to attract them."

Hold on. If my parents were *in* the book club, and Sabina was *with* the book club, then why hadn't they recognized her when they came over to my house over the summer? On the other hand, it was three and a half decades later, and she seemingly wouldn't have aged a bit. Upon meeting Sabina, Mom had said, "I feel as if I've known you all my life," which now took on a whole different meaning. At the time I had not given it a second thought. Now it seemed as though Mom and Dad *had* known Sabina, not for their whole lives exactly but for a long time—longer than any of us had realized. I'd have to ask them about it when I got back.

Some spying is in order, Abigail had said. I understood the plan without needing an explanation. I was well versed in organizing campus events and knew how much discussion it took to get any group to agree on anything, no matter how small the group or the matter. The timing of the trip, the destination, and the other associated details would all have been hashed out in advance by the book club. All we needed to do was to jump back to the last meeting and eavesdrop.

The place where the club met each week, the recreation room of St. Olaf's, was on the ground floor at the end of the hallway, Xave explained. "There's a Ping-Pong table and some chairs and a couch. I don't go there much."

"Their last meeting would have been Friday the twenty-ninth," Dr. Little said, and reached for his duffel bag to get the equipment out and calculate coordinates. "Mooney—"

"You're kicking me out again? Well, I suppose I do need to show my face at the lab, or my advisor will think I'm slacking off."

I had reset my watch yet again. "It's past 9:00 p.m.," I protested, unwilling to see him leave and quite certain that I wouldn't see him again until we got back to 2012. (From his point of view, the next time he would see me would be on my first day of work in the science dean's office. It was an odd thought.) "How will your advisor even know if you're in the lab this late or not?"

"Oh, he'll know. Dr. Eatchel already thinks my time-travel idea is an embarrassment to the department and would probably be happier if I just…left. I wish I could introduce you to him. Oh, how I would love to see his face after you showed him that little smart phone."

"I bet," Dr. Little said.

"Will I see you three again?" Xave asked from the doorway.

"Yes," I answered for all of us.

"Thanks for the sandwich."

Once the door had closed behind him, Dr. Little briskly unzipped his duffel bag. "I'll run the necessary calculations for the Slingshot—I'll send us to the Open Book, and we can walk over from there."

For the first time since we'd stepped into 1976, I was optimistic that everything was going to work out just fine.

14

A jump of three days back got us to October 29, the day that Dr. Little had originally planned for his run and the very day when Sabina had arrived on campus. We found the ground by the Open Book muddy from a light drizzle. The green area on which the sculpture sat was empty except for a few students crossing it, their forms shadowy under the sparse streetlights. Sabina was presumably inside the warm, well-lit cafeteria, but we had no way of getting to her—this day was already in her past and could not be changed.

Still, I tossed out the idea of one of us trying to sneak up on Sabina to slip a note into her pocket for her to find later, with instructions not to do anything foolish such as stow away on a transatlantic liner, but the plan was waved away. Neither of my companions thought it would work.

Abigail pulled her coat closer around her thin frame as we strode across the plaza to St. Olaf's Hall. Assuming there had not been any unexpected minor adjustments by History, it was just about eight thirty, and the book club meeting had already started. Dr. Little reminded us that bold was occasionally the way to go, and we strode up the brick path of St. Olaf's Hall and toward its front steps as if we belonged.

It didn't work. We hit an invisible wall about halfway up the path.

"*Oof.* I wish there was some kind of warning about these things," I complained, rubbing my shoulder where I had smacked it against History's wall.

We regrouped behind the shrubbery in the dorm's courtyard. After a few minutes' discussion, we decided that trying to march in as a group had drawn too much attention and it would be better to send in a single person.

Dr. Little tried first. Having set his duffel bag on the ground, he left the shelter of the shrubbery and, still sticking to his theory that bold trumped stealthy, gave striding up the path another go. He came back in defeat, his hair matted from the light drizzle.

Abigail tried the opposite approach, stealth. Petite as she was, she made herself smaller by hunching her shoulders in and turning the collar of her coat up over her ears. She headed up the path, softly stepping on the worn bricks glistening in the rain.

"Well, that didn't work at all," she said, having stomped back without any further attempt at stealth.

"My turn." I remembered a rule that had been drilled into us before the Pompeii run—*Blend in.* We were trying to crash a book club meeting and needed to look the part. "Do either of you have a book, textbook, anything of that sort?"

There was nothing that would work in the two backpacks I had brought with me. Dr. Little retrieved a pencil flashlight from one of his pockets and rummaged briefly in his duffel bag. "Yes…here." It was the 1976 *Old Farmer's Almanac* (the Bicentennial issue, with a yellow cover and an Uncle Sam–featuring ad on the back that proclaimed *EVERYBODY AND HIS UNCLE LOVES SNOW'S CHOWDER*). I saw that Dr. Little had printed out the *actual* weather data for fall of 1976 and taped up the tables inside the pages. "Handy for checking the weather forecast on the go," he explained with a straight face.

It wasn't ideal as far as literary club reading material went, but it would have to do. Leaving the cover of the shrubbery, I tucked the almanac in one coat pocket so only the top of it was showing and set a course up the path and toward the front steps of the dorm. As far as I could tell, there was no one watching from any of the windows—it was too early for Friday night parties, and the only signs of activity inside were silhouettes in lighted windows and the sound of a door shutting somewhere. I guessed that the bottleneck was someone in the common area just inside the dorm door.

I successfully passed the halfway point of the brick path, where Dr. Little and Abigail had been stopped, and, turning up the collar on my coat like Abigail had, brainstormed wildly about what my next move should be. Would it be best to keep my head down?

Plaster what I hoped was an erudite, literary look on my face? Take the book out of my pocket and hold it in my hands?

Before I could decide I had pulled the front door open.

The hall monitor, a lanky and pimple-ridden student, glanced up briefly from one of the easy chairs. The TV was on, blaring fast-paced dialogue. "Close the door, it's cold."

I did and tapped the almanac in my pocket. "I'm here for the book club."

"Rec room. At the end of the hallway." He gestured with his head and went back to watching TV above the textbook in his lap.

"What's on?" I asked.

The student gave me the same look I might have given if asked what *American Idol* was by a contemporary. "*Hawaii Five-O.*"

"Right, right." As I continued past, I thought I heard him mutter under his breath, "Udo attracts them like flies."

The door to the rec room was open. The cigarette smoke (of both the regular and the less legal variety) was so prevalent that a fine fog engulfed the space. I stepped inside. A dozen or so students were sprawled on the room's couches and chairs or cross-legged on the floor. The Ping-Pong table had been pushed aside and under the window, leaving room for the speaker, who was standing in the middle of the cleared space. Fighting my twenty-first-century reflex to open a window to clear the air, I took a seat against the back wall, where there were several empty wooden chairs.

Udo Leland—for it could be no one else—was gesticulating with passion as he spoke. He was dressed all in black: a black turtleneck hugged his thin body over slim black pants and black shoes. His blond hair streamed over his shoulders, and he was wearing horn-rimmed glasses—black ones, of course. He looked so much like the artistic sort as to be a walking cliché, except that what was considered cliché in 2012 was probably fresh and exciting in 1976.

All of the female students—and some of the male ones, too—certainly appeared to think so. They were hanging on Udo's every word. For his bit, he was delivering his speech without making eye contact with his audience, as if humanizing his crowd distracted him from the topic at hand, which seemed to be Writing with a capital *W*.

"Forget the television sets in your parents' living rooms, the fancy cars in their yards. Forget their expensive clothes and watches. What the *true* writer needs is connections with his roots, with his community and friends...not the empty luxuries of the bourgeois life."

There were murmurs of agreement, though I thought he was laying it on a bit thick. It seemed to me that Udo was perhaps talking about his own family when he disdained fancy cars and clothes, like a trust-fund kid turning his nose up at his parents' wealth. Most undergrads at St. Sunniva are from within the state, both back then and in the present, and if there's one thing Minnesotans tend to be, it's thrifty. Though they were perhaps too embarrassed to say so, the students he was addressing probably came from hardworking families who had reached deep into their pockets to send their kids to college. This was certainly the case with my own mother and her family. She was at the foot of the couch, in a super-short blue dress and knee-high boots, her legs curled underneath her to one side. Like the others, she looked riveted by Udo's speech.

"The writers who *matter*...You know them—Vonnegut and others...Do they worry about being *liked*? No. Is their goal a house in the suburbs with a white picket fence, a TV set in the living room, and a station wagon in the driveway? No."

More murmurs of agreement. A patch of cigarette smoke cleared temporarily, and an odd, unexpected detail popped out at me. Udo's hair showed tinges of brown at the roots. So he had dyed it blond. It certainly stood out against his brown eyes and eyebrows and the all-black outfit. A lot of people in the state and on campus sported blond hair, courtesy of Minnesota's Scandinavian immigrant community. I was not one of them, and apparently neither was Udo.

"They wanted to write prose that would stand the test of time, words that would *transcend* time..."

My mind wandered a bit as he continued in this vein for a while. I was impatient for him to get talking about the important part, the tree he held in such high regard—and its location.

I couldn't help but stare at my mother. She seemed caught up in the moment, bedazzled by Udo and what he had to say. Was there a baby bump under her blue dress, or was the soft curve of her cheeks and arms just youthful pudginess? I wasn't sure how early that sort of thing showed. Once again there was a cigarette between her fingers, and this time there was also a beer bottle by her side. If she knew she was pregnant, was she...*ignoring* it? Is that why History had allowed me to come to 1976, because my influence, barely affecting even one person, had yet to be felt?

It was all a bit ego-squashing. I wasn't particularly swollen-headed or anything, but I wasn't immune to wanting to feel special...at least as far as my mom and dad were concerned.

I watched my mother watch Udo and a thought flew into my mind that immediately filled me with horror. Could the very man who had almost run me over and was even now delivering a hackneyed speech actually be my father?

I shook the idea away as being ridiculous and cleared my throat in an effort to forestall an emerging coughing fit. Speaking of Dad, there he was too, sitting in a chair across the room. He was in a tie-dye shirt and jeans, looking very young and in need of a good haircut and a shave under his large-framed glasses. He kept reaching for his handkerchief (fall was allergy season for Dad—ragweed—and the smoke probably wasn't helping.) He occasionally glanced at my mother, then quickly away, as if he didn't want to be caught staring. At one point his eyes shot to the broad-shouldered man sitting at the foot of the couch next to my mother. It was the man I'd seen her with in the cafeteria, the one with the strong-jawed profile and dark hair.

I tried to focus on what Udo was saying ("Every great novel is not about a single character, but Character...") but my eyes kept returning to my mother. She and the student next to her occasionally rubbed shoulders as they passed a cigarette back and forth in a familiar fashion. A good buddy of hers...or someone more important? My father certainly seemed to think so.

As did the student on the *other* side of the guy with Mom. The body language of the dark-complexioned woman in a sari revealed that she felt she should be on the receiving end of the man's attention, not my mother. She was pretending to read a book, testily turning its pages in the dim light.

Dad tried to stifle a sneeze and received a look of irritation from Udo, which I was proud to see he ignored. At least I knew the story had a happy ending. For Dad, not the other guy. I knew that all would turn out well and that he and my mother would end up together. Still, I wanted him to stand up, offer an arm to my mother, and lead her into their future life together.

As I tried hard not to keep my gaze fixed on Missy's belly—somehow I was very sure that Dad did not yet know that she was pregnant—I thought fondly of my previous time travels, which had flung me into life-threatening ghost zones but hadn't taken me anywhere near my family members. I was seeing potential fathers everywhere—first Udo, now the mystery man next to my mother. At least I knew that History wouldn't send me back, since I had successfully managed to blend in three days from now, on November 1. So, though I was starting to get a little light-headed, I figured History wasn't the culprit. Rather it was probably all the smoke. The dark-haired man passed his cigarette again to my mother. The strong line of the jaw, the somewhat large ears—who did he remind me of?

I felt a sudden sense of unease, like all of this was more than I wanted to know. I wasn't one for ignoring problems, preferring to deal with things head-on, grabbing a pint of ice cream or a glass of wine later if needed. I crossed my arms over my chest and locked my gaze on Udo and Udo only. I was here to do a job. Sabina needed me at my best, undistracted, single-mindedly focused on the task of finding her. That person by the couch—that person who was younger than me!—was not my mother, not yet...She was just Missy Donovan, a senior enjoying a literary Saturday night out. She was entitled to her privacy and it was far from fair for me to judge her actions. I wasn't likely to have offspring (kids just aren't my thing), but I certainly wouldn't have appreciated them spying on me in my youth and weighing my every move.

"We need to explore our souls in our writing," Udo was saying rather grandiosely. "Mine, yours, his, hers." He pointed from one member of his audience to the next and included me in his flock. "To seek goodness, wisdom, truth."

Get to it, I thought to myself. *I don't want to spend any more time here than strictly necessary. Where does the tree come in, and where are you going to look for it, Udo?* I considered raising a hand to ask the question but doubted it would work.

With a flourish, Udo pulled out a small stack of typewritten pages from a back pocket. He unfolded them, shuffled them a bit, and offered to share what he had been working on with the crowd. The idea was well received, and he launched into a story set in a dystopian future in which townspeople refused to throw anything out, down to the very skeletons of their late relatives, all because they valued material possessions so much. Udo was a good reader, lending emphasis where it was needed and holding back when that was the right way to go. It was an interesting tale, I had to admit despite myself—the skeletons had the power of speech and were starting to outnumber the living to the point where they were threatening to take over Eden, the town. Things were looking bleak for the townspeople...and then Udo stopped, for there were no more pages to read. He bowed theatrically, and hearty applause and whistles rang throughout the room. Calls for more erupted. Udo paused and said, "The rest is...not yet written. It requires inspiration, investigation, involvement. I must embark on my voyage of discovery to finish it."

"Not without us, Udo?" someone in the audience asked, and I sat up. It sounded like a discussion they'd had before, at an earlier meeting.

"*Everyone's* invited." He was not their teacher, of course, and he said it not as a natural educator might, with his students and what they might learn in mind, but as a performer who needed an audience. The monthly reading list aside, this wasn't so much of a book club as an Udo Leland fan club. The energy of the crowd was what kept him going, the feeling of importance and credibility it lent to his novel-writing aspirations. Or at least that's the way it struck me.

He continued the performance by saying, "The sooner we go, the better. Give me a moment." As if alone in the room, he closed his eyes and stood still for perhaps half a minute. Finally, he heaved a deep sigh, opened his eyes, and switched to practical mode. "Midterm week is done with, so it's a good time for a break. We will leave early Monday morning"—he was giving them only a few days' notice, but no one protested—"to seek the chrono-synclastic infundibulum."

His audience seemed to know exactly what he was talking about.

Was that a kind of a tree—the botanical name for it? No, that was dumb. I raised my hand. "I'm sorry, the what?"

Udo sent a glance of literary disdain in my direction. "You're new. Welcome."

"Thanks."

He repeated the term carefully, as if speaking to a child. "The chrono-SYN-clas-tic in-fundi-bulum."

"Uh, right, thanks."

I wished Abigail and Dr. Little, who would possibly recognize the scientific-sounding term, were with me. All I could do was try and remember the term by repeating it over and over in my head as people started getting to their feet and the book club meeting broke up. *Chrono-synclastic infundibulum, chrono-synclastic infundibulum, chrono-synclastic infundibulum…*

15

I rejoined the others behind the shrubbery. The book club attendees had lingered to chat with Udo and each other—and to, presumably, finalize their Monday travel plans.

"Well?" Abigail demanded. "Did they say where they are going?"

"Sort of. It sounds like they are on a quest to find the—what was it?—the chrono-synclastic infundibulum. Udo wants to use it as the setting for his book or whatever. Tell me you know what that is and where it is. Is it a tree, like Xave said?"

I saw Dr. Little wrinkle his brow in the soft light reaching us from the nearest streetlamp. It was still drizzling, and he wiped a drop off his nose. "*Chrono* implies that it has to do with time, of course. And *synclastic* denotes a positive Gaussian curvature."

"Say what?" I said.

"A surface that's curved toward the same side in all directions, like a beach ball."

"*Infundibulum* is *funnel* in Latin," said Abigail, whose working knowledge of that language had been enriched by her guardianship of Sabina.

"All righty," I said. "So not a tree but a time-related, precisely shaped funnel? It sounds oddly similar to our own spacetime warper, only more wormhole-ish."

Abigail tilted her head to one side. "Hmm…It does sound familiar—where have I heard it before?…How did people find answers to random questions before the Internet?"

I pointed across Sunniva Lake, dark and serene in the light rain. A well-lit building beckoned in the night on the other side. "They went to the library."

We circled the lake to the stone steps of the compact Crane Library, the predecessor to the as-yet-unbuilt Coffee Library. It wasn't named after a person, I knew, but rather the large bird. And there was no History Museum next to it, not yet, just a facilities building. Even though it was past ten, the library was still open—according to the sign on the front door, eleven was the closing hour on Fridays. It didn't surprise me. Most academic libraries keep extended hours to provide students with a quiet study space and access to research materials, a policy particularly needed in the pre-Internet era, I supposed.

We passed a couple of students getting their cigarette fixes out front and went inside. Dr. Little made a beeline for the science shelves. I explained to Abigail the purpose of the library catalog cabinet, with its drawerfuls of index cards, and left her rifling through them randomly as she tried to remember where she'd heard the term *chrono-synclastic infundibulum* before. I headed to the reference section to thumb through encyclopedias under the letter *C*.

The familiar scent that libraries always have of leather, must, and carpet deodorizer hung over the place. The library was sparsely filled with the more studious of St. Sunniva's students, those not out celebrating the end of midterms but taking this opportunity to catch up on projects or reading. I spotted a small sign showing a cigarette with an X through it on one wall; cigarettes and a flammable and valuable collection of books did not mix, which explained the smokers outside.

Having had no luck finding *chrono-synclastic infundibulum* in any of the encyclopedias under *C*, I gave up and went to the catalog cabinet, where Abigail was still thumbing through the index cards. Not slowly and haphazardly like before, but energetically now. "Julia, there you are. I've just remembered! *V-a...V-o...*Here it is, yes." She zeroed in on an index card, then grabbed a pencil from the cup that held a bunch of them and jotted the call number down on one of the paper scraps available for that purpose. "We need to find section 813," she informed me, holding up the paper scrap triumphantly, clearly proud to have figured out how to use the outdated (to the three of us, at least) library search system.

We pulled Dr. Little away from the physics shelves—he had been looking in the indices of a variety of textbooks—and over to section 813. I was surprised to see that the section held fiction. American literature from the twentieth century, to be precise. But perhaps it wasn't so surprising after all—I had heard the term at a book club, so the fact that we were now standing in front of a literary shelf was a good sign.

"I've remembered what it is—it's from one of Kurt Vonnegut's early novels," Abigail explained breathlessly, squatting down by a low shelf, where the *V*'s were. "Here, let's see—*Breakfast of Champions*, not that one...*Cat's Cradle*, no...*Slaughterhouse-Five*...Wait, I skipped over it. Here." She slid the book out of its spot and held it out like a prize. "It's this one. *The Sirens of Titan*."

"Never heard of it," I said, taking the book. "Is it science fiction?"

"The title makes it sound like a lighthearted, sexy romp through space. It isn't, not really. This one guy pops in and out of time and place, and this other guy gets sent to Mars against his will...Anyway, I don't want to spoil the ending, in case you decide to read it sometime."

"Abigail, this is no time to be worrying about spoiler alerts."

Dr. Little agreed. "I'm more of a nonfiction reader, anyway. Give me a nice solid book about the history of computing or code breaking, and I'll be happy for hours."

"So, the infundibulum?" I prompted Abigail.

"It's a term Vonnegut came up with. It's how one of the characters and his dog pop in and out of places."

A librarian was approaching, pulling a cart piled high with volumes that needed shelving, and we left section 813 to find a quiet corner. As we slid into an isolated table located directly under the *No Smoking* sign, I allowed myself a brief internal gripe. Why did STEWie incidents never involve matters on which I was an expert? I had read *Slaughterhouse-Five* in college, but I'd never even heard of *The Sirens of Titan*. I would have been a good person to consult on, say, seventies music—just yesterday I had been listening to a Carpenters album while trying to keep up with Nate's spaniel, Wanda, on a walk. At least this current STEWie problem didn't involve academic misbehavior bordering on criminal—or crossing into it—like the previous ones. The more we unraveled the situation, the more I realized it was unlikely anyone had given Sabina the security code for the lab door with evil intentions. And no one could really blame her for what she had done, not even Dean Braga.

There was one copy of the book and three of us. "I don't think I'll be of any use here, anyway. Let me know what you find," Dr. Little said, and went off to explore the library. Abigail and I settled in to figure out why Kurt Vonnegut's book had caught the attention of Udo Leland.

Abigail leafed through the first few pages and explained, "I read this one as a teen during my goth stage, when I was into being dramatic and mopey. Then one morning I got up, looked in the mirror, and decided that I needed to lighten up. And read some books in which women get to make decisions and stuff. Let's see now…Yup…yup…" She pushed the book, open to a beginning set of pages, across the table toward me. "Here, Julia. It's in the first chapter."

I took a moment to look the book over, as if its appearance might provide a clue as to the fascination it held for Udo. The book was hardcover and of medium thickness—319 pages. If there had been a book jacket once, it was long gone, leaving behind a matte black cover which carried the relevant information on the spine and a library sticker on the back. On the inside title page, the author's name was given in large letters over three lines—Kurt Vonnegut Jr., with the downstroke of the *g* pulled into service as the *j* in Jr. A smallish black circle listed the book's title. The original publication year was 1959, I saw, but the book in my hands was a 1970 reprint, according to its Library of Congress Catalog Card Number, which I knew how to interpret, since all the books written by our professors had them.

Of course, none of the physical details would have mattered to Udo. What was within did.

I leafed past the contents page, with its twelve chapters and one epilogue, to Chapter 1. Vonnegut's futuristic story opened in Newport, Rhode Island and flowed quickly, with snappy and somewhat cynical descriptions of characters. I learned that the person caught in the chrono-synclastic infundibulum for nine years was Winston Niles Rumfoord, a wealthy socialite who ended up there along with his dog, Kazak, like a fictional and more edgy version of Sabina and Celer. With Abigail patiently looking on, I skimmed some more…There! A definition, exactly what we needed, like she had said. It was several paragraphs long, but it seemed to boil down to this: there was more than one infundibulum—many of them, in fact, scattered throughout space—and they were places where "all the different kinds of truths fit together." I reread the passage to make sure I gleaned everything I could from it. They were places where you went to understand and be understood, it seemed; where people accepted each other's points of view instead of arguing, though I wasn't sure what the concept had to do with traveling though space and time. They also sounded a bit hazardous and somewhat like ghost zones in that you could get trapped in one.

I looked up from my reading. "The chrono-synclastic infund— Can we just call it the CSI for short? The CSI in the book is between Earth and Mars."

"Yeah." Abigail wrinkled her nose. "I don't think that's the one Udo meant."

"Let's hope not. So where, then? It could be anywhere really, depending on where Udo thinks truths fit together…" I set the book down and started to speculate widely. "People with different points of view coming together…let's see…the United Nations? The Olympics?…Or, to go in a completely different direction, Hollywood or Las Vegas? All right, that's dumb. Where does someone of a literary bent think various truths come together?"

Abigail gestured around us. "The library."

"Perhaps not just any library. How about the Library of Congress? That's sort of near the ocean, if you don't mind driving a couple of hours from Washington DC to the nearest beach. Or does Udo maybe have a place from Vonnegut's own life in mind? I wonder where he lives. Not Udo, Vonnegut."

"Not a clue."

There wasn't a biography included in the book—perhaps it had been on the missing book jacket. I got up to ask the librarian at the help desk. She was tidying up, as the library would be closing soon, but didn't seem to mind the interruption.

"You're wondering where Mr. Vonnegut lives?"

"Yes, for, uh…a book project I'm working on."

"Well, then. I did read a news article not too long ago—now where would that have been? Oh, yes. It was about Mr. Vonnegut's speech at the dedication of the new library at Connecticut College. They said that he suggested the name 'The Noodle Factory' for it." She chuckled. "They didn't accept his kind suggestion. But to answer your question, the article gave Mr. Vonnegut's residence as New York City."

I thanked her and went to rejoin Abigail. New York City matched the East Coast part, though it wasn't exactly the first place that came to mind when you said *tree*, unless that part had been wholly in Xave's inebriated imagination. I summarized what we'd found out so far. "Our best guess, then, is that they've gone either to the Library of Congress or Kurt Vonnegut's house in New York City. I'm not sure that narrows it down any. It would be easier if I just jumped back home and phoned my parents to ask them."

"Your parents were at the book club meeting together?" Abigail said as we got up to look for Dr. Little. "Aww, how romantic."

"Sadly, not in the least. My father was sneezing the whole time thanks to his allergies, and my mother was more interested in a tall, dark-haired stranger. Don't say it…"

"What?"

"That he might be the dark-haired ancestor I assumed was somewhere in my family tree."

"I'm sure that's not it," she said diplomatically.

"Well, let's hope it's not Udo, either. He's blond but he dyes his hair."

"Did your parents ever mention the book club to you?"

I shook my head. Had my parents possessed grander writing aspirations before their dreams were subverted by life's realities? Something else to ask them about when I got home. They had ended up happily running the town paper, the simply titled *Thornberg News*, writing articles that ranged from reports on the popularity of the September corn fair to birth and death announcements. I wondered what Udo Leland had made of the *Thornberg News*.

Dr. Little was by the library magazine rack, leafing through a *Popular Electronics* issue, his duffel bag by his feet, his coat draped over it. "Anything?" he asked at our approach.

"It will be a place where *all the different kinds of truths fit together*," I quoted from the book.

"Truths? Well, that's not very helpful." He slid the magazine back into place next to the others. "I don't suppose Udo said anything else of interest at the book club meeting, Julia?"

"Not really. He read a story about twenty-second-century skeleton hoarders. No mention of the tree Xave heard about from Jenny. I don't suppose there's a key tree in Vonnegut's book, Abigail?"

She wrinkled her nose in thought. "It's been a long time since I read it. There was a fancy fountain, some deep caves on Mercury, bluebirds on Titan…There may have been a tree, but I honestly don't remember."

"If we had current campus IDs, we could check the book out of the library and read the rest. But since we don't, you'd better put it back on the shelf, Abigail."

"Will do." She made a 180 and headed back into the stacks.

Dr. Little reached for his coat and duffel. "Hanging around reading books would be a waste of our time anyway. In this case, I mean, not in general, obviously."

"We could check in with Nate," I suggested as we left the library, Abigail having rejoined us.

"Why?" Dr. Little wanted to know.

I hoped that he didn't think I was eager to keep popping back into the present to see Nate. I was, of course, but that was beside the point. Like I'd told Abigail, I wanted to phone my parents and ask them about the book club, but I felt strangely reluctant to mention that in front of Dr. Little. I also *really* wanted to sit down and have a very frank talk with Dr. Mooney.

"Just to touch base," I said. "It could be that he's already found Udo and talked to him."

Dr. Little checked his wristwatch and did a quick mental calculation. "Only six minutes and fifty-five seconds have passed in the lab. It would be a miracle if Kirkland managed to contact Udo in that short a time. We need to give him at least a full twenty-four hours our time."

"In that case, let's jump to the previous book club meeting—I'm pretty sure the CSI was something they've discussed before."

On the evening of Friday, October 22, 1976, we found the campus under a clear night sky. This time all three of us were able to go into St. Olaf's Hall—the dorm monitor was missing from his post. We seated ourselves in the wooden chairs against the back wall of the rec room, just inside the door. A couple of students glanced in our direction, but only briefly. There was presumably nothing unusual about a newcomer or two listening in without contributing.

As before, a cloud of smoke hung over the space. The difference this time was that rather than Udo monopolizing the conversation, it was a free-for-all. We had walked into a discussion of the kind that really only can be had in college, before the everyday details of adult life take over: mortgage payments, meals, child care, laundry. More of the lights had been left on this time, and the students were sprawled on the couch, chairs, and the floor with well-thumbed copies of *The Sirens of Titan* in their hands. Words like *fate, free will,* and *determinism* were flying around the room. There never was an answer to these things. It wasn't there in Vonnegut's book, I guessed, and it wouldn't be hammered out by Udo's book club either. But they sure were trying.

Scanning the room, I saw that my parents were not present this time. Breathing a sigh of relief, I devoted my attention to the metaphysical questions occupying the students, which, I hoped, would soon turn into a discussion of where the book club would be heading in a couple of weeks.

I watched Udo as he occasionally partook in the debate regarding Vonnegut's *The Sirens of Titan* and read something in his expression. Not that I knew much about budding fiction writers, but I had spent almost eight years observing the academic environment from within. I suspected that the problems that existed in the ivory tower—jealousy, greed, narcissism, loneliness, unrealistic expectations—were all represented in this room as well. Udo was trying to figure out what elements in *The Sirens of Titan* spoke to the others in order to absorb them into his own work in progress. He wanted Vonnegut's success for himself.

I heard someone mention the infundibulum, and my ears perked up. It was the woman in a sari, the one who would form one fourth of the flirting quadrangle one week hence. She was wondering at the significance of the fifty-nine-day interval at which Rumfoord and his dog, Kazak, popped in and out of New England via their CSI.

A second voice said, "Gilberte, that's a great question," and I felt Abigail sit up in the chair next to me. Gilberte was who had taken Sabina in for the night. At her question, the discussion took off on a different tangent. Did the fifty-nine come from the year the book was published, or had it been chosen because it was a prime number, or perhaps because it was the last minute on the clock before it struck the hour, denoting inevitability?

Udo raised a hand. "Friends!" He was a natural speaker, projecting his voice without having to shout, and the conversation in the room immediately died down. "I have a thought. I propose we visit a chrono-synclastic infundibulum of our own."

There were gasps of surprise and approval in response.

"I have one in mind, as it happens. It's by the ocean, under a tree. The place has housed the rich, but no matter." He waved that issue away. "There we will find some answers perhaps."

I, too, wanted some answers. But it was not to be. I felt my breathing turn shallow, as if the very air was growing thinner. When I turned to look at Dr. Little and Abigail, I saw that they were already on their feet, backing out the door. I joined them.

Behind us, conversation had broken out again, voices rising and falling over each other as Udo's idea of a pilgrimage to a CSI took hold. We did not get to hear the rest.

In the hallway, we passed a couple hurrying into the room, late to the book club meeting. My parents. They were clearly in the middle of an argument—"I can eat dinner with *whomever* I wish," my mother was saying angrily; "I didn't mean it like that," my father countered, adding, "Are you mad because of what I said the other day?"

It was clear that their presence there meant that *ours* wasn't welcome. Would Missy or Soren have stumbled over our feet had we stayed in the rec room, thus interrupting their argument and halting the book club discussion? Whatever the reason, History propelled us as if we had a winter wind at our backs, and we passed out of St. Olaf's Hall.

16

"Too bad that couple had to come in just then," Abigail said after we came to a halt behind the now-familiar shrubbery in the courtyard of the dorm. Dr. Little gave an irritated grunt and pulled out his duffel bag from where we had left our things hidden—under one of the shrubs—but carefully so that none of the sensitive instruments inside would get damaged. Abigail continued. "Julia, were those your—"

"My parents, yes. Sorry," I said, feeling an obligation to apologize for their intrusion.

"They were having a lovers' quarrel?" Abigail said. "How cute."

"Poor timing on their part, though."

"I'm glad my parents are all the way in California," Dr. Little said. "I do *not* want that problem."

The statement was a touch insensitive—I was pretty sure Abigail would have been very happy to have the problem of running into her parents. It was too dark for me to make out her expression, but I decided it would be best to change the topic. "What do you think of Udo? Everyone in the club seems to hero-worship him, especially the women. He's more your age than mine, Abigail."

Abigail was an unabashed romantic, but she had a practical side. "He looks like he would faint if he had to wash a dish or mow the lawn. So the attraction—I don't know…the tight black turtleneck?"

We chuckled at that—a chuckle not shared by Dr. Little—and I brought up a thought that had occurred to me during the book club meeting. "Do you think it's odd that they're reading *The Sirens of Titan* and not *Slaughterhouse-Five*? That's Vonnegut's most famous novel, isn't it? I had to—I mean, I read it in college. And he's already written *Slaughterhouse*. We saw it on the library shelf."

"What was that one about, *Slaughterhouse-Five*?" Dr. Little asked. "It's not one I've read."

I remembered a bit about it. "It was based on his experiences in World War Two—Vonnegut survived the bombing of Dresden as a prisoner of war."

Abigail nodded. "Come to think of it, that one featured time travel, too…at least, of sorts. The main character, whose name I can't remember, jumped in and out of various points in his life. In one scene he'd be in a trench in Europe, and in the next he'd be an old man in an armchair back home, then he'd be back in the war."

"There you go. Udo never went to war," Dr. Little said. "He can't match Vonnegut's experience. The US pulled out of Vietnam in 1973—three years ago. He may have been called in for a physical, but he probably wasn't assigned a lottery number."

"A lottery number?" Abigail asked.

"To see who would be called up."

"Yes, I see…" I said. "Udo grew up watching those only a few years older than him be drafted—or go to Canada—all the while expecting that he himself might be called up, too. I wonder if he was relieved when that didn't happen, or if he was disappointed that he wouldn't get to serve, like his literary hero Kurt Vonnegut did."

"Udo could have enlisted in the army when he came of age," Dr. Little pointed out.

"Let's assume he was relieved, then. Either way, it makes sense that he's more enamored with *The Sirens of Titan* than with *Slaughterhouse*."

"There's a war part in *The Sirens of Titan*, too," Abigail said. "An interplanetary one. But I see what you mean, Julia."

We stuck around until the book club dispersed. I kept an eye out for my parents to see how their argument had turned out. The student my mother walked out with was not my father but the tall guy she'd sat next to at the book club meeting I'd crashed alone. Well, at least that probably ruled out Udo. It was dark, so I didn't get a good look at the man's face, but once again I had the feeling of familiarity—something about the way he carried himself and his walk. Had I met him before, in the present? If he was a student in

1976, that meant he was nearing his sixties in 2012. Perhaps he was a professor in one of the departments or maybe worked elsewhere on campus or in town.

Udo was the last to leave, with two female students on either side of him, but he seemed to be more interested in telling them all about his plans for the book than anything else. I heard him say, "I'm thinking of calling them *Richers*, my society of skeleton hoarders. What do you girls think?"

As we left the courtyard behind us and headed back to the Open Book, which we were using as our base of operations, I brought up the subject of Dr. Mooney once again—how he had never said anything about having met us in the past.

"That's not the only odd thing," Dr. Little said. "There's also the matter of the Slingshot."

The device was in the duffel bag on his shoulder, snug amidst the professor's sleeping pad, notebooks, and other belongings.

"What about it?" I asked. "To be honest, I've never understood how it works. I've been meaning to ask him to explain it to me."

To say I had no engineering skills would be an understatement, but I had hoped Dr. Mooney might be able to explain the main points with a napkin sketch or two.

I saw Dr. Little shake his head as we passed under a street lamp. "I'm not sure he even knows how it works, not really."

That was an odd thing to say. "How can Dr. Mooney not know? He built it," I protested.

"Well, we didn't actually see him do it, did we?" Abigail said quietly. Like before, her discomfort at saying anything even slightly critical of her beloved professor was obvious. "He just sort of…unveiled the Slingshot 1.0 when we were in Pompeii. But he could hardly have built it there."

"He must have brought it with him, then."

"But none of us noticed him working on it in the lab."

"Oh. I hadn't realized that," I said.

"And he's certainly been keeping things close to the vest since your return," Dr. Little said, which almost made me snicker, since he was the one prone to wearing vests, not Dr. Mooney. In fact, he had one on at the moment—the blue-jean one.

"Have you thought about what the Slingshot really represents?" Dr. Little went on. "It's not just a small, portable version of STEWie. It's a whole new paradigm."

Now that he mentioned it, I *had* wondered why the Slingshot didn't need the mirrors and lasers that served as STEWie's heart, or cryogenic equipment to prevent it from overheating. Dr. Mooney had breezily explained that the Slingshot used a power source more efficient than STEWie's expensive thorium-powered generator, and I hadn't given it much more thought than that.

As we crossed the plaza onto the green beyond it, Dr. Little added, "Even the conference presentations Dr. Mooney has done have only been demonstrations of the device in action, not explanations of how it *works*. I assumed Mooney didn't want to say more on the subject until he published"—not an unreasonable assumption, as publication was the academic equivalent of planting a flag on a mountaintop to stake your claim of having been there first—"but now I'm not so sure."

"And have you noticed," Abigail said, lowering her voice to almost a whisper, as if someone was listening in to our conversation, "how much better the device got between versions 1.0 and 2.0? Version 2.0 has a rechargeable battery and can go with or against the arrow of time. And who knows what the one he's been 'working' on, Version 3.0, will be able to do? For all we know, it'll be able to take us into the future."

"Hold on. I don't know much about inventions and design, but wouldn't you expect that each new version would be better than the previous one?" I asked.

"But for the innovation to happen so quickly? I mean, Mooney is a brilliant scientist, don't get me wrong," Dr. Little said as we reached the Open Book. The words, I suspected, had not been easy for him to say. "But he would need superpowers to have accomplished what he did in such a short time."

"So what are you suggesting, then?"

"What if Mooney's contribution to the Slingshot is only for show? That is to say, maybe he builds protective cases around devices that are provided to him."

"By whom?"

"Well, if *we* can jump into the past, then it makes sense that someone from further along in the future can jump into our present. In fact, we have to assume that it does happen."

"When you say it like that, it sounds a little creepy," Abigail said, wrinkling her nose. I was with her on that. I fought the impulse to furtively look around to see if anyone was watching from the shadows, judging us as I had judged my parents' actions and words just minutes before.

"You mean someone…sent the Slingshot to him?" I said to Dr. Little.

"My point is, there's a lot we don't know about Dr. Mooney. Like why he chose not to mention the fact that he met us in 1976."

"Well, he can't be from the future himself—he's here in 1976, just as he's supposed to be. Unless an older version of him sent the Slingshot back…But that's not possible, is it? Because that would mean Dr. Mooney was changing his own past." This was getting complicated.

Abigail tilted her head to one side, considering this. "Think about the times we've used the Slingshot. It helped us escape a ghost zone in Pompeii. It helped you survive the fourteenth century, Julia. For the most part, having it hasn't changed the past, only our own travels into it."

Drizzle had started falling all around us and was threatening to turn into a steady rain. Dr. Little brushed a raindrop off his nose and yawned. He and Abigail had been up for longer than I had, counting the hours that had passed when I went back to present-time to touch base with Nate.

"The cafeteria will be locked up by now. Should we all go to Xave's room in St. Olaf's?" I suggested.

Dr. Little shook his head sharply at this. "Let's not confuse matters further, Julia, by approaching Mooney even earlier in time than we already have."

"The library?" Abigail said. "We could go back there and find a quiet spot in the stacks."

I checked my watch, which I had carefully set to the correct time on October 22, 1976. "By the time we walk around the lake, the library will be closed. Unless you want to use the Slingshot to get us there faster, Dr. Little."

"I'm not opening up my laptop in this weather."

"We'll get in somehow," Abigail said. "Leave it to me."

Soaked from the now-steady rain, we stopped by the side door to the Crane Library, an industrial-looking one where I guessed book and other deliveries took place during daytime hours. Abigail eyed the lock. "Dr. Little, do you have a paper clip in your bag?"

"Why would I have one?"

"Just check," I said.

Sheltering the duffel bag under the overhang of the roof, Dr. Little unzipped it and rummaged around. The bag had an inner waterproof layer to protect the contents from inclement weather, such as the current downpour. "Will a pencil do? Pen? Wait, you're in luck." He pulled the paper clip off a thin stack of papers and passed it to Abigail, quickly sliding the papers back in to prevent them from being soaked.

"Give me a minute," Abigail said.

We did, and sooner than I would have thought it possible, not having any previous breaking-and-entering experience, we heard a soft click. Abigail pushed the door open. Her strange upbringing had led to some unexpected skills. "You're welcome," she said, pocketing the paper clip.

The night lights had been left on inside, bathing the quiet halls in a soft, ambient glow.

"Let's get out of sight in case campus security swings by for a check," I said.

We found a good spot away from the windows, a circle of easy chairs of the sort found in most libraries—that is to say, comfy and inviting. Dr. Little glanced at the easy chairs, then picked a high-backed wooden seat at a nearby table. He pushed a textbook left behind by a student out of the way, then retrieved his laptop from the duffel bag. As he did so, a page fell out and onto the floor, one of the ones that had been freed when he gave Abigail the paper clip.

I picked up the page for him, catching sight of a list of numbers on it as I did so:

4-9-33-36-39-47
8-21-32-35-36-38
20-30-32-43-44-47
5-7-12-21-32-45
4-5-18-41-47-48
11-16-21-26-27-47
2-10-19-23-26-30
15-18-22-24-28-49

. . .

"Oh, are these spacetime coordinates?" I was always interested in learning more about the mechanics of time travel. "Precomputed ones you planned to use with the Slingshot 2.0 to edge forward in time until you reached your birth date cutoff?"

"Something like that, yes," he answered a bit testily, as if not wanting to be bothered with having to explain things to amateurs. He opened his bag again, and the page joined its brethren within.

I plopped into one of the easy chairs. Well, he was right. I *was* an amateur when it came to time travel. But how was I to improve if I didn't ask questions? Deciding I wasn't going to let him brush me off so quickly, I said, "I've always wanted to learn how to calculate spacetime coordinates. Say I wanted to jump to a prehistoric time and place..." Kamal Ahmad's recent thesis defense, which I had attended, came to mind. "Neander Valley, 30,000 BC. Does the place and date of the destination somehow get woven into a sequence of numbers and that gets entered into STEWie or the Slingshot?"

Dr. Little bent down to plug the laptop charger into the wall. "It's complicated. If you're really interested in the topic, you should sign up for a class."

"You have to be a student to take a class."

"Yes, that is a problem."

Abigail had taken the easy chair opposite me. "STEWie uses light to warp spacetime so the point where you are meets up with the point where you want to go, like fingers pinching four-dimensional dough. You orient the STEWie mirrors just *so*, fire up the lasers and the generator...and there you are, fresh out of the basket, in Neander Valley. STEWie is the SUV of time travel—it's an energy-guzzling way to travel in time compared to what the Slingshot can do."

"And the Slingshot?" I asked.

"Let's see, what's the opposite of an SUV? Something slim, trim, and efficient that requires very little gas except for a starting push."

"A bobsled?" I suggested. "Never been in one, but I've seen them in the Olympics on TV."

"A bobsled, then. One that can go in both directions."

Dr. Little glanced up from the laptop, as if the current topic actually intrigued him, but said nothing.

"Like we said, though, we're not really sure how the Slingshot works, not really. Other than that it's prone to dropping travelers into ghost zones," Abigail said, trying out another of the armchairs.

"Well, at least we aren't likely to encounter many ghost zones in good old 1976." I wondered what was inside the device that was sitting there so innocently next to Dr. Little's laptop and whether he ever got the urge to just open it up and look. It was somewhat larger than the laptop, though it had a smaller screen and keyboard, and there were wire loops sticking out of it here and there. Not quite how I would have pictured a device from the future, if that was what it was.

Abigail curled up in the armchair. "You *should* sign up for a class, Julia. Even just to audit. I think you're good at this whole time-travel thing."

"I am? How so?"

"You don't let it mess with your head. Time travel isn't—you know—easy."

"It's not," Dr. Little concurred for once. He fought off a yawn. "Not computationally, physically, or mentally. I suppose we need to decide where to jump to next—to another book club meeting or Udo's room to see if we can find any clues."

"No." I decided an executive decision was in order. They both had bags under their eyes. "You two need some rest. There is nothing more we can do tonight. We'll regroup in the morning. That will give Nate time to track down Udo Leland in the present.

As for me, I'm going to fetch the copy of *The Sirens of Titan* and see if I can glean anything more from it."

Abigail pulled the book out of the pocket of her coat. "Here, Julia."

"You snuck a book out of the library? And then back into it?"

"I figured in the worst-case scenario we could return it when we got back home and pay a hefty fee."

"Hmm. I guess that's all right," I said, taking the book. "I'll keep an eye out for place-names, especially ones on the East Coast."

The others headed to the library restrooms to get ready for the night and, as Abigail said, "To check if there's a couch in there." The backpacks I had brought for us held a thin mat each, but a couch would certainly have been more comfortable.

She came back first—"No couch"—and pushed two armchairs together before stretching out on them and closing her eyes. Dr. Little came back and unrolled his mat—a thicker, more solid one— to one side away from us. He settled in after instructing me, "Keep an eye out for campus security. They make building rounds throughout the night."

"I know. They usually don't go inside buildings, though."

I found an armchair away from Abigail and Dr. Little and flicked on a nearby lamp. I had given up trying to keep track of the time-travel lag, deciding to eat and sleep whenever I felt like it and not according to my wristwatch, which I made sure to still carefully adjust every time we jumped.

I turned to the page in the story where I had left off, right after the CSI definition, and read on.

As the campus clock struck 2:00 a.m., I left Abigail gently snoring in the easy chairs and Dr. Little prone on his sleeping mat, and snuck out of the library. Not having Abigail's questionable skill for breaking and entering, I made sure to leave the door unlocked behind me. I hoped campus security wouldn't swing by to check.

I didn't have any particular purpose in sneaking out; rather, I just wanted to clear my head a bit after reading for two hours straight. I picked a destination at random—Hypatia House, where my office would one day be—and set a brisk pace. The rain had stopped. The night air was cool, but there wasn't even a hint of wind, which made the cold tolerable. Despite the late hour, I crossed paths here and there with a student on a bicycle or a couple intertwined in a dorm doorway. Occasionally I heard the unmistakable sound of a Friday-night party through an open window or glimpsed campus security as they made their rounds by car on the well-lit campus streets.

Seeing another of the intertwined couples—*not* my parents—made me wonder if their argument really had been about who was having dinner with whom, or if there was more to it. I hoped the issue wasn't my impending arrival, though I still had the feeling Dad didn't know about it yet, not at this earlier book club meet nor the later one I had gone to first. I had always thought that my parents seemed to get along very well, in a sort of cheerful, half-exasperated way, as though their very quirks and differences were what drew them to each other. Mom was chattier than Dad. Dad liked to be up and about early, while she liked to sleep in a bit. He liked spicy food, she preferred plain. And yet they had lived and worked together harmoniously for years, first running the Thornberg paper and now the retirement community. It was a situation that might have fractured the strongest couple, but all their rough edges and sharp points worked to their benefit. They were two irregularly shaped puzzle pieces that fit just right.

As I swung around the north end of Sunniva Lake, where the dock was, I found myself thinking of the Fourth of July picnic, the one that had been the source of the photo Sabina had taken along. Tonight the wooden dock was a dark strip in the calm surface of the water, and the reeds where it met the sand were bare and stark. On the Fourth of July the reeds had been tall and green, and we had all met up just before dusk, as it was a decent spot for viewing the town fireworks.

The day had started off on the wrong foot because of a morning dentist appointment for Sabina. It had been one in a long sequence of appointments intended to bring her teeth up to modern standards in health and appearance. By afternoon the Novocain had worn off and the puffiness of her cheek had subsided—she had been nervous that she would stay that way forever, with one of her cheeks unnaturally inflated—so her smile was back as well.

"Fire works?" she'd asked, sounding puzzled, as she and Abigail hauled the larger of the coolers out of the trunk of my Honda.

"Not two words," I explained, "but one. *Fireworks*. They're not really fire; they're more like shooting stars sent up into the sky." I winced, worried that everything I was saying must be reminding her of the Pompeii eruption. She didn't seem to mind. Still, I thought that it was probably good that we'd decided to watch the display from by the lake rather than opting for a more close-up view at the high school field, from where the town fireworks would be launched loudly and brightly.

Nate had pulled into the lot after us and parked his Jeep in a shady spot. As was his wont, he attended to a bit of campus business before coming over to help, advising a student who was trying to snag a visitor parking spot that all students needed to park in the orange zone. Wanda was trotting around excitedly at his heels.

Celer lumbered down out of the Honda, having decided that all the action was outside, and waddled over to where we were setting up our picnic on the tiny sandy beach that housed the dock. Wanda raced ahead of Nate to greet the older dog, who placidly submitted to her attentions. I unrolled a pair of oversized blankets and spread them on the ground. We were expecting four more people: two professors—Xavier Mooney and Helen Presnik; and two graduate students—Kamal Ahmad and Jacob Jacobson. Sabina was happy that Jacob wouldn't see her with one puffy cheek. She had a bit of a harmless schoolgirl crush on the ginger-haired second-year grad student, a crush he was oblivious to.

I waved a mosquito away and greeted Nate.

"Where do you want this?" He was carrying a case of gourmet ice tea.

"Put it in whichever cooler has more room."

"Lovely day, isn't it?"

"Yes, it is."

The exchange was not as insipid as it sounds, or maybe it was. But the Fourth of July picnic was before the incident with the runestone, before our first kiss in a fourteenth-century woodland. We were still in that equally awkward and exciting phase of things when all conversation, even that related to the weather, takes on a special meaning. I saw Abigail, whose hair was dark purple that day, wink knowingly at me.

Nate deposited the tea in one of the coolers and turned to Sabina. "How are the teeth?"

"Feel same. Look better."

"Are you excited to see the fireworks?"

"Yes," Sabina said in her distinctive accent. It didn't hide the combination of bravado and uncertainty that underlay the word. In moments like these I was reminded of how young she really was. An older person might simply have said, "Not really. It sounds like a loud and strange thing," but she was not only young but out of place, unsure of her surroundings or of what to expect.

"Just keep in mind that it's a happy occasion, a celebration," Nate said easily.

"Celebrate what?" Sabina bent down to rub Wanda's soft head, and the dog accepted the attention, rolling onto her back in the sand. Abigail smiled, as if to say, *Good luck with this one*, and walked off after announcing her intention to get some bug spray.

Nate scratched his head. "This country's independence from Great Britain—Britannia?—which we won many years ago. And independence...Let me see if I can think of a similar example from ancient Roman history...Can you think of anything, Julia?"

"I've been meaning to read up on my Roman history but haven't had a chance yet. We can ask Helen when she gets here. She would know." I tried to summon some long-buried information from my college studies. "Uh, didn't Rome have kings before it became a republic with a senate? There were seven of them, I think, weren't there? Not all at once, but in a row, one after another?"

This seemed familiar to Sabina. She nodded. "Yes. Seven—how you say?—kings."

"Well, there you are," I said. "Was the last one overthrown by the people, the seventh of these kings?" I tried to think of words she might know. "Overthrown means gotten rid of...done with..."

"Done with, yes."

The mention of Romans led us to Roma, which Sabina had never been to. Rome was the New York City of her day, and Abigail and I knew it had been a childhood dream of hers to visit it. Not to mention that she was set on paying respects to the goddess Diana, whose statue still stood in the Pompeii forum, something we could hardly make happen in the US. This was the conversation, the one where I should have picked up on her strong feelings about it. Instead, I had waved another mosquito away and said idly, "Maybe one day we could take a vacation to Pompeii and Rome," and quickly added, "Well, whoever wants to go."

I didn't want Nate to think I was hoping he'd want to travel with us. Or maybe I was, and that was why I had failed to notice how strongly Sabina had latched on to the idea.

Nate had simply nodded in agreement. "That's not a bad idea—I've never been to Europe. Well, not counting our few days in ancient Pompeii and that one stop in London on the way back…I suppose I mean I've never been to *modern* Europe."

"Who's going to Europe?" Abigail was back with the bug spray. Jacob and Kamal were with her, having walked over from the TTE building (empty-handed, I noticed, but I had expected that of grad students and had brought enough food to cover everyone.)

"We all," Sabina said.

"Are we going any place and time in particular? And when?" Kamal asked. "I've got so much preparation to do for my thesis defense."

"To Pompeii and Rome," I explained. "One day. And we're not using STEWie for it. Just airplanes and trains."

"I don't have a passport." Jacob was Dr. Rojas's junior student and lived with his parents in town, above their book-and-antiques shop. Sabina gave Jacob a smile that showed her new teeth. He didn't notice.

"Well, get one," Abigail said. She commenced spraying Sabina's arms after instructing her to stretch them out. "I'd love to go, but someone will have to fund me. I'm just a grad student—no travel money."

"Me too," Jacob said.

"I guess I could ask my parents for my share," Kamal said. "Maybe it could be a graduation present for me on their part."

I didn't remember inviting half the TTE grad student office. "I'm glad you're all on board with the idea. I suppose we could try to figure something out, get a group rate perhaps."

I had meant to look into organizing it, but I'd figured there was no rush—Sabina was still getting used to modern life, Abigail and Kamal were coping with thesis writing, and I was dealing with Quinn-related issues. For adults, the promise of doing something "one day" means a few years into the future, when a good opportunity comes up. I had even vaguely thought that once she was old enough, Sabina might join the Time Travel Engineering program and get to Pompeii—the past one—that way.

Young people sometimes need things to happen faster.

And so Sabina had taken matters into her own hands. But her plan had gone awry and she had landed here in 1976. When the opportunity to get to the ocean presented itself, which she knew was the first step to getting back to Italy, she took it. At times young people can be so blindly optimistic. I see it all the time with incoming students—freshmen arriving with high hopes that they'll choose the right major at once, ace all their classes, be popular with all their peers, and are then bothered when it doesn't all happen according to plan. Not that I don't still consider myself young, but for good or bad I was past that stage where everything seems possible. Not much in life ever happens according to plan, and usually that's okay. Granted, Sabina had more cause to know about life's turbulence than most, and, standing there by the still water with campus lights twinkling all around, I was happy she had managed to retain her youthful enthusiasm, even if it sometimes led to not-the-best decisions.

A disconcerting thought hit me as I left the dock behind me and turned back toward the library. I hadn't considered how Sabina would react when we did catch up with her. After all, we were planning to turn her right around and bring her home to St. Sunniva. I hoped she would be happy to see us.

She had ended up enjoying the fireworks after a few minutes of staring up at the colorful patterns, her eyes wide. And it was that image that stayed with me as I set a course back to the library.

"Julia, where were you?" Abigail asked sleepily.

"Wandering around. Never mind. Go back to sleep."

I was lucky to have made it back inside at all. I had almost been caught by Dan Anderson, the future chief of campus security. The young officer had been making his rounds of campus on foot, whistling a happy tune as he did so, and I'd had to duck under a dark stairwell until he passed, crossing my fingers for fear he'd check the library door. Luckily he hadn't. The last thing I'd wanted to do was spend the rest of the night outside.

"Did you see them?" Abigail mumbled, shifting a bit in her armchair setup.

"Who?"

"Your parents."

"Certainly not. Why would they be wandering around campus in the middle of the night?"

"Just thought you might have run into them at St. Olaf's or wherever."

I hadn't. But she was right, I had wanted to.

17

Nate and Dr. B looked up as I arrived on STEWie's platform. I was like Rumfoord and his dog, bouncing in and out of the lab, only without the dog.

"No luck yet?" Dr. B asked, waving a greeting at me.

Nate was at the workstation beside her, his cell phone pressed between one ear and shoulder, a pen in his hand. He nodded in my direction and said, "Uh-huh…I see…" into the phone. I wasn't used to seeing him at a desk; most of his campus security duties were done by car or on foot. But that wasn't why my step had suddenly faltered and I'd almost tripped as I descended off the platform. I had realized the identity of the man my mother had been keeping company with in 1976.

I hadn't met him in the present. I had met his son.

Nate's profile as he sat at the desk with the phone cradled in his shoulder was exactly the same as that of the man in the book club—they could have been brothers if not for the twist in time. I hadn't met Nate's parents yet—they lived on the North Shore, in Duluth—but I knew with certainty that the book club man could only be one person: Nathaniel Kirkland Sr.

Well, that was an interesting development.

I shook my head in response to Dr. B's question and set the Slingshot 2.0 down on her workstation. "Dr. Little asked if you could please recharge this," I said, adding, "I never realized how hard it could be to find a person lost in a particular year."

Dr. Little had not actually used the word *please* but I had thought it best to include it. (He had griped, "I budgeted for five small jumps on my original run and we've already done three. I don't know how many more we'll need.")

The third jump had brought us from the Crane Library of the morning of Saturday, October 23, 1976 to the Open Book of

November 2. We had jumped ahead so that we were once again parallel in time with Sabina. Dr. Little and Abigail were planning to head to Udo's room, which they were going to search one way or another. As I was preparing to leave, Abigail had started to throw out ideas, starting with picking the room's lock or bribing Sam, Udo's engineer roommate, to let them in. Dr. Little had looked a little aghast at her lawless approach.

"Hey, wouldn't it be funny if Chief Kirkland found Udo still on campus, teaching in the creative writing program?" Abigail had said as they prepared to send me back, in between breaking-in ideas.

"It would certainly be convenient," had been Dr. Little's reply.

Dr. B accepted the Slingshot and plugged it into its receptacle.

"Any new developments at your end?" Nate asked, hanging up the phone after thanking the person at the other end. Unlike my previous jump into the lab, when it had just been the two of us, he was all business in Dr. B's presence, which was fine with me—I needed to wrap my head around the implications of what I had seen in 1976. There weren't any, I was pretty sure—in 1976 Nate's parents were already married and very much together, even though little Nate was living with his grandparents, like I had mentioned to Abigail. So the fact that Nate Sr. was hanging out with my mother in book club meetings, and outside them, probably meant nothing. I was reading too much into it. Nate was not my half brother.

He wasn't.

"Julia?"

"Sorry, it's been a tiring run. There's been one new development. We found out that the book club is headed to a CSI."

"A what?" Nate said. "Sounds like crime scene investigation."

"The term is from a Kurt Vonnegut novel, *The Sirens of Titan.* Chrono-synclastic infundibulum, a place where people finally understand each other. We're calling it a CSI for short. The book club had been reading the novel, and Udo Leland wants them to go to a CSI of his choosing."

He wrote all this down after checking the spelling of *synclastic* and *infundibulum* with me. "So where is it?"

"We don't know. In the book itself it's in outer space. Udo's CSI appears to be on the East Coast, possibly by a tree."

Nate thoughtfully tapped the notepad in front of him, where he had scribbled down notes in pen. "That was the Registrar's Office. I called to get Udo Leland's contact details. I found out something rather odd. According to them, Udo Leland never completed his undergraduate degree here. He dropped out of St. Sunniva that semester—fall 1976."

"Huh," I said. "Maybe he left school to work on his novel, or to gain some life experience by backpacking around the world before settling down."

"That's the thing." Dr. B said. "We've been checking. He has no Facebook page, no personal blog, or anything like that."

"So he doesn't like social media," I suggested. "He would hardly be the only one."

Nate grunted in agreement. "You won't find much of an online presence for me, except what's required for my job."

"More to the point, he never did write anything," Dr. B said. "There's no published author by the name. No library listing, no Amazon listing, nothing."

"Pen name? Maybe he's a recluse author who works on an old typewriter in a cabin up on the North Shore," I suggested, before it struck me that such a scenario did not sound like Udo at all. Recluse living wasn't his style. He liked having an audience, unless he had changed a lot in the intervening years. "Didn't the Registrar's Office have his contact details?"

"No forwarding address, only his last known address—St. Olaf's Hall. I'm not sure where that is. It must be an old name for a dorm."

I pointed down at the ground. "It's here. Or at least it used to be here, before they built the TTE lab." I thought for a minute. "Whatever Udo ended up doing in life and wherever he ended up going, Sabina couldn't have had anything to do with it—it had all already happened before she went back. She was just a shadow in his peripheral vision—had to be, right, Dr. Baumgartner?"

"Yes, we can't change History, as you know. Although she would have hardly been a shadow—did you say she was in one of the vehicles with Udo and the rest of the book club? Driving for hours, maybe even days?"

I remembered Dr. Little's theory about boldness often trumping stealth in time travel, and mentioned it.

"It's not a *theory*, scientifically speaking," Dr. B said, distracted by the academic point. "That's a working idea on his part, a hypothesis. Contrary to popular belief, a theory is a hypothesis that's been generalized and verified—by observation, experimentation, or deduction. Like Einstein's theory of relativity, the theory of evolution, and many others…"

I didn't want to get sidetracked into a lengthy academic discussion. "But it could account for why Sabina was able to hitch a ride with the book club. She was just an extra passenger either in Udo's Ford Mustang or the art bus."

"Yes, I suppose it could."

After the briefest internal debate, I said, "I could give my parents a call."

"Your *parents?*" Dr. B said.

"To ask where the book club went. They were both members." I wasn't sure whether to mention that Nate Sr. had also been there, meaning Nate could call his father as well. A bit flustered, I covered it up by pretending to look around the lab. "Now where did I leave my cell phone?"

"In the lab locker," Nate said, staring at me. "With your purse."

"Right." I headed to the locker, retrieved the phone, and dialed my parents' home number. I received no answer and tried the main office of the retirement community next, even though it was late evening. Raul, their assistant, was still there. "¡Hóla, Julia!" I explained that there was something of an emergency afoot without giving any details, and learned that my parents were not back from their cruise yet. Getting in touch with them, he said, would be tricky—the aim of the cruise was to sweep its guests away from the pace of modern life, so no one carried their electronic devices on board. The first such cruise my parents had brought their retirees on—that one to the Caribbean—had been such a success that they'd immediately organized a second one to Key West. The best way to reach them would be through authorities, Raul suggested.

I left a message with him for my parents to call me when they got home and turned to find Nate still studying me.

"No luck getting through to your parents?"

I shook my head. "They're on the Floating Free cruise from Fort Myers down to Key West and possibly beyond. A vote is taken along the way to see what ports they want to call in."

"They should be reachable from shore," Nate said, reaching for his pen. "I'll get on it. Floating Free, you said?"

I hesitated. There was a faster option—Nate's father had also been at the book club meeting. Only bringing that out into the open might raise all sorts of other issues that I wasn't ready to handle. I watched Nate jot down the name of the cruise and decided this behavior was unworthy of me. "Wait."

"That's not the name of the ship?"

"I don't think it is—I don't know the name of the ship—but that isn't what I meant. Call your father instead and ask him. He was there, too, with the book club."

Dr. Baumgartner had gone to fetch her e-reader from her office for me—I figured it would be useful to have a biography of Kurt Vonnegut on hand, as well as copies of his books. In the meantime, Nate had left a message on his father's phone and turned back with the clear intent of drawing me into an embrace—not an amorous one necessarily, but as a gesture of support. Well, maybe an amorous one.

He looked surprised when instead of taking a step into his arms, I took one back.

"What, do I have bad breath or something?"

"No, it's not that." If anyone smelled bad it was me—I hadn't showered since we'd left for 1976, and the stench of the cigarette smoke we'd encountered everywhere we went clung to my clothes.

"Julia?"

"Really, it's nothing. I'm just out of my mind with worry about Sabina."

This was true, and also, what was I going to say to him—I think your father might be my father as well? Luckily Dr. B came back before he could ask any more questions. She handed me the e-reader. "It's recharged." Kamal and Jacob trailed in behind her. They waved a greeting at me.

Nate turned on them. "Did one of you give Sabina the door code to the lab?" he asked, sternly for him.

Both of them adamantly denied it. They hurried to explain that they'd been in the grad student office down the hall, spending their Saturday evening on thesis writing for Kamal and coursework for the younger of the two students, Jacob.

"The strange comings and goings in the TTE lab lured us out," Kamal said. "Did you say Sabina has gone somewhere?"

I brought them up to speed and underlined that they were *not* to tweet or post about any of this, even if they were used to sharing news, bad or good, online. "We don't need everyone on campus and beyond in our hair at the moment."

"We wouldn't do that, Julia," Jacob said, checking his hand on its way to the phone in his back pocket. "Can we come along and help look for her?"

"I'm not an expert on American history," Kamal said, "but I'd be glad to lend a hand."

I appreciated their concern, but we didn't need more boots on the ground. I instructed the pair to help Dr. B and Nate with the present-day research that needed to be conducted, then quickly downloaded a biography of Vonnegut's life onto Dr. B's e-reader. I did the same with all of his works I could find that predated 1977, up to *Slapstick*, published in October 1976, just in case.

"Thanks for the use of your e-reader, Dr. B. I may have run up a bit of a tab—I'll reimburse you when I get back."

"Don't worry about it, Julia." She was readying New York City coordinates—I was going to pop in quickly to Kurt Vonnegut's house there, before rejoining Dr. Little and Abigail on campus.

I took a step toward STEWie's basket, then turned back. "Dr. B?"

"Yes?"

"Sabina's presence cannot be what made Udo leave school...not even in a small way? That has to be right, doesn't it?"

She nodded without glancing away from the screen. "Correct."

"But the other way, that *could* happen? I mean, if Udo's plan all along was to leave school and disappear—for whatever reason—there's nothing to stop Sabina from also...disappearing."

She stopped what she was doing and looked up at me. "I suppose it's a possibility, yes."

"I've got a bad feeling about this," Jacob said as if quoting from somewhere—a *Star Wars* movie probably; he loved them.

"I don't. Sabina's smart," Kamal said. "She wouldn't do anything dumb."

"I don't know that any of us go out of our way to do dumb things," I said. "It's part of life."

Nate walked me to the basket. "I've got everybody in the campus security office working on finding Udo Leland. How has Dr. Little been?" he added, as if taking a stab in the dark about where exactly the problem might lie. The young professor was not exactly known for his interpersonal skills.

"Well, you know him."

"True. He did seem quite put out with what's happened—more than circumstances warrant, perhaps."

"Never get between a professor and his research, I guess."

"Still, I might take a look around his office."

"You don't think he had anything to do with sending Sabina into 1976, do you? He's been helpful—for him—really more overworked and overtired than anything. Maybe his long hours are catching up to him."

"That's probably all it is."

He offered me a steadying hand to climb STEWie's platform, and after the briefest of hesitations, which I'm sure he noticed, I accepted it. Once I was secure on the platform, he passed me the freshly recharged Slingshot. "I do wish I could come along. How's Abigail holding up?"

"You know her. She's very...resourceful. As for me, I feel I'm in 1976 on borrowed time—I expect to be sent back by History any second, my mother being, er, pregnant and all. Besides, I'm not sure I'm of much use. I don't seem to be an expert on anything that will help us catch up with Sabina, like seventies literature or the ins and outs of time travel."

"Nonsense. I trust Abigail—very much so—but Dr. Little is a professor, and she's a graduate student. I'm glad you're there—*you* can overrule him if it came to it. *She* can't."

This was somewhat true—there was a deeply entrenched power structure between students and professors, one I was outside of. I gave him a small smile. "I believe Abigail would be very much up to the task if it came down to choosing between antagonizing Dr. Little and helping Sabina. But I see what you mean—there's a power differential. My position doesn't depend on his goodwill…hers does." I had put my coat back on in preparation for 1976. I tucked Dr. B's e-reader into a pocket. The newly charged Slingshot was in my backpack, where it took up most of the space.

"Good luck in New York City."

"Thanks. Nate, I—"

But I didn't get to say more. Bright light filled the room, and STEWie's basket whisked me away.

The nineteenth-century brownstone stood inset a bit from the neighboring buildings on a one-way street. Ten steps led up to an ornate front door. A small chubby angel sat perched above it like a benevolent gargoyle. I set down my backpack and checked the house number—228. A cloak of noise lay over the city—car horns in heavy midafternoon traffic, sirens, construction. I had arrived in a quiet spot to one side of the steps, opposite what seemed to be a gated-off photo studio on the street level of the four-story townhouse. The black metal railing edging the front steps felt cool to my touch.

The upper levels had three windows each. There was no movement behind them.

If the pedestrians walking by briskly, as if they all had someplace to be, were surprised by the sight of me appearing out of thin air, none showed it. It *was* Manhattan, after all. And it was election day—the news blared from a TV through an open window on the neighboring building.

I moved from the railing to the curb to scan the cars parked bumper to bumper on both sides of the one-way street. It didn't take long. There was no sign of either Udo's red Ford Mustang or the art bus, which Xave had described as "colorful, very colorful." A few trees stood on each side of the street. City ones—spaced out, semi-healthy, and surviving as best they could in the urban shadows. Having checked a map back in the lab, I knew that 228 East Forty-Eighth Street stood a couple of blocks away from Manhattan's East River; a quick search in the e-book biography had yielded the address, and Dr. B had woven it into STEWie coordinates. It was hardly a location that anyone would describe with the words *tree* or *ocean*.

I felt a bit deflated. I had asked Dr. B to send me to Vonnegut's New York residence in the hopes that the book club had come to pay their respects to the famous author. But they weren't here.

I poked my head around a parked car to check again, and a yellow cab whizzed by with an irritated honk. I jumped back toward the curb but took one step too many and bumped into a fast-moving pedestrian. Both of us lost our balance, though a last-second acrobatic twist on my part made me land on my bottom and not on the backpack holding the Slingshot. We disentangled ourselves and I offered the fortyish-some woman sporting a leopard-print pantsuit a hand up. She accepted it, got to her feet, and helped me dust off the city grime that had collected on my coat. I picked up the purse she had dropped and handed it to her. It was all very civil and quite unlike the mental image I had of Manhattanites. I apologized for tripping us both, and she said, "No harm done, darlin'. Have you voted? Very important to vote." I nodded yes without meaning to, and she continued on.

I nursed my sore elbow and watched her walk away. My quick stop in Manhattan was turning into a bit of an embarrassing disaster. I tried to look on the bright side. At least I hadn't twisted an ankle or wrist—or crushed the Slingshot, which would have been the most disastrous of all possible scenarios.

A second taxi honked at me and I waved a *no* in its direction before retreating back into the shadow of the stairs, protectively holding the backpack with the Slingshot to one side. The question facing me now was whether to wait a bit in the hopes that the book club would choose this particular moment to arrive—granted, highly unlikely—or to type into the waiting Slingshot the coordinates Dr. B had prepared for me and jump to St. Sunniva campus to meet up with Dr. Little and Abigail. I did a quick mental calculation. Thornberg to New York could probably be done in a full day and night's drive if the students took turns at the wheel and made no long stops along the way. Given that they had left yesterday morning and it was now midafternoon, if they made good time it wasn't out of the realm of possibility that they were just around the corner, inching their way closer through Manhattan traffic. I decided sticking around an extra half hour or so couldn't hurt. Besides, I could use the time to leaf through the Vonnegut biography and see if there was anything in there that might help with our current problem.

I leaned back against the stairs with one of my feet crossed over the other and got out Dr. B's e-reader from my coat pocket. Luckily, it had been undamaged by my fall. Also luckily, Dr. B had it in a brown leather case, so at first glance it'd be mistaken for a hardbound book by pedestrians going up and down East Forty-Eighth.

I took a quick look at the contents and jumped to a chapter about the author's early life. I wanted to find out about his background, because I figured Udo probably identified with him for reasons other than just the desired fame. Apparently Vonnegut's parents (like Udo's own, I suspected) were wealthy...or had been until the Wall Street Crash of 1929. I jumped a bit further ahead and stumbled across something even more interesting. Vonnegut had left college midway through his studies.

In Vonnegut's case, it sounded like he had been pushed into studying the sciences by his father and older brother, and it hadn't been a great fit, and then the war had come. Vonnegut had left Cornell to join the war effort. I skimmed the Dresden part of the biography, which sounded like a positively awful experience for the twenty-three-year-old Kurt as well as everyone else involved. He had returned from Europe with a Purple Heart and a ceremonial Nazi saber, and re-enrolled in school, this time at the University of Chicago, but his idea for a master's topic (comparing Cubist artists in Paris with nineteenth-century Native American uprisings) was turned down by the anthropology department for being too ambitious, and he had left school for a second time.

I considered all this, pausing in my reading. If Udo was not coming back to St. Sunniva after the CSI visit, was he leaving school to follow in Vonnegut's footsteps? I knew that United

Nations Plaza, where I had once visited on a high school trip, was a short walk from here. Was he planning on joining the Peace Corps? *Did* the Peace Corps have anything to do with the UN? I had no idea, but Udo volunteering for it was as likely a possibility as any.

I shifted in my spot by the railing. The problem with Udo trying to emulate his hero Kurt Vonnegut was that it wasn't how life worked. Even if you have similar roots and try to take the same path, it doesn't mean you grow to be an equally tall tree. I had seen enough siblings come into the science departments and leave with very different outcomes, from successful PhDs to dropouts in the first semester, to know that. And Udo was trying to force his transformation into one of the American greats.

And it hadn't worked, had it? Because Udo was nowhere to be found in modern literature.

Realizing I had lost track of the time, I glanced up to see a tall man approaching from the direction opposite to the flow of traffic. I snapped the e-reader's case shut. The man had curly hair and a bushy mustache and eyebrows, like a Mark Twain look-alike. His pace was slightly impatient, that of a resident returning home. Was he was coming back from voting, a meeting with an editor, or an early celebration lunch for his upcoming fifty-fourth birthday?

My feet shuffled me out of the shadows of their own accord, not propelled by History but by curiosity. Kurt looked a little taken aback by my sudden appearance and flicked away the match he had just used to light a cigarette. He took a long drag off it, then offered me one out of the red-and-white pack of Pall Malls cupped in his nicotine-stained hand.

"No, thanks, Mr. Vonnegut."

"What can I do for you, young lady?"

"Uh…"

I was speechless for a moment, as (a) I had never met a famous historical figure before, and (b) I didn't know where to begin or what to say.

"Well?" Another drag on the cigarette.

"Have any students made a pilgrimage to your place today? They would have arrived in a red Ford Mustang and a painted VW van."

"Odd question." He took another long drag. "To answer it—no. They used to come more when I lived in Barnstable. Anything else?"

I shook my head, staring at this middle-aged man whose life story I now knew from beginning to end, having skimmed most of the biography. I could tell him what year his divorce would become final and how well his not-yet-written novel *Timequake* would sell. It was an odd feeling, to say the least. Had I told him right then and there that thirty years from now he would trip on a dog leash at the bottom of these very stairs and hit his head on the pavement and not recover, I imagined his reply would have been "So it goes," with an accompanying shrug.

But I didn't say anything, of course.

"You don't have a book you want signed? Or even a manuscript you want me to read?"

I shook my head again.

With a touch of disappointment, as if he took it personally, he said, "Well, then." He continued up the stairs, unlocked the door, and went in. The door closed behind him.

That was that.

I pulled my mind back to the reason I'd come. There was clearly no sign of the book club, and it was time for me to get going. Abigail and Dr. Little would be wondering where I was. Dr. B had written down the coordinates I needed to enter into the Slingshot—the first time I had actually been given the responsibility of doing so. I was a tiny bit pleased that I had been entrusted with the task.

The coordinates were in a small wallet, safely ensconced in one of my coat pockets. Or they should have been. I felt around for the wallet, then checked the other pocket of the coat.

The wallet was missing.

The leopard-suit lady so intent on getting me to vote hadn't been as nice as she'd seemed. I had been mugged.

18

It was cliché, getting mugged in Manhattan—unless getting mugged in 1976 Manhattan was not yet cliché. I didn't know, but either way I gave myself a mental kick for not being more careful. I had been so buoyed by the hope that the book club would be in Vonnegut's vicinity that I'd forgotten to be nervous about time traveling on my own. Now I felt panic rising up in my belly. I tried to take a deep breath, then another. Nate and Dr. B knew where I was. They would send someone to fetch me. I was not stuck here, doomed to roam the city like a displaced person forever.

Still, my quick stop in Manhattan could now *definitely* be considered a disaster. It was one thing to be held in place by History, or to accidentally fall into a ghost zone; it was entirely another to get self-stuck.

I slid down to the ground, my back against Vonnegut's staircase, to weigh my options. One, I could run after the pedestrian I had bumped into, although she was by now long gone, and demand the return of my wallet. She would have found it empty except for the sequence of numbers, so the disappointment she was bound to feel gave me a small sense of satisfaction. Two, I could knock on the door of the brownstone and enlist Kurt's help in calling the police and trying to get my wallet back. Three, I could sit tight and wait to be rescued by Dr. B.

Unless—

Leaving the backpack by the railing, I went back to the curb where I had fallen. There, on the edge of the road, among the discarded cigarettes butts, used bus tickets, and other trash, lay my wallet. The Slingshot coordinate note stuck out of it slightly, but it was otherwise undisturbed.

I picked up the wallet, feeling the red rise up my cheeks. The clichéd thing had not happened—I hadn't been mugged. My assumption had been the clichéd part.

I had much to learn about History.

"You did what?" A bit of spittle flew out of Dr. Little's mouth and landed on my neck.

I wiped it away. "I made a side stop at Kurt Vonnegut's place in New York City."

"On whose authority?"

I tried not to get defensive and to keep my tone even. "No one's—my own. I asked Dr. B to send me. She agreed that it was worth a try to see if the book club went there. Nate thought it was a good idea, too."

"Since when does Kirkland make decisions in the TTE lab? Last I checked, he was neither a professor nor a financial backer."

"I suggested a course of action, and everyone who happened to be in the lab—Dr. B, Nate, Kamal, and Jacob—agreed with me."

"To send someone with no formal training, someone unfamiliar with the subtleties of time travel, to a busy downtown…and to send them *alone*. Well, you're lucky nothing went badly wrong."

"It was just a short hop, cosmically speaking." I didn't think my wallet adventure counted as things going *badly* wrong. Still, I saw no reason to mention it. I had typed Dr. B's coordinates into the mini-keyboard of the Slingshot just fine—having triple-checked the numbers before hitting the Enter button—and had arrived behind the Open Book as expected. Once there I'd radioed Abigail and Dr. Little, and found them by Hypatia House.

Before Dr. Little could disagree that 1976 Manhattan was a short hop, cosmically speaking, I added, "Nate did find out one interesting item—Udo will leave school this semester. He may not return with the rest of the book club. Well, I imagine he will, if only to pack up his stuff. Did you learn anything at this end?"

They had. While I'd been to the TTE lab and the Vonnegut brownstone, they had searched Udo's room. Abigail told their story, pacing back and forth under the canopy of trees all the while; Hypatia House had a rarely used back exit, and the birch and oak trees offered the cover we needed. Dr. Little had taken up a leaning position against the brick wall, his arms crossed.

They had stayed out of sight, Abigail said, until Udo's roommate, Sam, the budding engineer, had left for a midday class with a book bag on one shoulder. He had locked the door behind him, but once again the lock proved to be no problem, Abigail explained without any false modesty. We all had skills that came in unexpectedly handy on occasion, and this was one of hers.

Inside, with the door closed behind them, she and Dr. Little had paused to take stock. Two beds—one made and one unmade—stood against opposite walls. There were also two dressers and two desks, one set for each side of the room. They could tell which side belonged to whom based on the posters on the wall—or the lack of them on Udo's side. Sam's wall was covered in science-related posters. Setting the scene for me, Abigail described one showing a Nikola Tesla lighting experiment. I vaguely remembered having seen that particular black-and-white photo before, of the famous inventor reading a book in a chair while large electrical bolts crackled and sparked above his head. The poster had apparently led to a discussion as they poked around, with Dr. Little claiming the photo was a publicity stunt, a double exposure, and Abigail suggesting that a STEWie run to get unaltered photos of the famous inventor might be in order.

"There were also posters of Edison, Faraday, and Hertz," Dr. Little said. I got the sense that he had been uncomfortable rifling through Udo's personal belongings, so he'd studied the wall posters while Abigail combed through Udo's neatly organized desk and dresser. The desk, she said, held a powder-blue Smith Corona typewriter with a blank page in it. She checked under the typewriter and also looked inside notebooks for anything Udo might have jotted down, such as a hotel name or the road routes the book club planned to take.

Her attention was then drawn to the side of the desk, where books were stacked all the way up to desk level. It sounded like Udo's reading tastes coincided with what I would have called *Books I was forced to read in school*.

Abigail then moved to the dresser, but before she could do more than open the top drawer, Dr. Little had turned away from the wall posters and tapped her on the shoulder. "I'm starting to feel light-headed—History might be getting ready to send me back."

But apparently Abigail had started to feel light-headed, too.

They heard the key turn in the lock and did the only thing they could do: hide.

"Typically the air under a bed isn't necessarily what one wants to be breathing," Dr. Little said, "but there were no dust bunnies under Udo's."

Abigail had taken refuge under Sam's bed. A pair of feet wearing brown leather shoes, presumably Sam's, passed her on their way to the messier desk. Their owner shuffled around a bit, found what he had forgotten, and left, closing and relocking the door behind him.

"Wow, that sounds like a close call," I commented.

"Not really." Dr. Little shook his head. "If he *had* seen us, most likely all that would have happened is that we would have been promptly propelled out of the room."

"So why did you bother hiding?" I asked.

"We weren't done looking through Udo's effects. I didn't want to waste the opportunity. Turns out I made the right call."

Abigail stuck her hand out. "This is what we found."

19

"It was with Udo's socks," Abigail explained. "Which were all black, by the way."

Whatever the paper was, it had to have been important for Udo to have carefully folded it and stashed it inside the top drawer of his dresser. The letter-size white sheet wasn't what I'd hoped it would be—a hotel reservation or a mapped-out route. A man after my own heart, Udo had typed up a list. There were only three items on it, about halfway down the page.

I could not make any sense of them.

"We had the same reaction, Julia," Abigail said. "It's almost like he really, *really* didn't want anyone to know where they were going."

She was right. The list read like a cheat sheet Udo might have used to work out the location of his CSI, or clues he had jotted down for his book club members to keep them guessing and invested in the location. He had typed up the following:

The chrono-synclastic infundibulum is…
1. …by a river. The animal KV wants to be lives in it.
2. …in a garden. The man at whose company KV worked built it.
3. …and beneath a tree. But not KT's money tree.

I assumed KV was Kurt Vonnegut (with the last KT a mistyping), but otherwise it was all very cryptic. I looked up from the list. "You had no problem walking out of his room with this?"

"I would have taken a photo, but my cell phone battery died," Abigail said.

"I brought you a charger," I said.

"Thanks."

"I suppose I could have taken a photo with my laptop," Dr. Little said. "It didn't occur to me. My runs usually don't require that sort of thing."

I couldn't imagine *not* wanting to take pictures of any past place and time, but to each his own. "Should we take a photo now or hand-copy the list, then sneak it back in his dresser? Though it would involve breaking into Udo's room again."

Dr. Little shook his head. "We don't need to. Udo will assume he misplaced the list, forgot where he put it. We wouldn't have been able to walk out with it otherwise."

Abigail wrinkled her nose. "Wouldn't it be funny if each time any of us lost something, it was actually a visitor from the future swiping it?"

"I don't know if it would be funny exactly," I said. "But it would be interesting, that's for sure."

Dr. Little looked from me to Abigail as if we were nuts. He shook his head. "We did ask around the dorm to see if anyone could make sense of the list, but no one could. We were just about to head to the library to do some research when you radioed."

I tapped a pocket. "We don't need the library—I came prepared." A postdoc or young professor came out of the back door of Hypatia House and gave us an incurious glance, then lit a cigarette (Was there anyone who *didn't* smoke in the seventies?) and I suggested, "Let's find a free bench."

"And do what?" Abigail asked.

"Research—twenty-first-century style."

We found a free bench table by the biology building. Students streamed around the Science Quad—classes were letting out for the day and people were headed to dorms, dinner, or voting. At the neighboring bench a love-struck couple had their books open but were not doing much studying. Some distance away, students were playing a late-afternoon football game on the green. A bird or two chirped in the trees. No one paid us much attention.

I slid onto the bench seat and took Dr. B's e-reader out of my pocket. Shielding the tablet in its brown-leather "book" jacket from the glare of the sinking sun with one shoulder, I turned it on, explaining, "I've been skimming through a Vonnegut biography. There are also copies of all his books published prior to 1977, just in case we need them." I readied the search function in the Vonnegut biography. "Abigail, read me the first item on the list again."

"The CSI is by a river. The animal KV wants to be lives in it."

"Searching for river…" I got a good fifty hits, from the Iowa River to the Elbe River, all connected in some direct or indirect fashion to Vonnegut's life. "Hmm…Maybe we better start with *animal*, as in Vonnegut's favorite one. Well, not his favorite necessarily, but the one he wants to be…" This was better and yielded only a handful of results. "Here we go. Dresden zoo, aftermath of bombing. No…Oh, here." I looked up from the e-reader. "It's from a *Playboy* interview, of all things."

"Well, what does it say?" Dr. Little demanded. He had slid onto the bench on the opposite side of Abigail and me, but couldn't see the text because of the angle and the sun's glare.

I skimmed the relevant passage. "Huh…Apparently Kurt wants to be an alligator."

"Why?" Abigail, quite fairly, wanted to know.

"Let's see…He gave the *Playboy* interview three years ago, in 1973. There's an excerpt—he talks about modern society, loneliness, how we lack the support of a community of like-minded people…Ah, here we go. He says he's tired of thinking and longs to live in a place where he doesn't have to think at all. Hence an alligator."

"I don't know if I'd have gone with an alligator for non-thought," Dr. Little said disagreeably. "Maybe a clam or something."

"I'd choose a tumbleweed," Abigail said.

"I'd probably just choose to drink a glass of wine. Speaking of like-minded people…" I recounted how Udo had read a chapter of his novel to the book club. "Udo needs the club not just for discussions of worthy books, but as an audience-in-waiting for his own work. It's *his* community of like-minded people—avid readers and wannabe writers. It sounded as if he doesn't get along with his own family very well. I got the impression that they're wealthy. Maybe Nate will send some information to us on that score."

Dr. Little turned the conversation back to practical issues. "Never mind Vonnegut's thoughts on communities. Alligator fits in with them going to the ocean, somewhere warm. Florida or Georgia probably."

Abigail found a pen in her backpack and jotted down *ALLIGATOR* in neat block letters next to Udo's clue #1.

"So we have a river with alligators, which would be neither the Iowa nor the Elbe Rivers. On to clue #2, then," I said. Twenty-first-century tools made research much faster than going to the library would have been. Using them in 1976 almost felt like cheating, but we needed every advantage we could get.

"Clue #2 is that the CSI is in a garden," Abigail read. "The man at whose company KV worked built it."

"Wait, I know this one." I made a few searches in the book text. "Oh, here we go. It says that after Kurt's thesis was rejected, he went to work at General Electric. His older brother, Bernard, had a job there as a research scientist. Kurt was hired by the public relations department, of all things…He wrote press releases about the research division's work and products."

"GE? Thomas Edison's company," Dr. Little said, as if he was thinking of one of the posters above Sam's bed. I wondered if that was where Udo had gotten the idea, too. "The original headquarters were in New York State."

"Could it be a garden by the company buildings?" Abigail suggested.

Dr. Little shook his head. "New York doesn't fit. No rivers with alligators. Interesting fact about GE—the headquarters in Schenectady have the zip code 12345. But, to get back to the issue at hand, Edison died in 1931, so it's hardly his company anymore."

"Could Udo have been referring to the army and a company there, like a military unit?" I suggested.

"No. He wouldn't have used the word *work*. You don't work in the army, not if you're a soldier," Dr. Little said.

"On to clue #3," Abigail said, penning in *EDISON?* next to clue #2. "The CSI is by a tree—which we already knew. But not KT's money tree. The T must be a typo."

I adjusted my position to better block the sun's glare and resumed my search. I looked in the biography for "money tree," then in *The Sirens of Titan*, but came up empty both times. I found the answer in *Slaughterhouse-Five*, Vonnegut's World War Two book. It was a tangential remark, one made by a side character Vonnegut had created, a struggling science-fiction author named Kilgore Trout. I read the relevant bit out loud. "'It had twenty-dollar bills for leaves. Its flowers were government bonds. Its fruit was diamonds. It attracted human beings who killed each other around the roots and made very good fertilizer.'" I put the e-reader down. "Well, that's a depressing, if not entirely inaccurate description of human beings. It fits in with Udo's dislike of money and possessions. So we need something opposite to that—a good tree, a healthy tree...a *real* tree."

Abigail recapped where we stood. "So we have an alligator-rich river, a garden with a possible connection to Thomas Edison, and some kind of nice, non-money-grubbing tree."

I glanced away, distracted as an exceptionally loud cheer from the football game onlookers reached us. It was an ordinary fall day on campus, a bit brisk but pleasant under the reddish setting sun. The loveliness of it gave me a sudden pause and had the opposite effect. I felt that we were caught in an unreal moment that wouldn't last. If I hadn't known better, I would have said that we'd inadvertently stepped into a ghost zone and an asteroid was about to come crashing down, smooshing us and the football players and the birds to bits. It was ridiculous, of course—if an asteroid had slammed into the biology green in 1976, I would have heard about it already.

"Julia?" Abigail asked.

"Sorry, my mind wandered for a bit. Just feeling uneasy for some reason."

But I knew why. It all seemed too pat—the list of clues, our quick and handy research tools to help us tackle its apparent randomness. I ventured a guess as to the point of Udo's list. "I wonder if what he's getting at is that much of what happens in life is just a random collection of coincidences."

Dr. Little frowned. "If the place they've gone to was randomly chosen, we will have a hard time zeroing in on it, even with this list of clues. Like I said, alligators strongly suggests Florida or another Southern loc—"

"Wait, that's it—Florida." I closed the e-reader and slapped myself on the forehead. "I know where they've gone."

∞

As we left the biology green, dodging a wayward football, I explained enthusiastically, "It's Fort Myers—it has to be. Edison had a winter home there."

"Yes, that sounds right. He was trying to find a natural source of rubber," Dr. Little said. "He owned a lab and garden, where he grew exotic plants."

"The Edison & Ford Winter Estates," I said. "It's a popular tourist destination."

"You've been there, Julia?" Abigail asked.

Since Dr. Little could hardly set up his laptop and the Slingshot in full view of the football game watchers and players, we were headed to the Open Book.

"I've been to Fort Myers many a time—my parents live there. As for the estates, uh, I've been meaning to go. Inventors and plants aren't really my thing. I've driven by it, though. Pretty palm trees lining the road."

"Is there a river?" Abigail asked.

"The Caloosahatchee."

"Does it have alligators?"

"It's not teeming with them or anything like that, but yes, I think so."

"And trees?"

"I expect the estate *is* teeming with those. Presumably, one of them is what Udo meant. We just need to find it." It felt good to finally have an idea of where the book club had gone. We had wasted enough time. I picked up the pace.

"I'll need a detailed map of Fort Myers," Dr. Little said, matching his steps to mine, "so we'll have to pop back into the lab again. Unless you happen to know the GPS coordinates of the estates, Julia."

"What? Of course I don't know the—*oof*. Oh, for heaven's sake."

A student fiddling with his bike had blocked our path, not literally but in the invisible-wall sense.

He was a bit down the campus path. We turned, but the opposite direction was blocked, too. We were stuck in a narrow space between two buildings. Sandwiched as we were, there was nowhere to go, and we were left to cool our heels as the bicyclist methodically applied a repair patch to one of the tires.

"C'mon, c'mon," I whispered to the student, peeking around the building corner. He was now waiting for the patch to dry. I wondered what possible disturbance the three of us could present—it wasn't as if we were likely to distract the student from his task merely by walking by. I could only assume that it was something intangible, perhaps a fleeting thought about to trickle through the scrawny student's brain—a thought whose arrival could not be disturbed. Whatever it was, I was impatient to get going. Not only had we finally figured out where to jump, but that underlying sense of unease was still with me, as if we needed to hurry for some reason. Abigail was fidgeting as well. Only Dr. Little seemed to take the delay in stride and had started calculating something on the back of Udo's list with a pencil.

He had said we needed a map of Fort Myers. I made a move toward Dr. Little's duffel bag. "That list of coordinates in your bag, could it help us any?"

"No," he said somewhat sharply, and I arrested my movement. "I didn't anticipate having to jump to Florida, obviously."

"Well, if there are alligators, we do *not* want to accidentally end up in the river. The Caloosahatchee did you say its name was, Julia?" Abigail said. "How long is the drive from here to Fort Myers? I wonder if they are there yet."

It turned out that's what Dr. Little had been doing—making an estimate on the back of Udo's list. "About seventeen hundred miles."

He could have just asked me. My usual method of getting there was a three-hour flight from the Twin Cities, but I had driven last time. "It took me three days, but I made sightseeing stops along the way and didn't have anyone else to take a turn at the wheel." Quinn had not come along. It wasn't that he didn't get along well with my parents—he was the type of person who got along with everybody—but things had really started going downhill for us by then. Was that why I had left early and taken my time driving?

149

But like I'd figured while waiting in New York City, the students were probably taking turns at the wheel and sleeping in the vehicles instead of paying for hotels along the way. Reaching Fort Myers would not take much longer than reaching Manhattan. "They could very well be there already. Probably tomorrow at the latest."

"But it's election day," Dr. Little pointed out.

"What of it?"

"If they're in another state, it means none of them voted. Irresponsible."

"Maybe they filled in absentee ballots."

"This is kind of a dumb question, but it *is* Carter who gets elected, right?" Abigail asked. "I moved around so much as a child, from foster family to foster family and school to school, that I have some odd gaps in my knowledge."

"Yes, Carter will win. And I think everyone has gaps in their knowledge," I said, though Dr. Little frowned briefly, as if unprepared to admit anything of the sort. "As you know, mine have to do with plants and cooking. I couldn't even tell you how to boil an egg."

Dr. Little wasn't interested in adding his own shortcomings to our discussion. Instead, he turned thoughtful as the scrawny student hunched over to pump air into the now-fixed tire. "So much happens in this decade. Seeing Mooney and Rojas attempting to birth STEWie reminded me of all the other innovations occurring right now: Wozniak and Jobs with their Apple I, priced at $666.66...the Cray I supercomputer...Microsoft..."

He sounded wistful, so I suggested, "Perhaps after we catch up with Sabina, you could work it into your research somehow and jump to the West Coast or wherever. Dr. Mooney manages to squeeze quite a lot of historical research into his experiments. And Dr. B as well."

"I just mean it's inspiring, that's all," he said. His brief moment of humanity was gone, and I remembered that he preferred to let his heroes remain that way, admired from afar.

Finally, the student slid the hand pump back into its place on the bike's frame, hopped on, and bicycled on ahead.

It took but a minute to reach the Open Book, which was deserted. Dr. Little asked, "Do we have all our things?"

"Two backpacks, one duffel," I counted. "We're all set."

Dr. Little readied the Callback, which would send us home at the touch of a button.

"Wait, Professor." Abigail said. "There's a note."

We hadn't spotted it at once because it was tucked under a rock, as if it and the rock had arrived together. Probably Nate or Dr. B making sure the note wouldn't blow off in the wind.

Abigail bent down and picked up the note and rock. The note had been taped in place, and she pulled it off, letting the rock fall on the ground by her feet. I saw her visibly flinch and thought for a second it had landed on her toes.

Dr. Little and I moved to look over Abigail's shoulder. The note was worded so that it wouldn't mean much to anybody but the three of us. Presumably, Dr. B had sent it, but Nate had written it— I recognized his neat handwriting. It said:

FORD MUSTANG IN ACCIDENT
SANIBEL CSWY, FL, NOVEMBER 3, 1:15 P.M.
UDO L. KILLED

We stood still, all of us frozen by shock. November 3 was tomorrow.

Dr. Little was the first to speak. "So *that's* why Sabina was able to hitch a ride so easily. Udo does not have long to live."

PART THREE:
THE
TREE

20

"That explains matters. Udo does not have very long to live," Dr. Little repeated.

I could have smacked him for saying it with such clinical detachment. Udo's book would never be finished. He would never see it in print, never have the opportunity to grow wiser and more jaded...*So it goes*, as someone I had spoken to recently would have said. Udo was not leaving St. Sunniva; he was leaving life. That thought was immediately followed by another one: *Not if I can help it.* Followed by one that pointed out just as firmly, *But History cannot be changed. It can't.*

Over the past several minutes I'd been feeling somewhat pleased that I had managed to contribute to this mission, even though I was not an expert in time travel or seventies US history or famous literary figures. True, it was merely a coincidence that my parents happened to live in Fort Myers and that's where Udo and his book club had gone, but so what? And now this...

"Well, this news about Udo is depressing. What's CSWY?" Abigail asked of the note.

"The Sanibel Causeway. It's a bridge that connects Sanibel Island to the mainland of Fort Myers," I explained distractedly. As a TTE professor had once pointed out to me—I think it was Dr. Mooney—everyone you met while time traveling tended to be dead already. It was always the case when you jumped to far time. But being in near time made it feel so very different. All the fresh-faced students milling about campus without paying us much heed—and

155

Udo, wherever he was at the moment—were *supposed* to make it to 2012.

"Hold on," I said. There was more to the note. Figuring that Nate had reused a scrap of paper from the recycling bin in the lab, I had at first glance ignored the text printed upside down at the bottom of the page. Now I realized that someone had fed the paper into the printer the wrong way after Nate had written on it. There was a sequence of numbers and a very short note—*BEACH, 8 p.m.*

"Beach, 8 p.m.," I said. "That's a bit cryptic."

Dr. Little took a look. "Not at all. These are coordinates."

Abigail clarified. "Dr. B made it easy for us—she gave us the coordinates to a beach we can jump to. Is Sanibel Causeway near a beach, Julia?"

"There are lots of beaches all around in the area."

"Well, we're heading to one of them." Dr. Little took the note from me and turned to ready the Slingshot. I wasn't surprised that he still found something to complain about. "I wish Dr. B had thought to send a grid map of the area, in case we need to make small adjustments. As things stand, we only have one data point in the timeline—Udo Leland's car will be nearing Sanibel Causeway just after one o'clock tomorrow afternoon."

"Perhaps that's all they had found out for the time being," I said. My watch said five o'clock. A thought occurred to me. "Can you tell from the coordinates if Dr. B and Nate are sending us to Fort Myers at 8:00 p.m. tonight…or tomorrow, November 3?"

"Not at first glance."

Tomorrow would be too late. Tonight there would still be time to do something. "I guess we'll just have to trust them." I bent down to pick up the rock that had accompanied the note. I turned it over several times in case there was some other hidden sign to be found on it, but the only significance I could glean was that I recognized where it had come from—the decorative garden in the courtyard of the TTE building. I slid the rock into my coat pocket. It seemed bad form to leave twenty-first-century detritus strewn around 1976.

Whatever they were feeling underneath, Dr. Little and Abigail did what we were supposed to do under the circumstances: focus on practical matters. However long Udo had left, our mission had to go on. "I've never been to Florida," Abigail said as Dr. Little started typing the coordinates from the note into the Slingshot in a furious staccato, much faster than I had done on the stairs of Vonnegut's Manhattan brownstone. I wondered if he would double-check them or if his belief in his infallibility would prevail. Abigail added, "I've heard it's very flat. Where exactly is Fort Myers?"

"On the gulf side of the state, roughly halfway between Tampa and Miami." I was keeping my fingers crossed that we would arrive at eight o'clock tonight, which would give us seventeen hours, and not *after* Udo's fatal accident had already happened.

Just as I'd thought, Dr. Little didn't bother double-checking the coordinates. "Ready," he said, getting to his feet.

Soft sand lay under my feet, and a warm, marine-scented breeze tickled my nose. It took a few seconds for my eyes to adjust to the new circumstances, helped by the light of the almost-full moon. I glanced around, trying to get my bearings. Dr. Little and Abigail were doing the same. Where had Dr. B sent us? And, more importantly, to what day? In one direction, silver sand met the pitch-black ocean; moonlight reflected off the waves crashing on the shore. In the other direction stood a line of beachfront motels and cottages with well-lit parking lots. Here and there, beachgoers sat intertwined on blankets or clustered around small bonfires, enjoying beer, cigarettes, and good company.

"Well, Julia?" Dr. Little demanded. "Where are we?"

"Couldn't tell you," I admitted.

"Nice beach," Abigail said, "wherever it is."

"Let's check for another note," Dr. Little suggested, ever practical.

We found one a few steps away by the expedient of me stubbing my toe on it. "Ow."

I picked up the rock and we huddled around it as Dr. Little turned on a pencil flashlight. This time there was a rubber band around the rock instead of tape, presumably in anticipation of the wet conditions on the beach. I took off the rubber band and removed the Ziploc bag that it had been securing. Several sheets of paper had been stuffed inside to keep them dry. I unfolded them. There was a printout of a newspaper story and also a year-appropriate grid map of the Fort Myers area.

"Ah," said Dr. Little, pouncing on the map. "That will simplify things. Pity we don't know exactly where we are."

"Is there an X on the map?" The rubber band, Ziploc bag, and the new rock joined the one already in my coat pocket.

Dr. Little pored over the map with his flashlight. "Nothing."

He turned his flashlight onto the news article next, and all of us gathered around to read it. It looked like it was from a small-town paper—I recognized the writing style, a mix of professionalism and gossip. Details jumped out at me: a freak accident...excessive speed or blown tire suspected...Ford Mustang flew over causeway guardrail...divers still searching for vehicle and its driver. There was a grainy stock picture of the bridge. The accident had happened near the mainland, on the first of the three segments that formed the bridge, with the vehicle headed toward Sanibel Island.

Body recovered two days later, Nate had written in the margin. He had added underneath, *Nothing to report on the other matter,* which I took to mean that he had found nothing out of the ordinary in Dr. Little's office.

The newspaper article included a short biographical bit about the missing driver. Udo's family was local and owned property both in Florida and the Midwest, the article said. His parents, Judith and Robert Leland, resided on Sanibel Island. Fort Myers was his place of birth.

"Poor Udo," Abigail said.

"At least he was alone in the Mustang," Dr. Little said. "There's no mention of any of the other students—or Sabina—being in the car. I'd say it was lucky for you, Julia, that neither of your parents was in the Mustang with Udo when he went over."

"Yes, that's true." I didn't even want to think about it.

"The article does give us one important fact," Dr. Little added, as if further emotionally detaching himself from the details, unhappy as they were. Or perhaps he thought nothing could be gained from dwelling on what was going to happen. History could not be changed. But we had to try. I would have to make sure the others agreed with me on that.

"What fact?" I asked.

"Didn't you see it, Julia? There, near the end." Abigail pointed over my arm.

My eyes skipped to the last paragraph. Focused as I was on the specifics of the accident, I had skimmed over it quickly.

The reporter had, somewhat judgmentally, written:

> One of the students admitted that the group had driven straight down from their school, St. Sunniva University of Thornberg, Minnesota, on what she called a midterm break. Rather than paying for a hotel here in Ft. Myers, the students spent the night at the beach, further adding to their sleep deficit. We will never know for sure if this contributed to the fatal accident, but can there be any doubt that it did?

The article writer finished with a call on the mayor to look into *the problem of seasonal incursions of students* as swiftly as possible.

They spent the night at the beach. This one? The article had said that Udo's parents owned a house on Sanibel Island, so perhaps that's where we were. In any case, the book club had to be here—it was the only reason for Dr. B and Nate to have sent us to this particular beach. We just needed to find the students, even if it took all night. The sandy shore stretched north and south of us, seemingly endless. It was impossible to make out the shadowy faces around even the nearest of the bonfires.

"Let's split up and head in opposite directions," I proposed. "Abigail and I'll go up the beach. Dr. Little, you go the other—"

He interrupted. "It might be faster to check the parking lots for the vehicles. There can't be that many cars with Minnesota license plates. And the art bus should be easy to recognize."

"That's not a bad idea," I said, irritated that I hadn't thought of it myself. "All right, let's walk over to the motel lot that's nearest, that one. We can check there first, then split up and head from parking lot to parking—"

"I know where they are," a husky voice said in the dark.

21

My first, wild reaction was that Xave had somehow followed us to Florida, but that wasn't the case, of course. An old man, older even than Dr. Mooney was in the present, stepped into the thin cylinder of light that Dr. Little's pencil flashlight projected onto the soft sand. Bare feet and bony knees stuck out from under ratty cutoff jeans; bony elbows jutted out of a tattered short-sleeve shirt that had been white once. There was a well-worn Havana hat on the man's head. In 1976 (and perhaps today) he probably would have been called a beach bum, the effect completed by the pungent odor of whatever he was carrying wrapped in an old newspaper.

I saw Dr. Little take a step back and fought off the impulse myself. Whatever was in the newspaper didn't mask the alcohol reeking from deep within an unruly beard.

"Can you tell us where we are, sir?" I asked.

"Of course I can. Don't *you* know where you are?"

"To be honest, no."

"Well, then. You're on Estero Island."

Not Sanibel Island, then, but nearby. It was good to have a point of reference. It had been disconcerting to land on a nameless dark beach. The Edison Estate was about twenty or thirty minutes by car over the bridge and inland; Sanibel Island was about the same, up the coast and across the causeway. Somewhere in between, the site that would one day house my parents' retirement community was probably still wetland.

Dr. Little grunted. "You've seen the people we're looking for?"

The man was staring at Dr. Little's shoes. "Most of them are very pale, yes? No tans. And Minnesota license plates."

"Yeah, that would be them," I said. "You know where they are?"

"Maybe."

"Either you do or you don't," Dr. Little said. "How can it be maybe?"

Abigail took a step forward and offered her hand for a shake. "I'm Abigail. What's your name, sir?"

He smiled a toothless smile at her. "Marlin."

She shook his hand. "Like the wizard?"

"Not Merlin. *Marlin*, like the fish. I used to fish—before."

"Got it. Pleased to meet you, Marlin. My friends' names are Julia and Dr. Little."

I shook his hand next—it felt leathery, as if he were wearing a glove. Dr. Little merely waved a short greeting in his direction.

"You can help us find the students, Marlin?" Abigail asked. "Ten of them who came here in two vehicles." That was the headcount she and Dr. Little had come up with by asking around St. Olaf's—nine members of the inner circle of the book club plus Sabina.

"Like I said, maybe…Let's just say that if they *were* here, they wouldn't be far."

"In which direction?" Dr. Little asked impatiently.

"Ah, that will cost you. A man's gotta acquire…things."

I hoped he didn't mean alcohol or drugs. Also that he *had* actually seen the book club and wasn't putting us on in the hopes of a handout.

I saw Dr. Little, who was the only one of us who had 1976 coins and bills, reach into his back pocket.

Marlin stopped him. "I don't want your money, man. Just…those."

I couldn't tell in the dark what Marlin was indicating.

Dr. Little looked down at his feet. "My shoes?"

"They seem mighty comfortable. And just about my size."

I heard Dr. Little heave a sigh. He bent down to unstrap his lightweight five-toed shoes, which were probably very expensive…and also *very* twenty-first century. "Don't know if it will work," he mumbled, as if Marlin had any clue about History and its constraints.

"Oh, they'll work," Marlin said. He handed his newspaper bundle to Abigail, who took it without even flinching. Dr. Little passed the shoes over with a resigned shrug. Marlin admired them for a bit, then slipped them on. "See, they fit just right. Like they was meant for good old Marlin. Do I tighten here?"

Abigail crouched down to help him with the shoes.

"Do you have a backup pair?" I whispered to Dr. Little.

"I have a backup of pretty much everything else, but not of shoes, no."

"Where to, Marlin?" Abigail asked once she helped the old man to his feet and handed him his paper parcel.

"This way."

Marlin, shuffling his feet experimentally in Dr. Little's shoes, set a leisurely course up the beach. We followed, and I watched his back, bent from age and a hardscrabble existence, bob up and down with his slightly uneven walk in the new shoes. Dr. Little shone his flashlight ahead so we could avoid stepping on rocks or intertwined couples.

"How well do you know Estero Island?" I called out to Marlin.

"I've lived here for twenty years now. Never seen you three before, though. Newcomers?"

"I've visited once or twice," I said.

"My first time here," Abigail said. "It smells lovely."

This was true, except for whatever was in the paper parcel with which Marlin seemed reluctant to part.

We walked about ten minutes up the beach, which was seven miles from tip to tip of the island, according to Marlin. He occasionally pointed out a good place to sleep, or an outdoor motel shower meant for rinsing sand off guests' feet but which came in handy for those like him who called the beach home. He certainly knew a lot about Estero Island and kept referring to it as "we," as if he and the beach were one. "We're part of the Gulf Barrier Island chain. A skinny, long island—that's us…Like I said, just under seven miles long, six feet above sea level, one and a half mile wide in the middle…Can't see it now, but that sand you're walking on is the whitest of white. Come morning when that sun comes up, keep an eye out for Fred."

"Who's Fred?" I asked, expecting to hear that he was a former fishing buddy.

"She's a bottlenose dolphin."

"You've lived here for twenty years, Marlin?" Abigail asked with just a shade of envy in her voice.

"Yes ma'am, from before they built the condos at the south end of the island. Now they're talking about replacing the swing bridge. I hope they don't—I like my bridge and my island just fine as it is."

There was no swing bridge in the present, its place having been taken up by a four-lane sky bridge, though I had no idea when the change would happen, except that it would and that more condos and hotels would go up, too. Marlin's island was destined for change, as was much of Florida. It's the way of things.

We had just passed a favored sand dune of Marlin's when he stopped and pointed. "The hippie bus and the other car are over in that lot. And that's them by that bonfire."

Dr. Little turned off his flashlight to let our eyes adjust to the dark. A wooden fishing pier jutted out into the water. Just beyond, a group of young people, merry and raucous, sat congregated around a bonfire, but it was impossible to tell if they were our students or not without going over and taking a closer peek. But I believed they were. Marlin had said so, and Marlin knew his island.

"You never did tell me why you're searching for them," Marlin said.

"To bring a girl home," Abigail replied simply.

"You do that. And tell them they shouldn't be lighting bonfires, not outside a proper fire pit."

"We'll try," I said.

"You're sure you don't need any money?" Dr. Little offered.

"The shoes will do."

And with that he was gone. I opened my mouth to call after him—I hadn't had the chance to ask him what was in that smelly parcel or what color Fred was, or to thank him for helping us. I settled on sending a silent good-luck wish to his retreating back.

All of a sudden everything clicked into place around me. Restaurants and small tourist shops began where the pier met concrete. This was the main hangout place on the island, where I had often stopped to grab lunch or pick up extra suntan lotion while visiting my parents. Of course, I didn't spend much time lying on the sand when I came to Florida—my week in Fort Myers tended to be spent on helping with mall and beach outings, volleyball tournaments, or whatever else happened to be going on in the retirement community, with its four buildings and sixty retirees. My parents were not much younger than their charges, but they kept themselves fit by staying active. The fishing pier was a great place to end a busy day with an ice cream while watching the sunset and the birds.

It was all completely recognizable, though it looked even more quaint than it did in the present.

"Let's go see if it's them," Abigail said.

We passed under the pier. Dr. Little swore under his breath as he stepped on a shell fragment or a rough patch of rock, and I felt something squishy underfoot and hoped it was just seaweed, but we kept the flashlight off. We stopped a stone's throw from the bonfire. Merrily crackling in the night, the fire sent sparks into the air like tiny Fourth of July fireworks.

I had a sudden doubt that it was them, a worry that we were wasting valuable time. Then a voice rose up, distinguishing itself from the general chatter flying around the bonfire.

"No, Vonnegut's *best* book is not *Cat's Cradle*—I *completely* disagree."

We had found Udo and his book club.

22

There was only one problem. How to get Sabina's attention? For she was there, her back to us, curled up between a couple of students. Simply approaching the bonfire did not work. We didn't even get close.

We regrouped back under the pier and took stock of the situation. Remembering what had worked in similar circumstances at St. Olaf's Hall, I suggested we try walking over individually and not as a group. Dr. Little waved a hand as if to say, *Be my guest*. He had lowered himself down to the sand to cradle one of his feet. I volunteered to go first.

Remembering my lesson from the book club meeting—*Blend in*—I discarded my coat, loosened my hair so it lay free on my shoulders, and took off my shoes. The sand still felt warm from the day's heat. I was just here for a leisurely stroll down the beach, that was all. My only goal was to inhale the scent of the ocean and feel the sand under my toes, letting those sensations wash my cares away.

I made an effort to believe it, all the better to blend in. I rolled up the bellbottoms above my ankles and set a course up the beach along the waterline, letting the larger of the waves wash over my feet. The water was cool and felt pleasant on my sore feet after all the walking we'd done. I paused to look out over the water, taking a moment to study the miniature lights of an offshore boat bobbing in the distance.

I was a traveler. We all were, in fact—every single person I had met or would meet. We were all moving forward in time, but that wasn't all. The ground under my toes—the very planet on which I was standing—was traveling, too, coolly circling our star, the sun, without any visible push or likelihood of stopping. And the moon grazing the horizon…Well, it was circling us in its own eternal dance.

I bent down to pick up a shell, whose curved contours my foot had encountered as I dug my toes into the sand. The warm gulf waters had carried the shell onto the shore, perhaps from as far away as the Caribbean. There was a bit of light further up the beach—a bonfire. Maybe it would be easier to examine the shell there. *Yes. I should move to where the bonfire is.*

I hit a wall again at about the same place as before: a stone's throw from the bonfire. The soft, wet sand had turned angry, abruptly becoming feet-grabbing quicksand instead.

I counted heads from where I was standing, immobilized next to an upright beach umbrella shuttered for the night. There were nine of them in a tight group around the fire, not ten as I had expected, their faces illuminated by the flickering flames of the driftwood and the cigarettes in their hands. I spotted Udo at once because of his lanky frame. He was flanked by two female students, one the woman who always seemed to wear saris and the other my mother. In a weird impulse, I almost waved to her, as if she was an old friend I had accidentally run into on vacation.

On the other side of Missy was Nate Sr. No, I didn't want to think of him as such—he was Nathaniel, a college senior. Now that I knew who he was, I had drawn another connection—the woman in the sari had to be Nate's mother. I should have recognized her from photos at Nate's house. I knew she was called Gigi Kirkland but hadn't made the connection between Gilberte Dubois and the married name. She was the Quebecois–Sri Lankan half of his roots, the other half—Nathaniel Sr—being the Dakota peoples and Scotland connection.

Dad was not there.

And finally, Sabina. She had dozed off, probably tired from the events of the previous few days. Her head was gently drooping forward as she sat next to Gigi with her knees drawn up and Dr. Mooney's old lab coat pulled tightly around her body. Gigi laughed out loud at something Udo said and Sabina shifted in her sleep. Both Gigi and Missy hung on to Udo's every word, leaning in to laugh at every point he condescended to make. They seemed starstruck. I saw Nathaniel yawn in an irritated fashion, clearly peeved that both women were giving their attention to Udo.

All of which in turn made me wonder if I had walked into not a love quadrangle but a love pentagon. Udo's blond hair came out of a bottle. *Could* he actually be my father? The thought was no less disturbing than attributing my parenthood to Nathaniel—all right, perhaps a *little* less disturbing, as the last thing I wanted was for Nate to be my half sibling. I had mostly dismissed the possibility of a shared parentage with Nate as soon as it had reared its ugly head. Nate's parents had been high school sweethearts; they were married and had a child who was up in Duluth with Mary and Duncan Kirkland, and it was all neat and tidy—at least on paper. I wondered if Nate—my Nate—had any questions to which he wanted answers, or if he'd at least want a photo of his parents. Something told me that Gigi and Missy had been good friends once, before various complications arose. I wondered if Gigi knew that her friend was pregnant.

This last year of college would be some kind of turning point for everybody. Come June, it would be time for Gigi and Nathaniel to pack up their college stuff, pick up little Nate, and start their family life in earnest. And for my parents, preparation for my upcoming arrival awaited them and then marriage.

Being young was no easy thing, I thought, remembering my own—and clearly unwise in retrospect—marriage to Quinn. Did I feel a little wiser now? Not really. Perhaps a little less blindly optimistic that everything automatically worked out for the best, but that was about it.

It struck me that, for all their interest in Udo's book club, none of the four—Missy, Soren, Gigi, Nathaniel—had become a novelist. My parents had ended up running the town paper before moving to Florida. Gigi worked as a biologist at the Duluth aquarium. Nate Sr. was a land surveyor. I didn't know for sure but figured that what had drawn them to the book club was not so much the desire to write the Great American Novel but the desire to discuss Life with a capital *L*. Was this midterm break, with its (let's face it, silly) destination their one last carefree fling before facing real-world responsibilities? Watching as Nathaniel passed what I hoped was a

Coke and not another beer to my mother, I crossed my fingers that it was a metaphorical fling and not an actual one.

Nathaniel yawned again.

It was clear that Udo's fan club didn't plan on sleeping any time soon. Since I was stuck a stone's throw away from them, inspiration struck, and I decided to toss the shell in my hand at Sabina's torso.

I lobbed it at her back and missed. Gigi flinched in the moonlight, my projectile apparently having found her instead. Rubbing her shoulder, she turned to look. A seagull chose that moment to swoop by, and Gigi grimaced and checked her shoulder for bird droppings. Satisfied that there weren't any, she relaxed and went back to listening to Udo, who was waxing on about his vision of a perfect community of writers. Ideas, housing, expenses, profits—all would be shared. It sounded very idealistic and very young, which made me feel middle-aged and practical in comparison. Still, the world needs both kinds of people: list-making realists like me and young dreamers like Udo. The thought occurred to me again: I wanted to save him. Perhaps once we successfully pulled out Sabina, we could turn our attention to trying to save the young writer, maybe even bring him back with us. I'd convince the others somehow that we had to try.

After tossing a second shell at Sabina, which also missed, I went back to where Abigail and Dr. Little were patiently waiting, seated by one of the pier's cement pillars.

"Why?" I demanded. "Why are we getting time-stuck everywhere we go? You said it would be easier to move around in 1976 than in Pompeii, Dr. Little."

"I wouldn't say we're getting time-stuck *everywhere*." Dr. Little had turned his flashlight back on and was trying to get all the sand off his feet. Realizing it was fruitless, he gave up and looked up at me. "Still, you may have a point. I've been thinking about it."

"About what?"

"Why we might not be able to pull Sabina out of 1976."

I lowered myself onto the sand next to him. "Why do you say that? It's not as if she belongs here."

"She doesn't belong in the twenty-first century either."

"Sure she does," Abigail said. She started ticking off the reasons on her fingers. "She has friends and family there—me and Julia, Chief Kirkland, Dr. Presnik and Dr. Mooney, Jacob and Kamal. She has a bed, schoolmates, a breakfast cereal she likes best, and an addiction to the Weather Channel. Of *course* she belongs in the twenty-first century. She's an immigrant to it, that's all. A time refugee."

"Exactly. The present is unwritten, so she has freedom of movement and no constraints by History," I said. "The life she'd lead here would be like Marlin's—the life of a loner."

"I understand all that, and of course we'll do our best to try to get her out of 1976. It's just that History may have other ideas. Just keep that in mind, that's all. Remember that tomorrow is no ordinary day for the book club, none of them. One of their own will be gone by the end of the day. They are locked into a course of events…and Sabina might be locked into it as well."

"You're saying there's no point in trying to pull Sabina out until *after* Udo's accident?" I said.

"Something like that," Dr. Little said.

I saw Abigail bite her lip, as if she wanted to say more but couldn't bring herself to do it.

We sat a bit in silence, then settled in for the night, though I didn't think I would get much sleep.

"I only have one blanket and mat," Dr. Little said, as if Abigail or I were going to snatch it away from him, just as Marlin had taken his shoes.

"We have our own in the backpacks," I said. "And some water and snack food, too."

While Dr. Little tried to select a spot well away from the rising tide for his sleeping mat, Abigail and I readied our own mats and blankets. I decided it was as good time as any to run my idea past them. "Since we have to wait to pull Sabina out anyway, I'll just toss this out there for consideration—why don't we try to save Udo?"

They both stopped what they were doing to stare at me. I saw Abigail shake her head in the dark.

"Have you heard nothing I've said? It won't work," Dr. Little said.

I tried to formulate my argument in a way that made sense, working it out as I spoke. "We were able to do it with Sabina, back in Pompeii. What if we stopped the Ford Mustang from going over? A blown tire might have been the cause of the accident, according to the article. We could check the road for nails or other—"

"Won't work," Dr. Little repeated. Having moved aside a couple of rocks and sharp-looking shell fragments, he unfolded his sleeping mat with a snap. "What would you have us do? Sweep the road? Warn Udo to drive more carefully? To wear a seat belt? Ask if he's had swimming lessons?"

I still did not want to admit defeat. "How about if, instead of trying to stop the car from going off Sanibel Causeway, we hid nearby and pulled him out of the water and into present-time?"

"You mean one of us should swim out to rescue him?"

"Yes."

"Again, no."

"Why not?"

"It's a busy bridge. If rescue had been possible, someone would have done it. Even if we waited in a boat or near the water's edge, bystanders would notice us diving in to pull him out. And then what? They would watch us all vanish into thin air? This is a whole different game than your experience in Pompeii—and I still have my reservations whether you did the right thing there, if you want to know the truth. But like I said, this is different. Sabina, to be blunt about it, would have died in the eruption along with most of the people she knew and who knew her. Hers would have been a cleaner death—not in its manner, obviously, but as it relates to the threads of History. Udo's death tomorrow won't be an isolated event that can be changed without consequences to History. There will be a police investigation, news articles, a funeral, people who will mourn Udo and miss him. For God's sake, Kirkland wrote down in the margin that the boy's body was found."

He was right, of course. I had pictured us bringing Udo back home safe and sound, helping him re-enlist in the creative writing department in present-time to finish his degree and his novel, one day reading the novel so I could find out how the skeleton hoarders had fared. It would have been good for Sabina to have someone like her, someone who was misplaced in time, too. A friend.

It seemed it was not to be.

It was the deepest, darkest part of the night, the moon having sunk under the horizon. The fire had gone out and the students were asleep, curled up in blankets on the sand. They remained tightly intertwined, with Sabina now sandwiched between Missy and Gigi, as if the two women wanted a buffer between them. Several times during the night we had taken turns sneaking over to the book club in our bare feet, but none of us managed to get close enough to arouse Sabina. Now it was my turn again.

I found Udo awake. He was some distance from the others, reclining on one elbow with his legs stretched out, taking an occasional drag on the stub of a cigarette as he watched the breaking of the waves. I wanted to tell him to get some sleep, that he needed it in order to be alert the next day. And I wanted to tell him the opposite as well, that he shouldn't sleep at all, because he had so little time left.

He glanced up as a nocturnal bird I had accidentally disturbed made a screech of complaint. I saw him stub out what was left of his cigarette and get to his feet. He headed straight for me. Not knowing how to react, I instinctively took a step back, as if he was going to accuse me of something. What, I didn't know. Of failing him? Of not having done enough? Although I knew I couldn't do anything to act on my knowledge about his future, the guilt I felt was very real.

Since secrecy and stealth were obviously out, I turned on Dr. Little's flashlight as he approached.

"Can I bum another cigarette? I'm out."

I couldn't even help him there. "Sorry, I don't have any."

"Pity. Do you often wander the beach at night?"

"No, uh—only when I can't sleep."

He was in his standard all-black outfit, sporting it like a uniform. He didn't seem to recognize me from the book club meeting, but the context was completely different, of course.

"I can't sleep either. My mind is full of thoughts. I'm working on a novel, you see. Do you have any interest in writing books?"

"I'm afraid I don't."

"Ah. Reading them?"

"I'd say so, yes." I wanted to ask him to wake up Sabina right then and there and send her to us, but the words would not come out no matter how hard I tried. Railing internally against History and its rules, I said instead, "I'd like to hear about the book you're writing."

It was an echo of something I wished I'd had the presence of mind to say to Kurt Vonnegut.

"Would you? In that case, ever hear—let's walk a bit—ever hear of the chrono-synclastic infundibulum?"

"From Kurt Vonnegut's novel, right?"

"Very good. Have you ever stumbled across one yourself? Such a place, I mean. I'm searching for it."

At least I could check whether we were right in our guess about the Edison Estate. I thought the best approach was to answer truthfully and thought about it before replying. "I can't say that I've considered where such a place might be—unless perhaps it's wherever you happen to be. Maybe it's up to each of us to make *that* a place where people understand each other."

"That's good. Yes, I like that. Make the place where you are the one where people understand each other…"

"What about yours?"

"I have one in mind."

The *"Where?"* would not come out of my mouth.

"My parents live over on Sanibel Island, you know," he added apropos of nothing. I had thought it a bit strange that Udo had taken his book club to Estero Island and not where his parents lived. "We don't get along. I'm a bit of a disappointment to them, you see." He gave a wry laugh at the words.

"I think most people are a bit of a disappointment to their parents. Or at least it seems that way when you're just starting out in life and have yet to accomplish much beyond getting passable grades in school, if that." I stopped, aghast. I had, without thinking, said what I usually do to students who were feeling overwhelmed by coursework and life decisions. I finished with an outright lie. "If there's one thing that's for sure, it's that things usually sort themselves out sooner or later."

I tried to remind myself that space and time were one, that terms such as *the past* and *now* and *the future* were human constructs, and that time only appeared to move in one direction because of our limited perspective. If I pushed for an additional STEWie roster spot, I could jump back into the mid-fifties and watch Udo's birth, or to eighteen years later to watch him graduate from high school, or to earlier in 1976 to listen in on further book club meetings in the rec room of St. Olaf's Hall. I could converse with younger versions of Udo on the very subjects we were discussing now—Vonnegut, interfering parents, college, books. Like Schrödinger's cat (a term I had picked up from physics presentations and lunchtime discussions, but which I was never quite sure I was using correctly), tomorrow Udo would be both alive and dead, if you looked at it from the cosmic point of view.

The thought didn't help one bit. Udo would die tomorrow.

We had strolled down to the water, which looked different now. Mysterious in its blackness, harboring who knew how many secrets and unwanted surprises.

Udo brought up his novel again. "I'm stuck on this one point, you see. My townspeople, they keep the skeletons of their dead relatives in their houses, around the dining room tables and on the TV couches. But I am undecided as to what happens once there are more dead than living, when the bony people outnumber the fleshy ones."

"You mean, would they get along or go to war with each other?"

"Something like that. The living need the dead, but do the dead need the living also?"

Again I answered truthfully. "I think they do. To be remembered by them, if nothing else."

"My skeletons, you know, they can talk…"

Tomorrow is no ordinary day for the book club.

Abigail was shaking my shoulder. "Julia, wake up, it's morning."

I groggily opened my eyes. It had been an uncomfortable night, and not only because I lacked a proper bed. After my conversation with Udo, I had stayed up to finish Vonnegut's *The Sirens of Titan* on Dr. B's e-reader, Udo's fate weighing heavily on me, only dozing off when dawn started to break.

I sat up and stretched. Abigail was gathering her things, and Dr. Little was munching on a granola bar as he carefully repacked his duffel. All around, the islanders and their tourist guests were slowly stirring awake and beginning their day, with a handful of early beachgoers setting up umbrellas in prime spots. It was a weekday, so the beach would probably stay sparsely populated most of the day, until after work hours.

A sudden worry shot through me and I whipped around.

The book club was gone.

23

I stumbled to my feet in a panic. Udo and the others had left. I would never see him again. All that remained was a black, ashy spot where the bonfire had been and a smattering of trash.

"It's all right, Julia," Abigail said. "They're over there."

And indeed they were—in the lot of the nearest motel, congregated in the empty parking space between their two vehicles.

I breathed a small sigh of relief and set about rolling up my mat. I tried to gauge how I felt about things now that the sun was warming everything up, spreading its cheerful rays on people and buildings alike. Out of nowhere, something Nate had once said popped into my mind. It was a discussion we'd had amidst Pompeii ruins, in the dark, as World War Two bombs fell all around us. He had jokingly suggested that once we passed, perhaps we embarked on a new adventure as alien life-forms. It was as good as explanation of the afterlife as any. It wasn't something I spent much time thinking about, as there wasn't anything practical to be done about it one way or another.

I hoped wherever Udo was headed, he would find the answers he was seeking. What was meant to be was meant to be. I felt something akin to acceptance settle over me.

I bent down to pick up the two rocks Nate had sent. Not surprisingly, they had dug into my side as I tried to sleep, so I had taken them out of my coat. Dr. Little saw me slip the rocks back into the coat pocket. "I'm usually a stickler for these things, but I don't think you need to bother. Plenty of rocks and stones all around the beach."

I mumbled a couple of words about not wanting to leave time-displaced trash behind. I certainly wasn't going to tell him the truth—that the stones, solid and grounding, felt like a connection to home. A connection to Nate. It was kind of silly, but there it was.

"If you folks need a bathroom, I can point you toward one," Marlin called out to us. He had appeared out of nowhere and was cleaning up the trash left behind by the St. Sunniva students. I was a little embarrassed for them.

We did indeed need a bathroom. I was hopping from one foot to the other.

"I paid to use the one at the motel," Dr. Little said.

Marlin approached with a selection of empty beer and Coke bottles hugged to his chest. The malodorous newspaper package, whatever it had held, was gone—another mystery lost to the sands of time. The bright morning sun revealed every leathery line above his scruffy beard, the result of both decades of Florida sunshine and age.

"The motel owner is a friend of mine. Let me put these in a safe place"—he was speaking of the bottles—"and I'll take the ladies over."

I stopped near Udo's Ford Mustang, whose red was dusty and bug-splattered from the long drive south, and bent down to pretend-tie my shoe. Marlin had accepted an offer of coffee at the motel from the owner, a middle-aged woman with beads around her neck, and Dr. Little had stayed by the pier with our things.

"That's a sweet ride for a college student," I heard Abigail say under her breath.

The students were in the empty parking spot between the Mustang and the art bus, eating breakfast, some in lawn chairs, others on their feet, leaning against the art bus. When Xave had described it as being painted many different colors, he wasn't kidding. Reds, blues, violets all swirled together like a fever-induced dream. The side door was open, revealing a messy interior—clothes, maps, bags, and other assorted belongings lay strewn on the seats. Soren—my dad, but he was too young for me to think of him that way—swung out and joined the others. So he had come along after all but must have spent the night sleeping inside the VW, probably because of his allergies.

I suddenly realized that I knew who owned the art bus—my father did. In fact, I had a vague recollection of seeing a picture of him and my mother in front of some van or other, but it had been a black-and-white photo, so the vehicle hadn't stuck in my memory. I hadn't made the connection until this very moment.

He offered Missy, who was in a lawn chair, a donut. She already had one, though, and had given half to Nathaniel. Some distance away Gigi was in a lawn chair pointedly reading a book (Anne Rice's *Interview with the Vampire*, I noticed; what did Udo think of that one?). Soren passed the pastry to her. She took it.

It was all, for want of a better word, irritating. No one was acting like they were supposed to be, and none of the future life partners were neatly paired off. The pentagon I thought I had detected last night went something like this: Soren was only interested in Missy; Missy was mad at him for some reason and flirted alternately with Udo and Nathaniel; Nathaniel and Gigi seemed to have had a falling-out over Missy's attentions, so Gigi was flirting with Udo; and Udo—he was like a eunuch, only interested in his art. He was draped over a lawn chair, not eating, silently studying the others, as if observing human behavior. There were bags under his eyes.

No wonder Sabina had been able to come along with the book club—not only did Udo have only hours left but the others were all busy with their own problems.

But where was she?

"You don't think she wandered away from the book club, do you?" I whispered to Abigail uneasily, having straightened up after taking as long as humanly possible to tie my shoelaces.

But Sabina had come around from behind the VW. She paused briefly, and for a hopeful moment I thought she might have seen us from across the parking lot, but it was not to be—not just then, anyway. She had stopped to take in the ocean view, as many a visitor to Estero Island did. Someone offered her a donut and she took it. She was still in Dr. Mooney's old lab coat and had unbuttoned it as the morning warmed up.

Leaving the ten of them—Sabina, Udo, Missy and Soren, Gigi and Nathaniel, and four other students whose names I didn't know—to enjoy their outdoor breakfast, we went to rejoin Dr. Little by the pier.

He greeted us with a frown on his face.

"What?" I said.

"I was right."

"About?"

"There does appear to be an impermeable bubble around the book club. I tried approaching them to ask for a cigarette light while you were using the restroom in the motel."

"You smoke?" I asked.

"It was a pretext. I carry a pack for occasions such as this. Like I said, I tried to approach with a cigarette in hand, but History had other ideas. So it appears I may have been right. Because of the gravity of today's events, the members of the book club are locked into their actions for the day."

Abigail and I had noticed the bubble, too. "Hopefully, there'll be an opportunity at the estate, assuming they head there right after breakfast," I said.

"I wish we had confirmation that the CSI is on the Edison Estate. We only have your guess to go on, Julia."

If he had made the "guess," he would have probably called it a deduction, or at least a hypothesis, but I didn't quibble.

Abigail gave a sudden peal of delight and pointed. "Is that a dolphin? I've never seen one except at the Minnesota Zoo. I wonder if it's Fred."

The dolphin, gray and smooth-skinned, frolicked in the water. Everything on the island seemed smaller and more intimate in the light of day—the motels and hotels, the cars.

Dr. Little noted, "We're not here to sightsee. Better check that we haven't left anything behind." He unfolded the map Dr. B and Nate had sent us. "The Thomas A. Edison Winter Home & Museum is not within walking distance."

"It's about twenty-five minutes by car, if we had one. We can hardly go on foot, so we'll have to use the Slingshot." As we finished packing up, I added, "If you're right about the book club being locked into their day, Dr. Little, why don't we skip going to the Edison Estate and jump to the causeway, *after* the accident?"

Abigail lost her smile. "No, we should definitely try before."

There was something in her tone I couldn't put my finger on. I assumed that, like me, she was disturbed about not being able to save Udo. Thinking it might help us all to bring it out into the open,

I said, "I know now there's nothing we can do for Udo. I wish there was, that's all. When I talked to him in the middle of the night, I kept brainstorming about how we could help him…but we can't."

"You talked to him?" Abigail asked.

"I didn't learn anything we didn't know already…except about him as a person. I wanted to grab your cell phone, Abigail, and use it to record his words, preserve a bit of him." I sighed. "Not much we could do beyond that, is there?"

Dr. Little zipped his duffel bag crisply. "I'm afraid it might be worse than that."

My own backpack was ready, too, so I swung it over one shoulder and went over to face Dr. Little. "What's worse than knowing somebody is going to die but being unable to stop it?"

Abigail's face crumpled. "He may very well take Sabina with him."

24

"Uh, no," I said in a brisk tone, as if this were an office problem to be dealt with and not a matter of life and death. Sabina's. "The newspaper story said they were still searching for the driver's body. There was no mention of any passengers."

Dr. Little spelled it out, though I already had an inkling of what he was going to say. "I don't know how deep the waters are by the causeway, but the authorities might not realize that there was a second person in the car. If Sabina's body is found weeks from now—well, she'll just be a Jane Doe."

I brought out the only counterargument I could think of. "Wouldn't the other students—Gilberte, at least, since she was the one who invited Sabina along—tell the police that there was a passenger in the car?"

"For all we know, the others may assume Sabina wandered off as suddenly as she showed up. They must know by now that she's not a student. Even if they mention it to the police, they may not be believed. After all, no such person as Sabina Tanner exists in 1976." He was silent for a bit, then added, "I hate to say it, but History may be about to right itself by letting the girl be lost forever. The scales of time need to be balanced."

History may right itself by letting the girl be lost forever.

I dropped my backpack on the sand in anger. "Did everyone see this possibility but me? Is that why Dr. B sent us to the beach last night, so we could try to save Sabina before it's too late?"

If Dr. Little was right, the cold, hard truth was that Sabina might perish in a watery death, from which we would need an abundance of good luck to save her. I had not come all the way here to let that happen. I said as much.

"I'm with you on that, Julia," Abigail said.

Dr. Little stared at us. "I'm not saying otherwise. What I'm saying is…Well, all we can do is try. Assuming they're heading over to the Edison Estate shortly, we should jump there and wait for a good moment to pull Sabina out. Why don't you two go back to the parking lot to see if you can overhear anything that confirms the location of Udo's CSI while I run the necessary calculations on my laptop?" Shielding the laptop from curious eyes behind the duffel, he bent over the Fort Myers map. "Let's see. It looks like there's a parking lot at the estate that would be a good place for us to jump…"

Gigi had put away the hardcover book. The students were done with breakfast and, I couldn't help but notice, had scattered more litter. How hard was it to find the nearest can and pitch your trash into it? Udo was already in the Ford Mustang, with the top down and the engine running. He revved the engine and, one hand on the leather steering wheel, waved Sabina over to the front passenger seat. It was a calculated decision, I thought, to avoid bad feelings between Missy and Gigi, who, with what could only be described as pouts, tumbled into the backseat. He took off, driving far too fast.

Nathaniel and Soren, having stared at the retreating Mustang, gave a shrug and started to fold up the lawn chairs. Abigail was still a bit puzzled as to which of the students was who, and I explained that the woman in the sari had been Gilberte "Gigi" Dubois, who was not yet using her married name of Kirkland. Abigail listened to what I had to say, then, perhaps in an attempt to distract me from the more pressing matter, said, "If you want my honest opinion, I don't think either of the women is attracted to Udo so much as what he represents."

"And what's that?"

"You know, writerhood. Besides, both Missy and Gigi are with other people, aren't they?"

"True."

"Speaking of being with people, are you and Nate thinking about marriage?"

"What? No," I said, a bit more loudly than I intended, causing Soren to throw a brief glance over one shoulder at us. Why was she even asking me this when I was out of my mind with worry about Sabina—and, I was sure, she was too? Besides, Nate and I had been dating only a few weeks, though admittedly it felt longer because of all the time travel. Plus my divorce from Quinn had only just gone through, not to mention the whole complication with Nate Sr. hanging out with my mother, which I was pretty sure meant nothing. I just wished I could be a 100 percent sure.

"Marriage is the last thing on my mind."

"The last?"

"All right, perhaps not the *last*, but it's at the bottom of the list, right along with clearing the house gutters and repainting the mailbox." Thinking that she might be a tad crushed to hear me speak of marriage that way (I knew there hadn't been anybody in her life since Dave, who had moved on during our five-month disappearance in Pompeii, having assumed, along with everyone else, that we were dead), I clarified. "Look, all I'm saying is that there's no need to rush into these things. Engagement, marriage, all that."

"Right, well, I guess that's a good philosophy."

Nathaniel and Soren had stashed the chairs in the VW, with the other four students, whose names we didn't know—two men and two women—helping. Everyone seemed excited to finally be heading to the CSI. Soon the art bus also pulled out of the parking lot, though it set a course in the direction of the mainland bridge at a far more moderate pace. Dad had always been a careful driver.

There was nothing further to be gleaned from the empty parking spaces with their trail of litter, and Abigail and I turned to go. At least we had one thing going for us: a hint that we had been correct in our guess about where the book club was headed. As he was pulling out of the parking lot, Udo had called back to the others, "Onward to Edison's tree!"

Abigail and I headed back to the pier.

Dr. Little wasn't there.

25

Abigail and I had been gone no more than ten, fifteen minutes, but apparently that had been long enough for History to send the professor back—Dr. Little had left behind a hastily scribbled note, tucked into the gap between the cement pillar of the pier and the sand, the checkered page ripped out of one of his research notebooks:

> *Starting to feel odd, light-headed. Shallow breathing. My birth cutoff. Will send the Slingshot back via STEWie. Good luck.* — Dr. Steven Little

Even though I was a month older, History had sent Dr. Little back first after all. Abigail and I concluded that he must already be home safe and sound, because we found the Slingshot nearby, wrapped in Dr. Little's blanket. The professor had also sent the Edison Estate coordinates, the grid map of Fort Myers, some cash, two bags of trail mix, and his laptop—presumably in case we (meaning Abigail) needed to calculate new coordinates.

"I wonder if he really did feel light-headed, or if the lack of shoes started to get to him," Abigail said half jokingly, unwrapping the Slingshot and blowing a bit of sand off it.

"I suppose I wouldn't blame him if it *was* the shoes. It's one thing to walk on the beach barefoot and quite another to do it all over town. Either way, I guess it's just you and me now."

I shook the blanket out in case we had missed anything. There was nothing from Nate—no note. I fought off my disappointment. He was probably too busy with things at his end.

I turned to Abigail. "If Dr. Little really did have to drop out and it wasn't his footwear, and I suddenly do as well…"

"Then it will be up to me to bring Sabina back."

"Count me in," Marlin said. " I got nothing planned for today. And I owe you for the shoes."

He was like a jack-in-the-box, popping up everywhere we went. I wondered if he had seen Dr. Little disappear into thin air and, just moments later, the Slingshot and other items reappear wrapped in a blanket, and if so, what he had made of it. I made a decision. If History was willing to let Marlin help us, who was I to object? There was no reason *not* to accept his offer of help. As familiar as I was with the future Fort Myers, he was obviously much more familiar with the current town.

And—maybe—Marlin being allowed to help us was a sign that History was on our side, that Sabina would not be in Udo's car when it went over.

Besides, if I *did* have to drop out as Dr. Little had, I didn't want Abigail to be in this alone.

"Thank you, Marlin. We're happy to accept your offer of help," I said. Abigail sent a surprised look in my direction but didn't say a word.

"We gonna try to follow your students?" Marlin asked. "You want me to organize transport? A friend of mine runs an off-the-books taxi service. He'd give you a mighty proper discount."

"Thanks, but we already have transport." So he *hadn't* seen Dr. Little vanish off Estero Island in a seeming violation of the laws of physics and reality after all. Well, he was in for a surprise. I thought I'd better warn him. "You're welcome to come along, Marlin. Just—well, be aware it's a bit unorthodox."

"Unorthodox suits me just fine."

"All right then. Abigail, are you ready with the you-know-what?"

She nodded and Marlin said, "Which way, ladies?"

"We aren't catching a ride. We're going to have to, uh, link hands—"

"Well, Udo didn't say they were going to come here directly," I pointed out. Having a faster mode of transport, we had arrived at the estate ahead of the book club. But it had already been half an hour. I checked the parking lot again, as if the Ford Mustang and the art bus could have somehow snuck in past our post on the sidewalk by the lot entrance. The parking lot held a handful of station wagons—to my modern eye, it seemed odd that there weren't any SUVs—and also a telephone booth tucked into one corner.

"Could they have stopped for ice cream or coffee or whatever?" Abigail suggested.

"But they just had breakfast," I protested.

"Nothing wrong with stopping for ice cream right after breakfast," Marlin said. He had taken our Slingshotting from Estero Island to the Edison Estate in stride, his only comment being "What will they come up with next?" He had shaken his head at the speediness of it all, as if we were messing with nature. Were we? Probably, but like with any technology, there was no going back. Abigail and I had told Marlin that the Slingshot was an experimental apparatus and held back the important detail about us being from the future.

"Could we have heard wrong? Maybe the tree is somewhere else?" Abigail asked after a few more minutes had passed.

"You heard Udo. He definitely said Edison's tree. It's got to be here on the estate."

There were certainly plenty of trees all around. In fact, we were under one. Tall, graceful palms lined McGregor Boulevard like a squadron of slender, top-heavy soldiers, swaying gently in the calm morning. The estate sprawled on both sides of the boulevard, and there were trees of all kinds to be seen on either side of the road.

As I had been doing periodically, I got to my feet to check for Udo's Ford Mustang—and the art bus behind it—shading my eyes from the bright sunlight with one hand. There was a steady trickle of cars on the boulevard, and a driver went past tooting the car horn in celebration of Carter's victory, the body of the car adorned with election posters. He waved at me, and I waved back.

"Maybe they stopped to pick up a newspaper," I suggested as I sat back down on the yellow-edged curb between Marlin and Abigail. "To read about the election results."

Abigail was chewing her nails. "Where's the fort?"

"What fort?" I asked.

"Well, it is Fort Myers, right?"

"Oh, that. I looked it up once. There used to be one on the shores of the Caloosahatchee River. It was built during the Seminole Wars but was taken down in 1876 and the wood reused to build the first houses in town."

"I like that word, *Caloosahatchee*," Abigail said.

"I looked that up, too. The *hatchee* part means river, so it's a bit redundant to call it the Caloosahatchee River." I got to my feet again to check the road. "The Calusa Indians lived here on the Gulf Coast for more than a thousand years," I added in a further educational note.

"You folks are very impatient." Marlin appreciatively stretched his toes out in Dr. Little's shoes. "Not everyone moves as fast as your—*thing*."

The Slingshot was in my backpack, taking up most of it, and Abigail was carrying the laptop in hers. We'd had to leave out the mats and blankets and a few other things, which Marlin had accepted and hidden back at the beach.

"We call it the Slingshot," Abigail explained, taking a break from chewing her nails.

"Abigail!" I chastised her.

"What? Julia, you were the one who invited him along. No offense. I'm very glad to have you here, Marlin."

"I'm glad to have Marlin along, too, but that doesn't mean we should spill everything."

Abigail gave a tiny shrug. "What's that old saying? In for a penny, in for a pound. I read it in a book once. It refers to British money. Besides, I figure History will stop me if I say too much."

This was true. My complaint wasn't really with her—it was the absence of the book club that had me on edge. Where were they? Had we misunderstood Udo and gotten everything wrong?

Marlin scratched his beard. "The Slingshot and History, you say? Well, I've seen a lot of odd things in my seventy-three years."

"And?" I prodded him.

"And that's it. I've seen a lot of odd things. Don't be thinking yours stands out."

Despite the circumstances, I chuckled. "Okay then. Nothing unusual about us. I suppose we just have to wait—probably the book club had to stop to fill up on gas and that's all it is."

186

A town bus whooshed by, dousing us with a noseful of polluted air. I checked my watch. It was just past ten. I decided we needed something to keep our spirits up, not a repeat of the granola bars we'd eaten for breakfast or trail mix; something more comforting, in the cookie or ice cream category, was called for. I sent Abigail to the gift shop to see what they had on hand while Marlin and I kept an eye on the road. She came back with a box of cookies, which we all shared. They had the desired effect of buoying everyone's spirits.

I noticed that a tour group had started to gather outside the gift shop and had a sudden brainstorm. "Let's buy tickets on the off chance that the book club parked elsewhere and are already on the estate."

The tour group consisted of a dozen or so people, from a very sunburned, sweaty man with a large camera around his neck, to three bored-looking teens there with their parents. After a few minutes' wait, the tour guide came out the gift shop and led us like dutiful sheep across McGregor Boulevard to where the historic Edison home stood. Seminole Lodge was actually two houses, a main house and a neighboring guest house, connected by a covered walkway. The twin houses faced the wide Caloosahatchee River as it flowed past, mellow and serene. A short seawall marked the partition between land and river. The place, from its two-story, veranda-encircled lodge to its palm trees and colorful gardens, was a taste of old, colonial-era Florida.

The estate looked a bit run-down, as if everything needed a good cleaning and a fresh coat of paint. I thought I remembered my parents mentioning on the phone that a renovation of the tourist site was just about finished in present-time, their way of trying to nudge me into a visit. Here in 1976, tourists milled around, clicking their cameras. None of them were our book lovers.

"Abigail," I whispered as we followed the tour guide down a path that led to the main house of Seminole Lodge, "keep an eye out for anything that might be considered a CSI."

"What's that you said?" Marlin asked quite loudly.

"Shh. A CSI. It's, uh, a good spot for people with varied viewpoints and backgrounds to come together and put their differences aside."

Marlin nodded sagely, as if what I had said made perfect sense to him.

I considered ditching the tour group so we could look around on our own, but History had other ideas—we shuffled along with the others in the tour group and stopped on the river-facing porch of the main house. The guide, an older woman with hair in a bun, embarked on a history of the estate. Under other circumstances, it might have been very interesting to learn more about Edison's life, but I shuffled my feet impatiently as she listed factoids—"Edison purchased the fourteen-acre property in 1885, when Fort Myers was nothing but a one-road cattle town, population three hundred forty-nine…Lumber was shipped from Maine to build the two red-roofed houses and a small laboratory…Edison, his wife Mina, and their children lived in the main house, on whose porch we're standing. The guest house had many visitors, including President Herbert Hoover, and Henry Ford of the car fame…After Edison died in 1931, Mina deeded the property to the city of Fort Myers for one dollar."

One of the teens on the tour yawned. The guide gave a vague wave to her right. "Ford purchased the neighboring property, The Mangoes, in 1916."

"Are there mangoes at the Ford house?" Marlin asked.

"I'm sorry? Yes, there are, in the garden."

"Does the town have any plans to acquire the Ford house, too?" one of the tourists, the man with the bad sunburn, asked. He peered around a porch column and snapped a photo of the Ford house. The Mangoes wasn't part of the tour.

"I suspect they will," I said, knowing that the name of the tourist site in 2012 was the Edison & Ford Winter Estates.

The guide shot me a withering glance. "I wouldn't know anything about that," she said, seemingly annoyed by our wavering focus, and went back to her spiel as though it had never been interrupted. *There's a way to do it better—find it!*" She waved her arm to encompass the estate—only the Edison part, of course. "That was the great inventor's philosophy. He sketched out the estate in great detail, including the gardens, before building commenced…"

She continued on in this vein as Abigail and I tried to zero in on something, *anything*, that might indicate where on the estate Udo had envisioned his CSI. Marlin simply seemed to be having a good time and occasionally raised his hand with a question, most of them odd ones that stymied the guide.

"There's a way to do it better—find it. That's a good saying," Abigail whispered as we filed into the house through a french door, moving past Mina Edison's case of stuffed birds. Once inside we saw the dining room, with its elegant table and hand-painted china, and the parlor. The guide explained that Thomas Edison had been mostly homeschooled by his mother and could read a book in fifteen minutes. I couldn't help but think that documenting the inventor's early life would make for a perfect STEWie project, something for the History Alive exhibition at the campus museum.

The parlor, with its books and easy chairs, presented the most natural place for a book club to congregate. Granted, there was no tree, which had seemed to matter to Udo for some reason, but otherwise the location, a historical node of invention, felt like a perfect CSI for our students to meet up at. They weren't there.

We moved on to the guest house, after which the guide took us past a gnarly fig tree that grew on the line between the Edison and Ford properties. Udo's tree? I had no idea. Still stuck with the group, we followed the river wall under more trees, past a narrow wooden pier that jutted out into the water, and over to a banana tree–lined swimming pool that was original to the property. "Florida's first pool," the guide said. One of many to come. The pool was about fifty feet by twenty feet and reflected the foliage around it. We learned that it was made of cement and bamboo, had waterproof electric switches, and had apparently not leaked since it had been built in the early years of the twentieth century.

I had half expected to find the book club students frolicking in the pool, but it wasn't open for public use and, more importantly, it hardly seemed like an appropriate literary destination. I was starting to get itchily impatient, partly from the warmth of the sun in my coat, but also because we were wasting valuable time. I checked my watch again. It was nearing eleven…We were but two hours away from the car going over the bridge.

After the tour guide had answered several questions about old-time bathing suits asked by the teens on the tour, the pool finally having roused their interest, Marlin raised a hand. "Can we swim in it?"

The guide threw him a look of exasperation. "I'm afraid not. There are tropical fish in it."

"That's all right. I don't know how to swim anyway."

"Is this where the best trees on the property are?" Abigail asked, glancing from a nearby banana tree to a coconut palm and back.

"I'm afraid I don't know what you mean by *best*, my dear."

"You know, the most important ones."

"They're all important."

"If you had to pick one," I took over, "which one would it be?"

"I like the lily pond."

"That's not a tree," Marlin pointed out. "The ladies asked for a tree."

"The most exotic one," I said. "The most interesting, the most unusual—"

"If it's *unusual* you want, well, that's where we are headed next. The research garden."

Having taken us back across McGregor Boulevard (whose royal palms had been imported from Cuba and planted in a configuration designed by Edison, we learned) the guide led us into the experimental plants part of the estate. Instead of going directly into the garden, she pointed first to the botanic research lab and the museum next door.

Doubting that the book club was to be found inside, I said in a low voice to Abigail and Marlin, "Let's try ditching the tour group so we can nose around in the experimental garden."

"We could pretend we work here," Abigail suggested.

Marlin shook his head. "Won't work. You two are like the inside of a banana—not tan enough."

Whether that was the reason, or something else, we were shuffled into the botanical lab with the others. The guide explained that the lab had been built by what she called "the three"—Edison, Ford, and Harvey Firestone (of the car tire fame). "World War One had inflated the price of rubber and they wanted to find a domestic substitute for car tire production. Many latex-producing plants—more than two thousand species—were grown and tested." She explained that the yellow-flowering weed goldenrod worked the best. "Unfortunately," she added, crisply wrapping up the story, "goldenrod wasn't suitable for commercial use."

"Isn't there a quote from Edison about how there was nothing wrong with failing ten thousand times, because it showed you ten thousand ways how *not* to do it?" Abigail asked.

"That was about lightbulbs, dear," the guide said, as if plants were a completely different matter.

She led us past Edison's phonographs, a whole lot of them displayed along one wall. We were also shown his Stock Ticker, the first talking doll, a nickel-alkaline storage battery, the oldest electric lamp still around, and a Model T Ford personally gifted to him by Henry Ford, which sported the goldenrod tires. The cot in Edison's office, where he had taken fifteen-minute catnaps, his deafness helping tune out unwelcome disturbances, was still in place.

Abigail seemed to be drinking it all in despite the circumstances, which made me feel for Dr. Little—he would have enjoyed this part and no doubt had a lot to say about the correctness (or not) of the exhibits. Certainly a STEWie run, perhaps with a grad student or two disguised as gardeners, would yield much information about Edison and his work, helping to sort myth from reality.

"Too bad Dr. Little isn't here to see this," I whispered to Abigail.

"He's more of a Tesla fan than an Edison one."

"Oh."

"The research gardens are next," the guide said, and my head shot up from the turntable-mounted replica of Edison's New Jersey movie studio. She added in our direction, "You said you wanted trees? Well, we're about to see the Australian sea grape, the Chinese golden rain tree, the pincushion tree, the pudding pipe tree, the African sausage tree…"

All of those sounded worthy of hosting Udo's CSI.

"…And, of course, the pride and joy of the estate, the banyan. We passed under its roots on our way into the museum."

"We passed *under* its roots?" I said.

"Under its aerial roots. It's the banyan tree—*Ficus benghalensis*, a gift from Harvey Firestone. Brought over from India in a butter tub in 1925. It was only four feet high and two inches wide when planted, and is now more than three hundred seventy-five feet all around. It's where we'll end our tour."

"Can we go there first? To the banyan tree?" I asked.

"Certainly not. The garden tour does not begin at the banyan, it ends there."

But we were able to give the tour group the slip on the way out of the Edison Museum. The tour guide didn't seem very sorry to see us go.

We stepped over a short wooden fence and found ourselves under the banyan.

The tree was immense, sprawled like some exotic organism between the museum and the estate parking lot. As the guide had said, we had passed under its aerial roots on the way in, but I hadn't noticed, since the tree didn't obey the standard algorithm of a single trunk with traditional branches. It was hard to tell where trunks began and branches ended. There were multiple trunks—dozens, too many to count—and thick branches with their own gnarly roots shooting down into the ground. The words *sprawling* and *majestic* didn't do it justice. The tree had an almost alien quality to it, as if it had existed since time began and would remain in place eternally. It was one crazy tree. If there ever was an object that embodied *living connections*, this was it.

The ground beneath the banyan was mostly bare, devoid of grass below the extensive canopy. And there, under its twisty branches, on the side abutting the parking lot, was the book club.

26

The book club must have just arrived. They'd formed a loose circle, with some of the students on their feet and others cross-legged on the ground. Udo was passing out pages.

Abigail grabbed me by the elbow and drew my attention away from the banyan. She pointed. Sabina was in the parking lot, leaning against the Ford Mustang and studying the banyan from there, as if unsure she wanted to approach it at all. I didn't blame her. Like I said, it was one crazy tree.

"That her?" Marlin asked, nodding toward Sabina. She was not in Dr. Mooney's lab coat anymore—it was now warm enough that she didn't need it—and her simple Roman dress and sandals made her look like a sixties flower child. She was still frowning at the tree under a hat someone had given her, a straw one with a pink band.

"It is indeed," Abigail said in a voice that revealed her relief.

"Let's go get her," I said.

It was all very well for me to say the words, but it was not to be. We tried the most straightforward route, through the tree's branches. And when that didn't work, we went *around* the tree and past the restrooms to the parking lot, even going so far as to return to McGregor Boulevard and try the car entrance. No matter what we did, we were gently propelled backward, as if an invisible hand was firmly saying, *No.* Always we ended up back where we'd started. Like Edison's ten thousand tries, we now knew how *not* to get to Sabina.

I thought Marlin might comment on the strangeness of it, but he only said, "Well, now" a couple of times, as if he, too, was trying to figure out the puzzle.

Maddeningly, Sabina had glanced in just about every direction other than the one where we happened to be. We watched as she cautiously shuffled to the banyan and entered its shade. She took a seat on the ground with her back against one of its many tree trunks, her legs folded to the side.

Meanwhile, the book club had embarked on a reading of Udo's work. I overheard bits of dialogue, enough to realize that he had written an ending. He must have stayed up as a crisp and cloudless dawn broke over the beach, scribbling down pages. I guessed that the students had stopped to photocopy the handwritten pages, and that was why it had taken them so long to get here. It was a dialogue-heavy scene, a council meeting of skeletons to determine the fate of humanity, with a hierarchy of roles: some of the skeletons—Missy and Gigi among them—had more lines than the others. Soren was the narrator and Nathaniel didn't seem to have a role at all.

As to Udo himself, he stood off to one side, arms in an L, his thumb and forefinger framing his chin as he watched and listened, like a one-man audience.

We were by a bench, concealed by some ornamental (and, no doubt, exotic) shrubbery. Abigail frowned and suggested, "Maybe we're the problem. I mean, you and I, Julia. Marlin, why don't you give it a try? Tell Sabina that Abigail and Julia are here to bring her back home. We'll wait."

It was worth a try.

She and I took seats on the bench. Marlin's back bobbed up and down as he stepped around the shrub and over to the tree. We could see what was happening through the thin gaps between the shiny green leaves of the shrub. Abigail shook her head and said to me, "I don't want to be a downer, but if the bubble is still here, Dr. Little might be right that Sabina's options are locked in because of Udo's fate."

"Nonsense," I said as firmly as I could.

"Julia—"

"We're just having a bit of bad luck. Marlin will get to her. Look, he's almost reached her."

But just then Nathaniel's voice rang out, in his first line of dialogue: "I'm the Oldest Ancestor!" He hadn't been thrilled about tagging along with the book club, but he gave his all to the character and had said the line in the same voice of authority his son would later use when he wanted to get everyone's attention. It certainly made Marlin take note: he stopped in his tracks. I wanted to will him to keep moving.

It was warm, and beads of sweat had broken out on Nathaniel's forehead. "I do not speak often, as these bones are a thousand years old, my flesh gone a millennium ago."

"The Oldest Ancestor's joints and bones creaked as his bony body slowly shuffled to its feet," Soren read out.

Nathaniel got to his feet as instructed. "The judgment is mine to give," he intoned.

"Before he could do so, a fuller, flesh-heavy form approached. The twin skeletons heralded the Living One's arrival."

"Look, it's a Living One," Missy announced from Nathaniel's right.

"Yes, the Living One," Gigi said from Nathaniel's left. "Vulnerable, transient, soft."

"Living One, show yourself to me, the Oldest Ancestor."

"The Living One stepped out of the shadows and into the light. He was here to plead humanity's case..."

Marlin suddenly remembered his task and took a step forward, but it was too late. Udo had waved Sabina up. She was to be the Living One. She did not receive any pages as she softly stepped into the middle of the readers' circle, so it was apparently a nonspeaking role.

"The Living One, open your ears and prepare to receive the wisdom of your elders."

Sabina seemed to understand what was going on—Pompeii had featured a lovely theater, two in fact (I had walked up their stone steps). She opened her arms with her palms turned up toward Florida's sky, pale blue with its blazing hot sun.

I wondered who would have played the Living One if Sabina hadn't jumped into the past, if none of us had been here. Perhaps Udo himself.

"Oh Living One, here is what we say to you..."

Marlin returned to where Abigail and I were waiting, on the garden bench. He shook his head at us. "I take it back. This *is* the oddest thing I've seen in my seventy-three years."

∞

Defeated for the time being, we sat waiting as the club acted out Udo's pages. For thirty long minutes, the Skeleton Ancestors conducted a lively discussion, which we could hear from where we were sitting, out of sight behind a flowered shrub. Sabina had been allowed to leave the circle before the Ancestors started their argument. The Ancestors, who had the upper hand, were bickering about whether to banish the living out of their town, Eden. Udo listened carefully, as if making mental notes about what needed to be changed. His turtleneck, out of place in the warm sunshine, seemed to be itchy, and he occasionally pulled at its neck.

"What time is it?" Abigail asked.

She had asked the same question maybe two minutes ago. "It's five past noon," I said. "Do you want to take my watch?"

"I want Sabina to look this way and see us."

I wanted that as well. I craned my head to see around the shrub—Sabina had been called forth as the Living One again, to learn what the Skeleton Ancestors had decided. She shuffled into the center of the circle once more.

"The accident won't happen until one fifteen," I said, "so we still have plenty of time. Besides, that was probably just an estimate made by the police. It could have happened a bit later."

Marlin was on the other side of Abigail. "What accident, ladies?" He had one tanned arm draped over the back of the bench. Abigail and I were perched on the very edge of the wooden seat, ready to spring up as soon as History allowed it. "Who's going to be in an accident at one fifteen?"

Abigail opened her mouth to answer. I figured I'd better speak up before she said too much, but in an ironic turn of events found myself saying exactly what I had wanted to stop her from saying. "We're from the future. Udo—the tall one in the black turtleneck—is going to drive off Sanibel Causeway. There's nothing we can do to stop it from happening, but we need to make sure Sabina doesn't get into the car with him."

I avoided Abigail's eyes.

Marlin, one arm still draped over the back of the bench, spoke as if he were stating that the weather in Florida tended to be pleasant—that is to say, easily and conversationally. "Then we'll make sure that she doesn't get into the car with him."

"I'm going to ready the coordinates for us to jump to Sanibel Causeway in case that becomes our only option," Abigail said, as if looking for something to do. Marlin raised an eyebrow in response to the laptop Abigail pulled out of her backpack. He said, "Well, okay." Apparently a beach existence accustomed you to seeing strange things.

"Julia, do you have that map of the area?"

"Here," I said, drawing it out of my bag.

"If you're doing your crazy jump thing again, that's a good spot, just past the first segment of the bridge," Marlin said, pointing to a spot on the map. "There's a beach."

"...*The Oldest One was ready to pronounce judgment.*"

"The Ancestors shall have voting rights, too, same as the living..."

So Udo had decided on an optimistic ending after all. The skeletons had chosen to put a "fleshy person" in charge, at least provisionally. There would be an elected government. A new era of bone and flesh cooperation would begin.

The readers took a bow and gave a round of applause, both for themselves and for Udo's work. Laughter and digs at particularly good or bad performances followed. They didn't high-five each other or tap fists in a congratulatory manner as students did in the present; the men gave Udo hearty thumps on the shoulder as the pages made their way back to him in a messy stack.

Next came a moment of awkwardness. They had done what they had come to do—read and perform underneath The Tree—and now everyone seemed uncertain about what to do next.

Udo himself appeared lost in thought, as if digesting the performance of his work.

"I have to make a phone call," we heard him say. We watched as he headed for the public phone at the near end of the parking lot.

The rest of the book club, after a few minutes' conversation, settled on doing the out-of-towner thing—they split up to look around the estate. Sabina stayed with Gigi and a couple of other students, Nathaniel trailing behind them.

We would have followed, but our bottoms were History-glued to the bench. Instead we watched Udo put coins into the phone box. He greeted someone at the other end in a gruff fashion, judging from his body language. I strained to hear what he was saying—after all, these had to be some of the last words he had left—but the booth was too far from our bench.

"Do you want to know what he's saying?" Marlin offered.

"You can hear?"

"I can lip-read. Lost my hearing for a couple of years. Turned out to be earwax."

"Yes, please do it," Abigail said.

"All right, let's see…He just said that he's not skipping classes, it's midterm break—Writing is an art, Father, and art is not a foolish pursuit. Just because you have a law degree doesn't mean I must as well…"

It was the classic scene, one that played out between many fathers and sons. Udo's father did not approve of his son's choice of a career. I guessed that Udo was being told that writing did not pay well enough, that a man needed a steady job to support his family, and so on. The usual way these things went was for the parent to threaten to cut the child out of the will—and for all I knew he might have, since Udo's face was turning very red. He glanced around for his book club, as if to draw strength from them, but the others, unaware of the importance of this particular moment in Udo's life, were paying more attention to the exotic plants than their leader.

Udo seemed to come to some sort of a decision. He straightened his shoulders. Receiver pressed to one ear, he stretched the phone cord so far that I thought it might snap and dumped the pages of his novel into the nearby trash can. In they went, all of it—the handwritten parts, the typewritten ones, the photocopies.

The CSI was supposed to be where everyone finally understood each other, but this was not the case today—not for Udo and his father.

He was still visibly angry. I half expected him to slam the phone back into its cradle, but instead Marlin revealed his next words to us. "Tell Mom I'll stop by for lunch, yes."

Udo had hung up the phone after delivering that parting line. The others, Sabina in tow, were by Edison's lab, reading an informational sign out front. Instead of walking over to join them,

Udo turned on his heel and headed straight to where the three of us were glued to the bench.

"All right, what's going on? Why are you following us? I recognize *you*. You were on the beach last night."

Abigail and I looked at each other. We had to try.

"Your car," I said. "The Mustang. Don't—"

But that was all I could get out. And Abigail got no further than opening her mouth.

"Well? What about my Mustang?" Udo demanded.

Abigail gave a sigh of acceptance. "I wish we could tell you, I do. But we're really here for her." She pointed over the shrub, in Sabina's direction.

He crossed his arms over his chest. "Julia? Why?"

For a second I thought he was addressing me, had somehow learned my name, then realized that Sabina had for some reason given my name as hers.

"To bring her home," Abigail said.

"She's not a student—she looks mature for her age, but she's actually only thirteen," I explained.

"So you say. But if you really know Julia, why have you been lurking in shadows?"

I knew how bizarre our behavior must appear to him. "It's hard to explain."

"So you claim."

"If you could tell her we're here and—"

"Sounds to me like she doesn't want to see you. Look, *something* made her run away from home. She hasn't explained what, but that's her right. I'm certainly not going to force her to go back."

"If you could just tell her we're here," I tried again.

"I don't think I will."

"I know it must seem like you're doing her a favor, but—"

"But she's not safe with you," Abigail finished for me.

"What? Nonsense. Of course she is. Who are you people, anyway?"

With that, he walked off to rejoin the others.

∞

NEVE MASLAKOVIC

It was maddening and ridiculous. There Sabina was, under the straw hat, close enough for one of us to call out her name to get her attention if only History would let us. We were, to all intents and purposes, invisible to everyone but Udo. I hated the feeling of powerlessness. At least we had finally been able to detach ourselves from the bench.

The students had streamed across McGregor Boulevard, the three of us trailing behind them. Sabina was in front, as if Udo had placed her there so he could keep an eye on her. She made a left at a fountain in the direction of Seminole Lodge, and Missy and Udo followed, with Soren a few steps back. Nathaniel, Gigi, and the others continued past the fountain in the direction of the wooden pier and the river.

Abigail said with a note of hope in her voice as we too made a left at the fountain, "Can Udo even make it to the Sanibel Causeway by one fifteen? It's a quarter till. Maybe it's some other Udo Leland who dies on the bridge."

"He can only make it if he drives like crazy," I said. It was a good twenty-, twenty-five-minute drive. "But how many Udo Lelands can there be? It's not a very common name. Plus the newspaper article said that he's a St. Sunniva student."

I watched as Soren, who was a few paces ahead of us, blew his nose and put his handkerchief away. He picked up his pace to catch up to Missy as the four of them climbed onto the veranda of the main house. Seemingly annoyed by Soren's trailing after her, Missy pulled him aside by the elbow. The pair remained on the porch while Sabina and Udo went inside. "What is it now?" we overheard Missy say to Soren.

"Why don't you stay here, Julia," Abigail said, "in case Sabina and Udo come out another exit. Marlin and I will go inside."

She knew how badly I wanted more information about my parents—even now.

They headed into the house and I stayed where I was—just around the corner from where my parents were about to have some kind of showdown on the veranda. Despite the circumstances, my curiosity got the better of me. I had to know what the argument was about.

"Look, I just want to explain," I heard Soren say. "When I said what I said, I wasn't talking about *you*—I was talking about *me*. That it would be a farfetched dream for me. Being a novelist, I mean. Do you see what I mean?"

Missy had been keeping her gaze on the river, steadily and unflinchingly. After he had said his piece, she turned to face him. "Don't you want to be a novelist?"

Soren blew into his handkerchief again. "Not really, no. I can't imagine sitting at a typewriter all day alone, not talking to a soul. Besides, it seems like a lot of work."

"I thought you liked being alone."

"When did I say that? But if you want to be a novelist, that's great," Soren added quickly. "I think you'd be fab at it."

A crack had appeared in Missy's stern countenance. "You really think so? That I'd be good at it?"

"I'd be honored to read anything you wrote."

"Gee, thanks." Though those words were often said sarcastically in present-time, I could tell she meant it. "Want to hear the truth?"

"Always."

"I don't want to be a novelist either. I don't think I could keep up the necessary aloof attitude. I like talking to people and finding out about their actual lives. I'd rather write about that."

"Yes, I feel the same way. But if that's the case, why did you join the book club?"

"Because you seemed to think it wasn't a good idea. Why did *you* join?"

"Because you did."

"Oh." Missy appeared flustered by his answer and she quickly changed the subject. "I mailed off a letter before we left—*Thornberg News* ran an ad for a job opening, and I applied. Reporter."

"I sent in an application, too!"

There was a moment of awkwardness as they realized what that meant—that they were in competition with each other.

"I'll withdraw my application," Soren offered chivalrously.

"Nonsense. That wouldn't be fair or right."

"Oh. Then may the best, er, person win."

"May the best person win. I think we better not mention this to Udo. He'll say working for a small-town paper is too bourgeois or something."

"He will, won't he? Mum's the word."

As they went inside to rejoin the others, I thought I heard Missy say, "By the way, I have a bit of good news."

I didn't get to hear the rest.

So their argument hadn't been about me, or even Missy's interest in Udo and her flirtation with Nathaniel. It had been about non-earth-shattering stuff, though when you're in your early twenties, most things seem vitally important.

I waited where I was until Abigail and Marlin rejoined me. Udo, Sabina, and my parents exited the lodge after them, talking about what would happen if someone accidentally fell into the river, according to Marlin, who was lip-reading again. How quickly would an alligator show up?

"If you see one, you should make noise and try to poke it in the eye," Marlin quoted Soren, and then stopped. I saw that Udo was checking his watch. He said something to the others.

"What did he just say, Marlin? Did you see?"

Having a lip-reader as a helper was useful, and I made a mental note to suggest that our time-traveling researchers be trained in the art. Handheld electronic listening devices could be cumbersome to carry and were hardly discreet.

But Marlin shook his head. "No, he's facing the wrong way."

All at once, things were happening. Udo, Sabina, and my parents were striding in the direction of the parking lot. We followed more slowly than we would have preferred, History's hand keeping our pace down. We found that our path was temporarily blocked by McGregor Boulevard traffic. I tried to dart across the road, but Marlin caught my arm and stopped me. "You'll do her no good dead."

I pushed his hand aside—"I won't be killed, don't worry"— and Abigail and I darted across.

We were too late. Udo's Ford Mustang was pulling out of the parking lot. I scanned the heads by the art bus, which was still parked. My parents. Nate's parents. The other four students, whose names I didn't know.

Sabina's dark-haired head was not among them.

Marlin's mouth dropped open as Abigail and I took off after the Mustang on foot, dodging several cars to much honking. We would catch it, I was sure we would—a red light at the nearest intersection halted its progress briefly. I glimpsed Udo's blond hair above the seat headrest and Sabina's straw hat in the passenger seat. We were almost there...

We didn't make it in time. There was a break in the traffic, and the car sped off.

27

I struggled not to sink into the cold seawater weighing down my clothes, battled to blink the sea out of my eyes so I could get my bearings. Abigail was next to me, treading water and holding the Slingshot high above her head. We were within swimming distance of shore, near the narrow sandy beach abutting the middle, sea-level segment of the causeway, just past the elevated portion where the accident would happen shortly. Abigail had sent us here as quickly as possible. We had elected to leave Marlin behind, since he'd told us he didn't know how to swim, and it turned out the precaution had been warranted—we'd aimed for the causeway shoulder but had missed.

I swam in the direction of shore and my feet found the bottom. I turned to see Abigail do a sort of backwards foot paddle, the Slingshot still held high above her head. An elementary school-age kid who had been playing in the shallow water was staring at us with his mouth open. An inflatable dolphin was bobbing away from him. The adults who were playing cards in the shade of an umbrella while ostensibly keeping an eye on the boy had not seen us.

I waded in the direction of shore, hoping we wouldn't get time-stuck because of the boy. We had minutes, if that.

I stumbled ashore, my clothes streaming water. Abigail joined me and spit out a mouthful of the sea. "History must have nudged us a bit—*cough*—hopefully only in location, not in time. We should have a good ten minutes or so."

Like hers, my eyes were on the bridge. It looked different—a drawbridge rather than the high-span bridge that was there in the present, and lower in the water. But still high enough.

The boy, more driven by curiosity than social norms, as is common with kids, had come out of the water and was giving the Slingshot a frank stare. The card players hadn't yet registered our presence. I started to get to my feet to walk over to them and confirm the time, worried that History had nudged us in that direction, too, but never got the chance.

When the sudden screech of brakes filled the air, the boy lost all interest in us and the strange device Abigail had dropped on the sand. He turned to look.

We were too late.

There was nothing we could do—we were too late, too far, too powerless to do anything but watch.

I was thankful that our view of the bridge—we were below it and off to the side—was obstructed. I wanted to cover my ears to stop the *sound*—the screech of tires, the heavy *thump* of metal hitting cement, the shattering of glass—but they all melded into one never-ending moment. Time stopped. Abigail and I, still on our knees on the sand, only saw a mercifully brief glimpse of sunlight reflecting off a car-shaped red object streaking into the choppy water. We did not see Sabina and Udo fly out. We did not see their soft bodies hit the cold, unforgiving water.

And then, as quickly as it had happened, it was over.

The adults onshore had dropped their cards and were on their feet, hurrying across the road to see what had happened and if they could help.

Words escaped my mouth, unheeded, unstructured. I didn't care what the boy would make of it. "Abigail, what if we jumped back home and returned with scuba diving gear? I think Dr. B has some—she's gone scuba diving in the past. She could give the equipment to Officer Van Underberg, he's young enough to jump to 1976. He could help Sabina swim out and to—"

Abigail put a hand on my arm. "Julia."

"Sabina would catch on quickly, I'm sure. She'd let the officer help her."

Where were the ambulances, the police cars to come to their aid? Did we need to call? I frantically looked around for a public phone booth.

Abigail tugged on my arm again. "Julia, it's over. We need to go," she said softly.

"Right," I said.

I was distantly aware of being in a state that can be only described as shock, going through the motions of what needed to be done. Following Abigail's example, I picked up someone's beach towel and dabbed at my wet clothes. The sun would finish drying us off soon enough. We needed to head back to the Edison Estate to fetch our backpacks. That was what we needed to do.

The boy—practical, as kids tend to be—had gone back into the water to retrieve his dolphin, not wanting to lose it to the ocean current, and was dragging it ashore.

Abigail had pre-calculated the estate coordinates. They were written on a piece of paper tucked into the Slingshot where the casing had come slightly loose. She didn't bother getting out of sight as she propped the Slingshot open and wiped sand off it— everyone on the beach and bridge was gathered on the north-facing side, watching as a passing boat tried to reach the spot where the car had gone down. Of course, we knew it would do no good.

I laid the towel back down where it had been, only a bit wetter. The sun would soon dry that off, too. I had been so sure, up until the very end, that we would be able to save her. But she was gone. History had corrected itself.

And Udo was gone, too.

Bits and pieces of a monologue from the end of *The Sirens of Titan* took over my mind: *I am not dying…In the grand, in the timeless, in the chrono-synclastic infundibulated way of looking at things, I shall always be here.*

"Ready, Julia?"

28

In our haste to get to the bridge, we had stuffed the two backpacks into a container holding discarded garden clippings back at the Edison Estate. They were still there. Marlin wasn't. I was in a downer sort of mood and imagined what would happen if we left the backpacks there, let them decompose into nothing during rainy season after rainy season on a trash dump or a field somewhere. Still, as Abigail pointed out, Dr. B wouldn't be happy to lose two go-bags on a single time-travel run, so we retrieved them and wiped off the assorted trash stains as best we could. It was a good thing Dr. Little wasn't around to see it.

I pulled myself together and searched my mind for something ordinary and comforting to say. I reached for my usual tool in dealing with problems, which felt so inadequate now. "Want a snack, Abigail? We could get another box of cookies or a Coke from the gift shop."

"No, thanks."

"I don't want you to think we failed her."

"Except that we did, didn't we?"

We had, but it hurt too much to face the truth.

"Do you mind if we stick around for a bit?" I asked. "I want to gather my thoughts before we break the news to everyone in the lab." Perhaps Nate, Dr. Little, Dr. B, and the others knew already; maybe by now they had heard from Nate's parents that the girl they'd known as Julia had not returned. A thought struck me—had I been named after her in some weird circle-of-life thing? Surely not. Wouldn't my parents have told me the story if that was the case? It must have just been a name they liked, that was all. Anything else was just too much to process.

"No," Abigail said when I brought up the possibility after we had squished over in our wet clothes to the bench we had occupied earlier. We sat down to try to process what had happened and to let the sun dry us before heading back. "Your parents didn't name you after her. Your name was chosen first, before we ever rescued her in Pompeii, before she went to 1976—then, for whatever reason, Sabina gave it as her own."

"Odd that she used the modern pronunciation." *Yoolia* was what she had called me back in Pompeii and since.

"Once she saw that she wasn't back in ancient times, she probably decided that it would be better to keep a low profile and give a modern name. In any case, whatever made your parents choose Julia, it wasn't because of Sabina."

We hadn't been gone that long—my parents, along with the rest of the book club, were still at the estate, unaware of what had happened to their leader. They were all perched on the curb of the parking lot by the art bus, paired off and sipping Cokes in the shade. The palm tree fronds above their heads danced in the soft breeze.

I couldn't help but notice that something had changed between my parents. They were holding hands now. But that wasn't all. Missy glanced at Soren, and in the glance I read not just contentment and happiness but *readiness*—readiness to move on to the next step in life. They had not discovered Life with a capital *L*, the way Udo had wanted to; they had rediscovered each other. Missy reached over and snubbed out her cigarette. Dad gave her a friendly wink.

A bit down from my parents, Gigi and Nathaniel were sharing a Coke.

There was no mystery here after all. Dad was my father—always had been.

An unexpected wave of something hit me. It was grief about Sabina, but not only that. My mother had come to terms with her pregnancy, and now Soren knew as well. I was about to take my place on the stage, which meant there couldn't be a second copy of me here in the past. It was time to leave 1976.

Through a sort of shallow-breathing mental fog I said, "Abigail." My voice sounded odd, distant, weak. A fresh tour group had emerged from the Edison Museum and were admiring the banyan. I tried to quell the rising sense of *not belonging*.

"What's up, Julia?"

"We need to head back, I think."

"I guess we're dry enough. Let's get out of sight. Hey, we could go into the telephone booth—you know, like Superman, only not to change into an alter ego but to pop back to the present."

I knew she was trying to cheer me up. "How about the public restrooms instead? Besides, someone's using the phone already—the phone…What on earth?"

"What's *he* doing here?" Abigail said.

29

The person in the phone booth was Steven Little, who had penned a hasty note to us saying History was forcing him to go back. Yet here he was, still in 1976 in the flesh. Using the pay phone. We watched him fumble in his jean pockets and pull out the necessary coins. Receiver to one ear, he dropped the money into the machine and dialed. He greeted the person at the other end. I wished we had Marlin there to lip-read for us, but he was nowhere to be seen. Whatever adventure he had headed off to, I wished him the best of luck.

Dr. Little bent down to retrieve a couple of sheets of paper from his duffel bag, which was by his feet. He readied the first page and opened his mouth to read into the receiver. There was no need for Marlin to lip-read for us after all—even through my mental fog, it was clear to me that Dr. Little had been stopped by History from reading from the page, whatever was on it. He opened and closed his mouth like a fish several times, then shook his head and hung up irritably. He slipped in a new coin and redialed.

"Well, this is odd," I said, my own words distant to my ears.

Abigail was equally puzzled. "I wonder if he managed to come back to do some kind of follow-up experiment for his research."

"Why don't we go ask him what he's up to?"

We shuffled over to the phone booth, passing within half a step of my parents, who were too busy ogling each other to look up, and approached as cautiously as if we had spotted a ghost, even though he was obviously real enough.

The young professor didn't see us, as he was too busy mumbling to himself while he dialed yet again. The words penetrated my brain like stones thrown into mud, one occasionally making a bigger splash than the others. "I'll try the *numbers* one more time. If it *still* doesn't work, I'll tell them about Microsoft and

Apple and IBM…Oh, and perhaps diversify with Starbucks, Beanie Babies, and such…"

Abigail nudged me in the side and pointed. Dr. Little was barefoot. He hadn't jumped home, then once more back to 1976. He had never left.

When whoever was at the other end of the phone picked up, Dr. Little said, "Do you still have the pen and paper? I'm going to try to read you the numbers, starting with October 18…No, it doesn't matter *who* this is—call me a well-wisher. Let's see if I can read them out—and if I can, then I'll tell you what they are…No, I *know* it's odd…"

"Professor?" Abigail said.

The phone receiver dropped out of Dr. Little's hand and clanged against the glass and steel of the booth on its cord. He swore under his breath and retrieved it. "Hello? Hello?"

He turned to face us and said accusatorily, as if we had ruined an experiment, "They hung up."

"Dr. Little," I managed to ask, "do you want to tell us what's going on?"

He didn't. He grabbed his duffel and wordlessly took off across the parking lot, the pages still in hand.

"Dr. Little, wait," I yelled, or thought I did. It might have just been a whisper.

Abigail seemed torn between running after the professor and helping me, as I was starting to feel a bit unsteady and probably looked it, too. She offered me her elbow for support and together we stumbled in our wet sneakers in the direction Dr. Little had gone.

The book club students, startled, had glanced up at the commotion, as did a gardener who had been digging around a potted plant when Dr. Little dashed by her. The professor was about to disappear into the foliage when a scrawny body in cutoff shorts and shirt stepped into his path. The two men fell to the ground in a tangled mess of limbs.

We hurried over. Abigail made sure I was steady on my feet, then turned her attention to Marlin. She helped him up and dusted gardening mulch off his shoulder.

"I'm too old for this," Marlin said. "Much too old."

The gardener shook her head at all of us in disapproval, then went back to work.

Dr. Little was still down on the ground on his back, his notes strewn all around him, his duffel bag knocked off his shoulder and to one side.

"Why did you stop me? What's it to you?" he said to Marlin.

"Looked like the ladies wanted to talk to you."

I slid a foot over to where Dr. Little's page, the one he had wanted to read over the phone, was threatening to blow off in the wind. I picked it up, steadying myself on a wooden post so as not to lose my balance.

"We thought you went back home, Professor," Abigail said, and offered Dr. Little a hand to pull him to his feet. He did look pathetic as he lay on the ground, his bare feet scratched up and dusty. He accepted Abigail's hand. "I was hoping to get this done in private so that no one would know. Obviously it made no sense for me to run. I don't know why I did," he admitted. Then, noticing our faces, "Is it bad news about Sabina?"

I sighed. "I'm afraid so."

"Sorry. That's awful." He said it like he meant it.

"Oh, no," Marlin said. A large tear rolled down one age-sculpted cheek.

With a sigh, Dr. Little dusted off his jeans and picked up his duffel bag and dusted that off as well, then glanced around, as if searching for some way to explain his continued presence in 1976. But I knew the truth and so did Abigail—he had some kind of agenda of his own; he'd had one all along. Dr. Little finally said, "I just needed to make a phone call. That's all."

"We figured as much, Dr. Little," I said. "But *why*?"

"Not in front of Marlin."

Abigail moved over to Marlin's side. "Marlin has been very helpful. We owe him the truth."

"Fine, then. That really is all I was going to do—make my call. To my parents. I waited at the beach inside one of the motels until you and Abigail left. After I was finished, I planned on rejoining you. I was going to tell you I'd been to the lab and back and my feeling of light-headedness was just an anomaly. But I was unable to use the public phones at the beach—I tried several—so I caught a bus over here, figuring maybe History didn't like that we were all scattered. You weren't here, so I figured you were elsewhere, on Udo and Sabina's trail." He digressed again. "It's...it's hard for those of us who are expected to use a time-travel machine only for lofty goals such as documenting History and exploring the physics of spacetime. I am as human as the next man. I tried not to succumb to temptation—for the birth cutoff research study, I made sure to stay on campus, far away from my family in California...I think now that approach was wrong, that we might need to observe our parents to gauge the cutoff moment. It's likely a personal event, one governed by emotions and not an equation."

That look on my mother's face when I watched her finally accept the pregnancy...and now the very air felt thinner, and I knew my time in 1976 was nearing an end. Dr. Little was right—there wasn't a hard and fast rule about when a newcomer's presence on the stage was noticed. It was different for each of us.

I looked down at the page Dr. Little had been trying to read to his parents. It was a printout from the lab, and I had seen it once before, in his duffel bag. At the time I'd assumed the numbers were Slingshot coordinates. "So...these aren't spacetime coordinates?" I asked.

4-9-33-36-39-47
8-21-32-35-36-38
20-30-32-43-44-47
5-7-12-21-32-45
4-5-18-41-47-48
11-16-21-26-27-47
2-10-19-23-26-30
15-18-22-24-28-49

. . .

Abigail glanced at the page. "They aren't, no."

Dr. Little turned his palms upward, as if it was a relief to tell the truth. "They're lottery numbers. *Winning* numbers for the California Super Lotto, starting with the first week the game began—October 18, 1986. See? Four, nine, thirty-three, thirty-six, thirty-nine, and forty-seven. I was going to read them over the phone to my parents so they could buy a ticket. There was only a negligible chance of it working, but it was still a nonzero chance. I felt it was worth a try."

Money. So that was it. Nate had been right about there being more to the professor's reaction than mere annoyance at the interruption to his research. I should have seen it.

"But it didn't work, did it?" Abigail said.

"Can I have that paper?" Marlin asked.

"Certainly not. No, it didn't work. My mother answered, but I was unable to read anything out. I was calling a second time to try again. If I was unable to use the lottery numbers, I was planning to tell my parents to buy stock in Apple…" He trailed off with a glance at Marlin, who said, "I like apples. Is it an orchard? A juice maker?"

Dr. Little went on: "The ethics are murky perhaps, but after all, if it *did* work, that would by definition mean that no one would be affected or harmed by it in any meaningful way." He said it as if grasping for a way to justify his actions. "It could even be called an experiment in History and the limits of its changeability."

Abigail asked the question. "You wanted your parents to be rich, Professor?"

"I didn't grow up poor—solidly middle class, really. But a junior professor's salary and my wife's website design freelancing do not go very far when you have a young one and another two on the way."

"Two?" I asked.

"We're having twins."

"Congratulations, Professor!" Marlin said.

"I wasn't expecting…quite so many—and quite so soon. Worries about their college tuition and all the other bills keep me up at night. I wanted everything for Piper and the new kids. And this appeared so easy, so clean. Just a simple phone call. I think I lost my head."

Nate had once said that everyone had a personal flaw. Dr. Little's turned out to be that he was human just like the rest of us; he was guilty of the very thing he was afraid of discovering if he looked too closely at his heroes. It wasn't greed but parental love that had made him risk his career. The twins that he and Mrs. Little were expecting had already reserved their place on the stage.

Dr. Little wasn't accepting defeat just yet. "Do you want to call anyone in your family, Julia? We could all share the winnings, perhaps."

I wouldn't even have to call. Just slip the printout to Dad, over where he and the other students were getting back into the art bus, having finished their Cokes. I thought I heard the words *beach*, *shrimp lunch*, and *swimming* mentioned.

I shoved the printout back at Dr. Little and said no sharply, more sharply than I'd intended. I was fighting the realization that I might have been tempted if Sabina were still alive. The money would have covered a trip to Italy, her college tuition, whatever else she might have needed.

Abigail looked like she'd had the same thought, but all she said was, "You're lucky you had someone to call in the first place, Professor. And Piper and her siblings are lucky that you care so much about their future. But even if it had worked, it would have been—"

"Wrong." I finished the sentence for her, watching the art bus pull out of the parking lot. "It never would have been the right decision."

The gardener had been glancing in our direction, as if she wanted to send us on our way. We gathered our things and headed toward the far end of the parking lot, where a couple of picnic tables, meant for tourists partaking in gift shop snacks, were clustered. Lunchtime had passed and only one table was occupied, by a sightseeing family. I noticed that someone had forgotten their things at a second table. It took me a moment to register what was on it. Whoever had retrieved Udo's novel out of the trash bin had arranged the pages in a neat stack. I was more interested in what was on top of them, keeping the paper from blowing off in the light wind.

A lab coat, neatly folded.

Then a person stepped into the sunlight from behind a palm tree.

30

I held back, letting Abigail run up and hug her first.

"We thought you were dead—don't ever do that to us again! Ever!" Abigail pulled back to let Sabina breathe but was still holding on to her, as if afraid to let go. She swatted at Sabina's dress ineffectively. "Oops, I got you a bit wet. Sorry."

"Why wet? Sunny day."

"It's ocean water. Never mind, it's a long story. We'll tell you all about it later."

"But why you and Yoolia here?"

"We came here to find you, of course."

"You want me back?"

"Are you kidding? Of course we want you back. We *need* you back."

I had so many questions for her: Why had Udo pretended she was in his car? Why had she gone back in time in the first place? And was she happy to see us? But none of it mattered. I noticed Abigail had tears streaming down her face just as I wiped them from my own eyes. I rather thought that Dr. Little had something in his eyes, too. I saw him glance in the direction of the phone booth as if he wanted to give his plan one more try, but he said nothing. He shook hands with Sabina and said awkwardly, "Glad to have you back."

"Sabina, this is Marlin," Abigail introduced them. "Marlin, I'd like you to meet a person who's very important to us."

"Pleased to meet you, miss," Marlin said.

I cleared my throat and gave Sabina a great big hug of my own. "Let's go home."

PART FOUR:
HOME

.

31

I didn't get a chance to talk to Nate alone until the following morning, Sunday home-time. There was too much going on—the happy reunion after we got back to the lab; the lengthy account we gave the others of our time in 1976; the fussing Abigail and I did over Sabina once we got her home...I tumbled into bed, exhausted and in need of a good eight hours. I'd given Nate a cheery wave as he drove off (he'd followed us back to the house in his Jeep to pick up Wanda) in the hopes that it would convey that everything between us was all right. While he had been very glad to see the four of us step out of STEWie's basket, he'd been more reserved than usual. Not that he had ever been particularly demonstrative toward me while others were present, but I'd given him the cold shoulder earlier, and he had no idea why.

A honk outside the house woke me up, and it took me a moment to register where I was, back in my own bed in 2012 and not tucked into some out-of-the-way alcove in 1976. Sunlight streamed in; I had forgotten to close the curtains. I grabbed the clock—it was nine. I had slept in for the first time in, well, years. I threw on a sweatshirt over my pajamas and padded outside in my slippers to see that Nate had pulled his Jeep into the driveway. His grandmother was in the passenger seat, and Celer was in the back. A rush of warmth flooded my chest. He must have realized how important it would be for Sabina to see her dog today. To be here now, he must have left for his grandmother's house as the sun rose.

Sabina, who was dressed in a crisp white T-shirt and light green shorts, had already rushed outside to greet Celer. It wasn't the modern clothes that made me heave a sigh of relief but the expression on her face as she squatted down next to Celer and rubbed him all over. She was back for good. I knew it in my bones.

It turned out that, while Quinn's blackmail may have been the catalyst that had sent her into STEWie's basket, she had been motivated just as much by a desire to find out what had happened to her father, Secundus, and her grandmother, Faustilla—if they had survived the eruption or not. We could offer no more than a promise to try to find out, but I had sensed acceptance on her part. I guessed that her unexpected foray into 1976 had helped her see the difficulty of any such undertaking. Her focus now was on the future, not the past.

Celer waddled up the house steps and inside, as if exhausted from all this coming and going. Sabina grinned at Nate, then followed with a polite greeting to Mary Kirkland, whom she hadn't met before. She and Mary shook hands. Sabina thanked the older woman for taking care of her dog, and I had to wipe something from my eye.

I wasn't the only one. Nate coughed and said with a catch to his voice, "Well, now everyone's met everyone. Shall we go inside?"

"Most certainly," I said. "Judging from the delicious smell, I believe Abigail is making pancakes."

Celer shuffled over to his favorite spot behind the TV, and the rest of us joined Abigail in the kitchen. Nate rolled up his sleeves and offered to crisp the bacon. His offer to help was accepted, but Sabina's was waved off. We pointed her to the seat of honor at the kitchen table and directed Mary to a chair as well. As I got the coffee going, I heard Mary ask Sabina how she'd liked the seventies. They launched into a discussion of disco pants. I suspected the two would get along very well, which gave me a good feeling. The more people in your life who care about you, the better. I wanted Sabina's support network to be vast.

I set up the coffeemaker and readied several mugs. When Abigail walked away from the counter to bring the stack of pancakes to the kitchen table, I said quietly to Nate, "Good news. We're not half siblings."

He was methodically lining up bacon slices on a napkin to drain them. "We're not—what did you say?"

"It's a bit of a long story. I'll tell you all about it later."

Speaking of later, I had decided to do what I should have done long ago: make an appointment to talk to an expert in the genetics department. The expert could tell me more about hidden traits, and perhaps I could even volunteer for a genetics study to trace the dark-haired ancestor from whom I'd inherited my looks. There was always the chance that a TTE run to the relevant time period would open up, whatever century it was, and I could tag along.

There was only one problem. Dean Braga had left a message on my voice mail. She needed to talk to me as soon as possible.

There was no deep meaning to the location of Udo's CSI in the end, not the way I'd thought there would be. According to Sabina, who had been inspired to join the book club's journey more by the Latin word *infundibulum* (she'd hoped it might lead to home somehow) than by the prospect of catching a boat ride, Udo had wanted to show the others that much of life was just chance and coincidence. The chain went something like this: Udo wanted to be a writer; Kurt Vonnegut was the person he looked up to most in that quest; Kurt had written PR releases for General Electric; GE had been founded by Edison; Edison had owned a winter estate in Fort Myers; Fort Myers was where Udo had been born. I didn't know if the phrase *six degrees of separation* existed in 1976, but that's what Udo had done. He'd linked Kurt to his own birthplace. The actual location didn't matter much—Udo could have picked any spot and probably connected himself and Vonnegut to it—but he'd chosen the banyan as a symbol.

History itself, it occurred to me, is like a large, never-ending game of six degrees of separation—or better, six degrees of connection. A lattice links everybody and everything. Time and geography. The past and the present, and the future as well.

Sabina had called the pages in her possession "Udo's book." She pronounced the name with a long *u* and a softer *d*: *Ooo-doh*. Hating to see anything go to waste, she'd recovered them from the bin after Udo's departure. He had told Sabina it was time to part ways and that she should wait in the art bus. Not understanding why we were on her trail, he hadn't wanted Abigail and me to find the girl he knew as Julia, so he'd stuck her hat onto the passenger-side seat of the Ford Mustang to mislead us.

After some time spent waiting in the art bus, Sabina had peeked out and seen Dr. Little get off the city bus. Something about his manner had made her uncomfortable, and she'd hidden in the garden until spotting Abigail and me once we jumped back from the causeway.

Udo had been headed to a final showdown with his family, I guessed, perhaps to make a grand announcement that he was leaving school for good. He never got the chance. The pages Sabina had saved, and we had brought back with us, were all that was left. In a way it was a childish gesture—throwing the story pages away because he hadn't found any support from his family. But it was what had saved his book for posterity.

"How did you get along with the others?" I asked Sabina as the mellow Sunday rolled on. "Did you recognize any of the book club students?"

"Missy...your mother, yes? And Soren...father?"

I explained about Gigi and Nathaniel being Nate's parents, but she already seemed to have figured that out, too.

"You gave your name as Julia?"

"Udo ask," she explained. Apparently the others had stuck to calling her Lab Coat Girl.

"But why my name?"

"Rule of time travel—blend in. Julia a nice name and you nice to me."

Seeing my parents there had kept me in her mind.

Speaking of my parents, they returned my call around lunchtime—the ship had pulled into port—and I had a chance to ask if they remembered meeting Lab Coat Girl. The answer was they did, vaguely—Lab Coat Girl had spent much of the drive down to Fort Myers staring out the window, my Mom said—but it was the memory of Udo that had stayed with them all these years. I filled them in on the facts as they both listened in on the speakerphone. After Mom's exclamation of surprise, followed by "I thought Sabina looked familiar," there was a moment of silence on their end when I mentioned that we had rescued Udo's manuscript.

"Get it published in his name, Jules," Dad finally said. Mom heartily agreed.

"I will," I promised. "Just as soon as things get back to normal here."

I didn't ask about their college friends Gigi and Nathaniel in case there were still some hard feelings there even after all this time. My parents were driving up soon and it was best to bring up the issue face-to-face. It was time I introduced them to Nate, anyway.

Dean Braga pointed me to the chair across from her desk. Dr. Little had passed me in the hall on his way out, his cheeks bright red. My guess was that he'd told the dean everything, though I wasn't sure if that included the truth about how Sabina had come to be with us. I took the chair. Before I could say anything, Dean Braga spoke. "Dr. Little told me about the lottery numbers and his breach of conduct."

"Is he staying on?"

I hoped the answer was yes. Dr. Little and I didn't get along very well, but he was talented, and he cared deeply for his family.

Dean Braga sighed. "He did offer to quit, but I didn't accept. He said he lost his head and that it won't happen again. I believe him. I'll think about what the consequences of his actions should be. Now, about what prompted this madcap run to 1976…"

"I'm not even sure where to begin."

The dean leaned back in her leather chair. "Sabina is Abigail's charge, right? And the two are renting the mother-in-law suite in your house? I'm afraid I don't know very much of the backstory beyond that. Was Sabina acting out for attention, as teens do, having somehow figured out how to get into the TTE lab? Or is there something here that I'm missing?"

I was suddenly at a loss for words. How to explain why we had plucked a thirteen-year-old out of the Pompeii ghost zone and brought her into the twenty-first century, why we had violated time-travel protocol? I took a deep breath and the story came tumbling out. It wasn't so difficult to explain after all. "We met her on that run to ancient Pompeii, the one that was orchestrated by Lewis Sunder. Her father was Secundus, a fish sauce merchant with a small shop in town. He entrusted his daughter to our protection when the eruption started…We couldn't just leave her there." I slumped into the chair. "Sorry, we should have told you before."

The apology felt inadequate.

Apparently she agreed. In a rare moment of unprofessional snippiness, she said, "You think?" She tapped a pencil, then said more mildly, "I apologize for my outburst. I suppose I can understand why you kept it secret. Making the details widely known would have cast a shadow on the TTE program and the school, not to mention the girl's life here in the twenty-first century."

"I—we just wanted her to have a little more time to get accustomed to her new environment. In retrospect, it may not have been the best plan. It was why she used STEWie. She was trying to go back to Pompeii because she thought she was a burden on us, and to find out what happened to her family."

"I see. You understand that this is one secret that cannot stay that way?"

"I do."

"Well, what's done is done. I'm not heartless—of course I'm glad you were able to rescue her from Pompeii. But we can't allow anything like this to happen again. I'll have to give some thought to how to handle the PR angle, which will require some finesse on our part. There'll be those who will argue that it's not our job, our right, to play God. They'll be right of course, but they can hardly make us send her back."

We both knew that there were many who thought using STEWie was messing with the natural order of things and that the past was best left unexplored. But growing pains were to be expected with any new technology, especially one as groundbreaking as time travel. Things would sort themselves out. I sat up and opened my notepad to start a list of what needed to be done, but she held up a hand.

"As I said, we can't allow anything like this to happen again. You bringing her back from the Pompeii run and hiding it, this weekend's events—it all reinforces what I've been considering for some time now. The STEWie program must be shut down. I'm going to make the recommendation to Chancellor Evans."

The pen almost fell out of my hand. Dean Braga wasn't fond of time traveling herself, but I knew that that didn't enter into her thought process. "Shut it down? Surely that's an overreaction."

"Julia, think about it. If there is one thing that has become abundantly clear, it's that human nature and time travel *do not get along very well*. We're not ready. Since STEWie's first successful run, we've seen a sequence of inappropriate behavior from one researcher to the next—Dr. Mooney, Dr. Sunder, Dr. Holm, and now Dr. Little...and that's only the actions we know about. What other secrets has the time-travel lab been privy to? I realize that some of the researchers had good intentions—"

"And some didn't, that's true."

"But this cannot go on."

"Still, to shut down the lab..."

"I share your disappointment, but for now it is the only course of action we can take. We'll have to let the other schools know." She meant MIT, the University of Beijing, and the two other schools that were building their own STEWies. "We can't make them halt their lab construction, but I think public pressure might increase after Sabina's story hits the news." She pointed at the blank page in my notepad. "Let's start by notifying everyone on the STEWie roster that I'm putting all runs on hold. Then we can release an official statement and see about scheduling a media Q&A and a meet and greet with Sabina."

"If you don't mind my saying so, you know there will be considerable opposition to shutting the program down from within the school. Unfinished research. Students unable to wrap up their PhDs. Unused funding. Upended work schedules."

I'd dealt with angry tenured professors before. That's what tenure guaranteed them—the right to speak their mind without the worry of being fired—and boy, did they use it on occasion.

"That can't be helped. It's the right course of action. I feel that strongly." She shifted in the leather chair, as if uncomfortable. "Do you know what finally convinced me that it was impossible to separate personal issues from scholarly ones in time travel? The unsavory sides that surfaced in our researchers—these attempts at murder, blackmail, fraud...I could have put all those down to having bad seeds in the lab. But when I came right down to it, there was *one* matter I couldn't ignore."

"What was it?"

"Despite my dislike of the physical act of time traveling..."

"Yes?"

"I found myself fantasizing about going back in time. To, er, fix a small math error in my thesis."

32

The few steps from Dean Braga's office to my smaller one next door felt like a lifetime. I knew what *temporarily on hold* usually meant in academia—not days, not months, but *years*. Things did not move fast, especially where labs were concerned. Delaying the crafting of the message announcing the "temporary" shutdown to everyone on STEWie's roster, I slid into my desk and put my hand under my chin. I couldn't believe it. We were just on the cusp of finding out so many things about History. I scrolled through the rainbow of topics filling the STEWie roster: photographing art that had been lost in World War Two; recording Neanderthal speech; then a very challenging one—a jump to the moon and back, space suits and all, which would truly count as *space*-time travel...

There was so much we didn't know about History, about ourselves.

I glanced up and was surprised to see a blank spot on my wall right across from the desk, where there hadn't been one before. When she'd gone back to 1976, Sabina had taken not only the Fourth of July group photo and Dr. Mooney's lab coat, which she said had reminded her of him, but Abigail's purple hair extensions. All of her meager possessions, except the lab coat, had been in the Ford Mustang when it went into the water. I hadn't noticed anything missing besides the photo—not that I'd had time to notice, really, as we raced to find her. Besides, she might not have taken anything at all to remind her of me, which would have been all right, of course. I was just Aunt Julia.

But if I'd had to venture a guess as to what might represent me, I might have gone with (a) a blank yellow legal pad from the stack in the drawer of my desk; (b) one of the many gel pens that populated my shoulder bag; or (c) a list from her room—perhaps the first one I'd made, of things everyone was expected to do in the mornings: brush teeth, shower, put on a fresh set of clothes, make the bed, and so on.

It wasn't any of those things. She had taken the world map poster that was normally tacked to the corkboard on the wall of my office just under a row of vintage St. Sunniva photos. I stuck a blue pushpin into it for each successful STEWie run made by our researchers. There had also been two red pins, representing the places where I'd spent some time myself—Pompeii and the fourteenth-century Minnesota woodland. I had been about to reach for a new red pin, for 1976, when I noticed the map was gone. Sabina had left the pins in a paper cup on my desk. The two red ones sat among the blue ones like unwelcome guests.

The map, with its little punctures all over, had by now decomposed in the salty waters lapping Sanibel Island. I automatically made a mental note to buy another one, then remembered there would be no need. The program was to be shut down.

I glanced at the blank corkboard again. In a swap that neither she nor Udo could have anticipated, Sabina had lost her treasures to the sea but rescued Udo's story. If I had anything to say about it, *The Skeletons of Eden* would see the light of day.

I might have done some introspection on why the map had reminded Sabina of me, or gotten started on the e-mail letting everyone know about Dean Braga's decision. But I suddenly couldn't wait any longer to demand answers from someone.

"Why didn't you tell us you met us in 1976?"

Dr. Mooney was at his workbench, soldering something on the new Slingshot 3.0. At my words—I had tapped him sharply on the shoulder before uttering them—he turned off the soldering iron and set it aside. He blew gently on the wire connection he'd just made before speaking. "It was all so long ago, Julia," he finally said. "I could make little sense of it, either at the time or after. I gave up on trying to figure it out, perhaps even started to believe I'd imagined the whole episode—the visit Gabe and I received from three people from the future. Then, one day years later, you showed up in the dean's office, Julia. Not long after, Abigail enrolled as a graduate student and Steven wrote to apply for a junior professorship. It was all happening. I brought it up with Gabriel, but he didn't remember meeting you all those years ago. When we brought back Sabina from Pompeii, I wondered…and then she disappeared into 1976 and it all came back clear as day. My three visitors and the missing girl they were searching for. I didn't think Sabina was the name you had given me, but everything else fit. Only—"

"Only what?"

He was still wearing his safety goggles, behind which he looked rather like an unhappy fish. "Only I never found out what happened to her in 1976. None of you ever came back to campus to tell me. You were just…gone."

"Oh."

"So what could I have told you? That I was going to try my best to help you in 1976, but I had no idea if you'd find her or not? Would it have helped?"

"I suppose not."

He slid off the goggles, mussing up his hair, which was grayer, shorter, and thinner now than it had been when he was a young man. He ran his hand through it. "There was a sense of familiarity when I first met Sabina in Pompeii, but I couldn't figure out why. In retrospect, I must have recognized her from the photo you showed me all those years ago. I just didn't make the connection. I'm ashamed to admit that I paid more attention to the smartphone with her picture on it than the picture itself. Then Steven started the experiments bringing him to 1976 and I began to wonder. Still, what could I say? I had two options, if I had them at all. One was to keep Sabina away from the TTE lab at all costs, and the other was to teach her about STEWie technology so she would have some tools at her disposal when and if she *did* get stuck in 1976. I chose the second. Or maybe I didn't really have a choice at all, since I knew it had all happened already. The thought struck me then, you know."

"Which one?"

"That some strands of the future must be as firmly fixed as the ones in the past."

"You mean key future events are inevitable no matter what we do?"

"Not key events, necessarily…just *some*."

I let the remark pass unchallenged. "It wasn't our fault somehow, was it? Udo crashing his car?"

"You know it wasn't. Four people—Sabina, Abigail, Steven, you—slipped into the past like a raindrop finding its way down a tree trunk, no more able to disturb History than the raindrop could harm the tree. Is anything bothering you? I am very glad Sabina is back. I only wish I could have helped more."

"You did help, Xavier. That's not it."

I sighed and explained that Dean Braga was shutting down the STEWie program. He nodded, like he had expected it.

STEWie's mirrors towered over us accusingly, as if pointing out that we had not treated what they represented, the grand things they could do, with enough respect. With the lab closed down and the STEWie program halted indefinitely, the mirrors and their companion lasers would be left to gather dust. For a second I had the wild idea of asking Dr. Mooney to send me into the past one more time, to a location of my own choosing. I could step into STEWie's basket to find that dark-haired ancestor, or to get some answers about Abigail's parents, though I didn't think she would have wanted that, not like this. Or I could use STEWie to answer a question for the ages. An entry from STEWie's roster popped into my mind, one made possible by Kamal's recent thesis defense—he had found safe landing zones in Eurasia of thirty-some thousand years ago. Yes. Neanderthals. There was so much we didn't know: Did they speak? Were they beefy and taciturn, as modern stereotypes would have it? What did they think of their artistic cousins? I would instruct Dr. Mooney, "Neander Valley, thirty-five thousand years back," and he would give me a frank look, then reach for Kamal's catalog of safe landing zones. "It's a risky run for an untrained traveler, even one with experience," he would point out.

"I'm not going to do anything foolish, just take a look around to see if I can spot a few of them."

"Who?"

"The cave painters and their chunkier cousins."

"Well, all right then. Bring back video footage and photos."

And I would.

The professor's voice broke through my fantasy. "Julia? When is Dean Braga halting all runs?"

"Immediately."

He gently flicked a metal shaving off the Slingshot 3.0. "I expect she'll ask me to hold off on my work on this as well."

"It didn't come up in our talk, but I expect so. Where did it come from, Xavier? The Slingshot? Version 1.0 that you had back in Pompeii, and Version 2.0? And that one? Did you really design and build them?"

"I never said I did, not exactly," he said, his voice quiet. "As a matter of fact, I found the blueprints for the first one in the lab the day I made the decision that I would go to Pompeii. There, on that chair. The blueprints had a note on them that said, *Build and take me along.* I obeyed. At first I thought it was meant for me, as an aid in my plan to document the ancient Roman lifestyle. I tested it up and down the Pompeii coast, trying to figure out how it worked— discovered it had a propensity for dropping me into ghost zones if I strayed from the handful of destinations I had programmed into it, like Rome."

"You said the engineering department had designed the battery."

"They probably did, just in the future."

"And that you had figured out how to splinter off a Mooney-shaped piece of STEWie's basket to get it to work."

"I decided it'd be best for everyone if I sounded like I knew what I was doing, rather than the truth, that I was winging it. I later realized that the Slingshot generated a basket on its own. In any case, we ended up using it to get out of Pompeii. I think we were meant to."

So someone had come up with a rescue plan—for us to use the Slingshot to jump to Rome and in due time meet up with Dr. May and return to St. Sunniva that way. But I had needed antibiotics— fast—and so we had done the foolhardy thing and used the unfamiliar device to jump all the way home. "And Version 2.0?" I asked.

"The blueprints arrived during the summer. It was an improvement. I discovered that Slingshot 2.0 was more stable and could go with or against the arrow of time, as you know."

"So all this while, when you've been tinkering with the Slingshot…the tests around campus…what were you really doing?"

"Trying to figure out why it works, with little luck so far. I think what it does is let travelers glide along the links that exist between the past and the present—and the future." He turned his palms upward, as if physically admitting the limits of his knowledge on the matter.

The Slingshot 1.0 was lying in bits and pieces on the worktable in front of him. I carefully touched a small half sphere, whose function I couldn't begin to guess at. It was simultaneously squishy and very smooth. "When you said you were trying to build Version 3.0 for us take along to the fourteenth century, was that all a farce?"

"It would have been a duplicate of Version 2.0. I think—no, I'm *guessing*—that it's all Abigail's doing. I don't know for sure."

My head shot up. "Abigail sent you the blueprints for the Slingshot?"

"Not our Abigail, the future Abigail. The one who has her degree. The one who's perhaps a tenured professor in charge of the lab. As I said, I don't know anything for sure—it's just a feeling. But I figured one of us from Pompeii had to have sent me the Slingshot in the first place. You know, to rescue us."

I scratched my head, somewhat stunned by his words. "Are you saying future Abigail saved herself and us by getting the Slingshot into your hands? But that doesn't make sense." I clutched the sides of my head, trying to reason it out. "If Abigail and the rest of us *had* been killed in Pompeii, there would have been no future Abigail to rescue us."

"I think she was the only one of us who originally made it out of the town alive, on foot, and got home safe after meeting up with Dr. May's group on their STEWie run to Rome."

"Even if that's the case, the future Abigail couldn't change History—you know that. It's more than a rule—it's an unyielding cornerstone."

"Is it? *We* can't change History, but *they* may have figured out how to. I'm talking about the next generation of occupants of this lab, or whatever stands in its place." The professor gestured around him. "Besides, if my hypothesis is correct, Abigail would have only been changing *our* role in the past, not the past itself. We didn't belong there anyway." He added thoughtfully, "I wonder if the older Abigail anticipated that we would bring Sabina back."

"And Version 2.0?"

"I think that was meant for fixing what happened this week, to find Sabina in 1976, and whoever sent it didn't expect that it would get used for a joyride to the fourteenth century by Quinn and Dr. Holm."

I stared at him wordlessly. Could it be true? If we hadn't had the Slingshot 1.0 in Pompeii, we wouldn't have made it out alive. If we hadn't had the Slingshot 2.0 in 1976, we wouldn't have been able to jump around Fort Myers so easily, instead relying on the unstable Version 1.0. Even with the Slingshot by our side, it had been a close call.

As for the designer of the Slingshots…he or she was a serious out-of-the-box thinker. Abigail had shown herself to be inventive when needed. She had the same cheerful disregard for rules as Dr. Mooney and was as fearless as he when it came to taking the unbeaten path. It's where she felt most comfortable.

"Do you have any proof of this, Professor? That it's Abigail, or any of it?"

"None whatsoever. But there's a familiar touch to the design of the two Slingshots. The simultaneous elegance and scrappiness of it is all Abigail, if you will."

I sighed. "I guess we'll have to be patient and wait to find out what happens. Will happen."

"Unless we're dead by then. I suspect I will be. If so, I'm content to know that Abigail will carry the torch and the lab will continue to thrive."

We left it at that. I turned to go, pondering that it was like knowing we were all headed toward a real-life CSI, one where all truths would finally become known. I stopped with one hand on the lab door. The professor had slid his goggles back on and recommenced tinkering with the Slingshot 3.0.

"Anything else you know that the rest of us don't, Dr. Mooney? Was 1976 the only time we unexpectedly popped up in the past?"

"Hmm? Yes, Julia—you know everything I know," he said without looking up.

"Well, all right then."

∞

I took the lakeside path from Time Travel Engineering back to Hypatia House, lingering to watch the ducks waddling on the shore. I found myself reluctant to go back to my office, to do what had to be done.

Hold on—

Did it have to be done? If Dr. Mooney was right, the lab would reopen one day with Abigail in charge. Maybe that meant we needed to fight to keep it open *now*. Maybe it meant *I* needed to fight to keep it open.

But how?

A student texting as she biked along almost ran me over and I called out after her, "Don't bike and text!" as much for her safety as mine. I don't think she heard.

I had been as guilty as the others. Like Dean Braga, I'd wanted to use STEWie to settle a personal concern, an issue important only to me. What on earth had led me to conclude that digging around in the past was a better course of action than asking my parents outright? I had wanted to save them some embarrassment—and myself as well—and I'd thought the answer would be easily found in 1976. Answers rarely were, of course.

There was nothing we could do about human nature. But there *was* something we could do about the way we approached time travel. The focus thus far had been on funds, academic merit, how to soothe wounded feelings over who would get a roster spot and who wouldn't. There was a fourth side to the square, one that had been overlooked. Because what did we, as a society, do to counter human nature and the tendency to make bad choices, cheat, steal, or take more than our share? That unexciting enemy of chaos—laws— usually boiled down to the administrative and bureaucratic enforcement of them. And administration was a job in which I had a lot of practice.

Feeling suddenly energized, I ran up the path of Hypatia House, passing Dr. B, who gave me a startled look on her way out, and burst into my office.

I slid into the desk and grabbed a notepad and a pen.

(1)   *Pairs.*

A single professor and his or her grad students just did not cut it, because of the power imbalance. Professors would have to go on STEWie runs in pairs, like Dr. Mooney and Dr. Rojas originally had. No one would approve of the arrangement, especially not the senior professors, who were tenured and used to being free of oversight. I foresaw much arguing and many wounded egos. It had to be done, however.

(2)   *An oath.*

Having travelers sign an oath of professionalism wouldn't guarantee that there wouldn't be any shenanigans, but it was a step in the right direction. I assumed that new police officers at campus security had to do something similar. I'd have to ask Nate about it.

(3)   *Retiring the Slingshots.*

That one made me pause for a bit, but I felt it was the right course of action. If the two versions had been sent from the future to help us out in Pompeii and 1976, then we shouldn't be repurposing them for other matters. Simple and straightforward meant using just STEWie, the method we had earned. The Slingshots would appear in their proper time; Dr. Mooney would have to find a new subject matter to focus his talents on.

I sat back and eyed the short list. It was not a groundbreaking idea, but it was a start. And it might just work, I thought.

Now I needed to sell Dean Braga on it.

I called Nate to enlist his help.

He agreed at once. "There's also a security loophole that needs fixing—I've long thought that too many people know the code to the TTE lab door. How did Sabina get in anyway?"

"She figured out the four-digit code from watching Abigail and Dr. Mooney go in and out of the lab so many times. She said it wasn't hard."

"That's what I mean—we need a system in which the equipment can't be accessed by a single person, per your *Pairs* point. Two sets of codes—or two lab keys—will help. The two-man rule."

"Like for personnel who oversee nuclear launches."

"Exactly."

"I'll add that to my list as (4)."

There was another point, (5), one which I had been hesitant to add. "I also think we need an independent observer on each run—an overseer—someone who's along for the ride only to make sure nothing goes wrong. Perhaps not another academic but a layperson. I was going to put it down on my list, only…"

"Only what?"

"I couldn't tell if it belonged on the list or whether I merely wanted to put it there."

"Because you'd be very happy to volunteer to serve as an overseer."

"Well, yes."

"Put it on your list."

I did.

"Do you think this is the right thing to do, trying to continue on with the program?" I had never asked him his opinion on time travel. I wasn't so foolish as to assume everyone was on board with it, even if he had never said one way or another.

He thought about it for a moment. Through the phone I could hear background chatter in the campus security office. He finally said, "The genie is out of the bottle, so I don't think it matters what I think. But I'd say in general it's better to know *more* about anything rather than less. Even if what's revealed is not easy or pleasant or perfect, and that includes the world and our past." He summarized: "Paired teams of professors, two sets of door codes to the lab, an overseer on each run…it sounds like an organizational nightmare. You're looking forward to it, aren't you?"

"You bet I am."

Epilogue

Nine months was how long it took to get everything sorted enough to satisfy Dean Braga, Chancellor Evans, and the board of trustees. It was longer than it took for the media interest in Sabina to die down, her story long since replaced by the latest celebrity scandals.

We'd implemented all the rules on my list. I had been given a promotion and was now heading an oversight committee. I thought that Time Travel Overseer had a certain ring to it, but my official job description was a little more mundane—and longer. I was the Time Travel Engineering Laboratory Oversight Committee Chairperson. There were six of us—none of us academics, purposely—and our job was to tag along on runs to keep everyone honest. I was in charge of organizing things.

My first run—the first run to be conducted in nine months—was to be tomorrow, with Dr. Baumgartner. We were going to Marie Curie's childhood home in Poland. Perhaps not as exciting as a Neanderthal visit might have been, but exciting enough. There was a lot to get done before then.

Everyone was getting together at my house for a little celebratory dinner. Sabina's first year at the Thornberg high school was over—she had done well despite all the publicity that had ensued after our news conference. We still had reporters calling about it once in a while, but the high school students had reacted much more levelheadedly than I had expected and had rallied around Sabina. Nate had been at the news conference, and he'd been an invaluable support system for Sabina when she needed it. He'd helped so much in getting the overseer program up and running that I felt he deserved an honorary title.

As for Sabina—she had turned down offers to be a guest on various news and talk shows, and even an offer to cowrite a tell-all book. She *had* accepted a visit to the White House, during which the president had complimented her on how nicely her English was coming along. At home we had celebrated a cheerful Saturnalia-Christmas, and Sabina had started dropping in at the Latin wing of the ancient languages department—time she spent going through their dictionaries and correcting mistakes. She was finally at home in the twenty-first century. It was lovely to see.

Abigail had been offered a spot in the TTE lab after graduation. She was a postdoc, and, if all went well, the position would lead to a junior professorship down the road, then a senior one and tenure. She and Sabina were looking for a place of their own. I was going to miss having them around the house.

Kamal Ahmad had accepted a research fellowship at MIT, where the new STEWie was nearing completion. He would take along the lessons we'd learned from the implementation of our overseer program here at St. Sunniva. Jacob Jacobson was doing well, too, making great strides on his thesis topic on the life of Sunniva, the school's namesake and patron saint of Western Norway. I saw a teaching position in his future.

Xavier and Helen had gotten remarried. Abigail and Sabina kept telling me that Nate and I were next—and I thought I had spied Nate through the window of the town jewelers one day, buying something, when he was supposed to be off fishing. I was not about to ask him, but the anticipation was making me giddy in a non-girlish sort of way. I had my answer all ready.

I still didn't understand how the Slingshot blueprints had made their way into Dr. Mooney's hands to save us on the Pompeii run, which now seemed like a long time ago, but I forced myself to put the thought aside. I would find out one day.

I tried to picture Abigail gray-haired and with a slight slump to her shoulders. In my imagined scenario, she had finally met her parents on one of her runs, during her long and productive career at the lab. In that future, the only Science Quad building lacking the name of a scientist now had one: The Abigail Tanner Time Travel Engineering building. Perhaps she had done it all with Sabina, a professor in her own right, by her side.

I believed it.

THE END

Acknowledgments

An author isn't supposed to have favorites, but this final book in the series might just be my favorite of the three—it was great fun to go back to 1976, a time when I was but eight years old, even if only in my imagination. How things have changed since then, globally, technology-wise, and for me personally. It's a brave new world this one of ours, and like Julia, I can't wait to see what the future brings.

A recommended biography of Kurt Vonnegut, though not the (fictitious) one Julia leafed through, is Charles J. Shields's *And So It Goes: Kurt Vonnegut: A Life*; I consulted the Kindle edition (Henry Holt and Co., 2011). Vonnegut's *The Sirens of Titan* is widely available, from a paperback edition (Dial Press, 1988) to an e-book edition (RosettaBooks, 2010).

My grateful thanks go out to those who provided feedback on various versions of the manuscript or parts of it: John Baron, Richard Ellis Preston Jr., and Jill Marsal. Angela Polidoro wielded the editor's red pen with good humor and a sharp wit; Marcus Trower, copyeditor extraordinaire, pored over the manuscript with a magnifying glass; theBookDesigners turned my vague word-sketch into an eye-catching cover; and Rob Kroese skillfully handled the practical matter of formatting the manuscript for publication.

Grateful thanks also are due to Westmarch Publishing and 47North authors, with a special shout-out to Joseph Brassey, Roberto Calas, Anne Charnock, Allison M. Dickson, Rick Gualtieri, J. D. Horn, Rob Kroese, Stant Litore, Amber McLelland, Angela D. Mitchell, Cynthia L. Moyer, Melissa F. Olson, Richard Ellis Preston Jr., Denise Grover Swank, and Roberta Trahan. Your support, good humor, and savvy advice provided an anchor in a rapidly changing publishing landscape.

The book is dedicated to John and Elizabeth Baron, awesome parents-in-law, in recognition of many great visits to Fort Myers. If you ever find yourself in the area, the Edison & Ford Winter Estates are well worth a visit. The banyan tree is still there and going strong.

Finally—and as always—my most grateful thanks go out to my husband, John, and my son, Dennis.

About the Author

Thank you for reading *The Bellbottom Incident*—I hope you enjoyed the book as much as I enjoyed writing it! You've just finished reading the third and final book in the series. The previous books in the series are *The Far Time Incident* and *The Runestone Incident*. I also have a standalone novel, *Regarding Ducks and Universes*.

To help other readers find this book, please consider leaving a review on Amazon, Goodreads, or another reader site. Even only a short line or two helps spread the word and is much appreciated!

If you'd like to find out about my future book releases, you can sign up for my e-mail list at www.nevemaslakovic.com or find me on Facebook at www.facebook.com/NMaslakovic or Twitter at @nevemaslakovic.

Before turning her hand to writing fiction, Neve Maslakovic earned her PhD in electrical engineering at Stanford University's STAR (Space, Telecommunications, and Radio-science) Lab. Born in Belgrade, Yugoslavia (now Serbia), Neve currently lives with her husband and son near Minneapolis/St. Paul, where she admits to enjoying the winters. Find out more by visiting her website, www.nevemaslakovic.com.

www.ingramcontent.com/pod-product-compliance
Lightning Source LLC
Chambersburg PA
CBHW020601180626
46810CB00007B/2595